I0628438

SUSPICIOUS ACTIVITY

SUSPICIOUS

ACTIVITY

DEVIL'S PARTY PRESS, MILTON, DE

SUSPICIOUS ACTIVITY

Copyright © 2018 by Devil's Party Press.
Cover design by David Yurkovich.
Compiled and edited by Dianne Pearce and David Yurkovich.
All rights reserved.
The works contained in this anthology are copyright © 2018
by the respective authors and are reprinted herein with the authors' permission.

SUSPICOUS ACTIVITY (and all contents within) is a work of fiction. Any
similarities between actual persons, places, organizations, corporations, products,
or events are entirely coincidental.

ISBN: 978-0-9996558-4-9

devilspartypress.com

SUSPICIOUS ACTIVITY

CONTENTS

Every murderer is probably somebody's old friend.

Agatha Christie

Introduction

WHEN I SET OUT to produce an anthology of crime, I was fairly certain of what I was going to get in terms of submissions. Picture me, anticipating being curled up with the collected works of Agatha Christie and a cup of tea, Earl Grey.

Then the manuscripts started to arrive, and each was surprising, engaging, emotional, and unexpected, as crime should be. As it turned out, I soon realized I had no idea about the vast scope of the crime genre.

For instance, when you turn the page, you'll be introduced to Fareed. I still cannot read Fareed's story without finding myself captivated and brought to tears. Fareed didn't say one untrue word to me, nor did he accuse the butler, or assemble a large group for the reveal. He didn't provide me with a trick ending, but he did take my hand, and, very insistently, very firmly, involve me in his life.

From there I found myself unable to put this book down. The tales of the future, stories from the past, works of love, of lust, poems that can duke it out with the big boys, descriptions of the dark underbelly we all have, the secret itch we all wish to have scratched–these works draw me in, rough me up, hold me hostage.

This collection came together so seamlessly, it almost didn't need curating, just a few small tweaks to determine the line-up. I can't offer enough thanks to the artists whose works appear in these pages. That they are able to write with such skill and imagination is a feat; that they are willing to share it with you is a gift.

Don't expect to put this book down. Do expect to be up all night.

Dianne Pearce
Milton, DE

PUZZLE BOX NO.1

Heidi J. Hewett

SHARP, POPPING SOUNDS. One eyelid pulled back, but no light enters.

"Fareed."

"Fareed."

"We don't have much time."

Go away, I'm dead.

"You're at St. Joe's, Fareed. My name is Hiro. I'm a detective and I need you to listen to me. The human brain has seven minutes of electrical activity after death. They're going to stretch that time as much as they can, but we'll need to work quickly. I have a video monitor here, and I want you to picture a green circle. Can you do that for me?"

There's something hard, painful, in my throat that I can't get out. Overwhelmed by dizziness and panic, I try to gasp, but I can't breathe. Then the sudden rush of air, forcing my lungs to expand, to bloat. I'm so cold. Even the blood seems to be moving sluggishly. I can hear it, moving in slow, reluctant waves, pushed through the arteries and veins. I can actually hear each individual blood cell lining up to squish through the narrow capillaries one by one, but only up above. There's a clamp somewhere, cutting off the flow downward. I can hear my heartbeat; it's too weak. Too fast. This feels all wrong.

"We've got to calibrate the imaging software, Fareed. Can you visualize a green circle? Fareed!"

Green. Green, I think. Air hissing out, releasing the pressure on my lungs. A relief. Waiting for the next influx of air. It's a split-second too long. Clawing for oxygen. Panic again. *Wham!* Here it comes. God! Green blobs, green dots, green bubbles. *Green, damn you.*

Another male voice: "Let's get his head into the machine. Hold the cords up. Watch out."

"Got it! Here goes nothing," Hiro's voice, tight, in an undertone. Louder, "They're going to send you back, Fareed. I want you to look for something to identify this man. Anything you see. Focus on the details."

I'm dazzled by sudden daylight. An unlit cigarette between my teeth. Right hand slipping the fresh pack into my suit coat pocket.

"Is that your car?" the woman asks.

My hand is on the door, but I turn around. Her expression is strange; she's not looking at me. She's looking at the middle-aged man in the shabby brown suit, standing at the counter. He ducks his head and pushes at the thick-framed glasses sliding down the bridge of his nose.

How did I get here?

Where am I?

"Ten on Number 8," he says.

"Is that your car, sir?" the woman repeats. Now the owner behind the counter looks up, alert.

I almost push open the door. I don't want to know what this is about. This isn't my business. But I hesitate, glancing back over my shoulder.

"Something's not right," the woman is saying. She takes one step away from the lottery machine, craning her neck to see past me out through the big front windows of the Mobil station.

Who are these people?

What am I doing here?

I start to turn to see what she's looking at, but the man in front of the counter has a small, silver pistol in his hand. I remember the pistol now. Shit. His hand is shaking.

"I really don't want to do this," he says in a soft, husky voice. He has to clear his throat before the words come out. "Just give me the gas. Number 8."

And I'm back. The gas station is gone.

"Show me the man, Fareed. Think really hard. Picture him for me."

It's dark, and I'm cold. So cold. What the hell's happening to me? I try to phrase a question, but I can't feel my lips. I can't make my jaws move.

"Fareed! Can you hear me? Did you see him?"

Green. Stooped. 5' 2" maybe? Could be because he was hunched over. Caucasian. Middle-aged. Forties? Face is lined. Brown hair falling over his eyes, like he's afraid to look at you. Thick glasses. Mus-tache. Not thin. Bushy.

"Is the image-processing software working? Are you getting this?" The detective's voice asks. He's worried. He can't hear my words. I try to think in pictures.

"Got it."

Hiro's voice: "You're doing good, Fareed. Keep going. We got video surveillance from inside the store. Tell me something I wouldn't see. Show me details."

Such an effort. I just want them to leave me alone. I force my-self to see the gun again. The hand holding it–weathered, covered with tiny creases and scars. Not grease. Dust. Dusty. Is this why I'm lying here? Are you trying to catch this bastard because he killed me?

"Tell the sergeant outside we're looking for a manual laborer of some kind. Mason? Maybe stone carver? Tell him to call around any stonemasonry companies in the area and see if someone's out today. What else, Fareed?"

A female voice, somewhere over my head: "His pH is falling."

Hiro's voice again, reluctant: "No help for it. Send him back again."

I'm lying chest-down, cheek pressed flat against the floor. At least I'm not cold anymore. Everything is sideways. I see the scuffed brown shoes moving across the square tiles, a pool of bright-red blood–my blood, I realize with a jolt–radiating outward. It's leeching into my silk tie, reaching out for my business card and the unlit ciga-rette that rolled away. More gray dust in the cuffs of the brown pants. The shoes step over me and my eyes follow them. There's a tear inside of me. Every time my heart beats, I can feel a wave of warm blood gushing out into my chest cavity. The door jangles, pushed open, and I can suddenly see across the expanse of concrete. Oh. There's a girl, a little African-American girl, in that pickup. I didn't see her before. She's banging her fists together against the window. Taped or tied. There's tape over her mouth. I can't hear what she's yelling. Now I can't see her. He's in the way. Someone is phoning 911 behind me. He gets into the pickup, and she disappears. Another spurt of blood. My mouth is slack, open like a fish. I'm trying to suck oxygen in, but eve-rything seems to be running out of me. The hole in my chest has stopped burning. I can't feel much anymore. My fingers and feet feel cold. Someone—it must be the woman behind me—is crying hysterically and talking too fast, and the hick gas station owner is standing next to me. He wants to kneel down, but he's afraid to touch me. Because I'm Muslim? No. He just doesn't want to get my blood on him. He's shouting something at the woman. I want to tell them to both shut up because I can't hear myself think, but everything is starting to look gray, and it doesn't matter anymore.

"Suction."

I'm dead. This is how I die. Thirty-five years and it ends in this stupid gas station because I stopped for cigarettes after I got gas on my way to a deposition. I didn't even get to eat lunch. The deposition! My meeting with Kyle this afternoon. Cynthia's going to have to reschedule everything. Reschedule! What am I talking about? Amir! I'm supposed to pick him up from school. Does Rasa know? Someone has to get a message to my wife at the clinic.

"I'm getting flashes ... some random images of a woman."

Rasa! Yes! I try to make my mouth work again. My head feels like it's pinned within a vise. I struggle to picture Rasa's face. How she looked this morning, tying her hijab in the mirror before she left for work.

"Part of the gas station?"

"No, the background's wrong."

Losing air again ... seeping away. I know there's another breath coming, but not in time. Not soon enough!

The nurse's voice cuts in: "Noradrenaline level climbing. EEG shows he's moving into Stage 3. We're losing him."

"How much more time do we have?"

"A couple minutes at the most. I stitched up the main hole in the artery, but there's too much damage. Everything we're putting into him is just draining into the abdomen."

"Shit. Let's go again."

Shock as I'm thrown back into the daylight world. I can feel myself standing. I'm standing in front of the door. John Doe, whoever he is, holds his pistol, not sure which one of us he should be aiming at. I'm still alive. I haven't been shot yet. I dart a look sideways at the woman in the blue silk blouse and dark skirt. She's got her hand in her purse, like she might be reaching for a phone.

"Just don't ... nobody make any sudden movements, okay?" I hear my voice say. I realize that I'm not really here, but they keep sending me back to this time. Maybe I have a chance here. Maybe I can change what happens. Maybe that is why they're sending me back.

"Focus, Fareed!" It's Hiro yelling. My mind opens back to the scene in front of me.

There's a click of a round being chambered in a semiautomatic. The gas station owner, a thirty-something white guy with a round, bald head, red and sparkling with sweat, brings up a gun.

"Whoa!" I say. He's pointing it across the counter at John, but if his aim's off by just a little, it could be me who gets shot here. "Just calm down. Everybody calm down," I say sharply.

"Is this a robbery? Are you in on this?" the owner demands, turning fully on me. "I have a gun!" I don't think he's seen the girl.

Off to my right, I hear the woman as she quietly starts to cry. A whimper or moaning sound, something so pathetic it makes me feel sick. "Whoa," I say again. "Nobody's going to get hurt. We can deal with this." I try to catch John's eye. Damp patches are soaking through the underarms of his jacket. I think he's just as scared as the rest of us. "I'm a lawyer. I'm not a criminal lawyer, but I know people who can help you. You just need to put the gun down, okay?"

"I can't," John says, somewhat pitifully.

"Drop your weapon!" the gas station owner barks at him. Coming out of his mouth it sounds like something he's seen on TV. I don't think he really knows what's going on with the little girl in the car. He's hyped up on adrenaline at this point. He keeps adjusting his stance and checking his trigger finger. It's his hero moment.

"Calm down!" I yell at him. My fingers have gone numb, my brain is racing, but I tell myself I can do this. I can fix this if I can keep my cool, so I refocus on John in front of me and make my voice steady. "Just, put down the gun. It's not too late to let the girl go and make this right."

There's a stifled noise from inside the woman's purse.

John whirls around with his pistol. The woman screams as she drops her purse onto the floor. We can all hear the tinny voice in the bottom of her bag: "911 operator. What is your emergency?"

"Please don't shoot me! Please don't shoot! I'm sorry!" she's sobbing.

"Don't shoot. Don't be stupid. I can get you out of this," I hear myself saying as I drop the cigarette on the floor and reach into the breast pocket of my suit coat jacket for my card. There's a deafening explosion.

The nurse's voice, sharply, warning: "V-fib. He's going into cardiac arrest!"

I just died. Again.

Now the surgeon's slippery, gloved hands ... God! They're inside my chest. Revulsion sweeps through me. I don't even know if they've put a sheet over my body. But it doesn't matter: I am more naked than naked. Some mechanical thing is forcing my ribs apart and he has his hands in my chest, squeezing my heart, and I hate him, even though I know he's trying to stretch out my life by a few seconds. I send Rasa's picture to Hiro over and over. Her dark hair. Her dark, bright eyes. *Please,* I beg, as the hands squeeze my heart unnaturally into rhythm. I'm never going to see my wife or son again.

"We're going to have to let him go," the surgeon is saying.

"One more!" Hiro says. "Give me one more. Fareed, are you listening? The girl, Fareed. Concentrate on the girl. I need you to tell me where he's taking her. He knows we're after him. We need to get this guy before he decides to kill her."

And just like that the cold and the pain and the darkness are gone. I'm outside, whole, breathing fresh air. Relatively fresh air, with the strong, sweet, suffocating stench of gasoline. The sun is shining and I can see the trees across the parkway: vibrant green and gold and brown like I've never experienced color before. There's a click and I turn my head to the left. The automatic gas pump has shut off. A beat-up white pickup truck pulls into the station as I replace the nozzle. The sound of the truck cuts out as it parks five feet in front of my car. The bed of the truck is filled with dust-covered stone saws and drills and portable tool chests. I see the Illinois license plate mounted below the front grill and the part of me that was not there when I was there thinks: *Got you, you bastard.*

The pickup cab door opens and a man in a worn, faded brown suit steps out, crumpling a Wendy's bag in one hand. I can't see the girl—I don't know she's there yet. He walks around the front of the truck, tosses the bag into the trash can, and heads into the store. I'm reaching for the door of my BMW while my left hand is feeling in my jacket pocket, and I remember the pack is almost empty: two cigarettes. I could buy more later, but I might as well get them here. I turn away from my car and start walking across the concrete expanse. I remember, rather than sense, that I am walking past a tan Ford Taurus, past the firewood and ice for sale, because all I can think about is the door in front of me. I try to push it away, but I'm already reaching for the handle. *No!* I'm screaming at myself, but I don't hear. This thing they have me in isn't a time machine; only a machine, extracting residual memories, the emanations of a dying brain.

There's a woman somewhere toward the back of the store by a wall of refrigerated drinks. I glance to where she's standing, but there's only a blank gray hole, and that scares me more than anything that's happened yet. Already I'm stopping in front of the counter to squint up at the signs. $34.56 for a carton of Marlboro. Unbelievable. My dad used to pay about $2 for a pack of Kents, less than a dollar if he bought domestic, at the crowded wholesale shops on Molavi Street, south of the bazaar in Tehran. *Well, it's only money,* I think.

Concentric ripples spreading out until they lose their shape. Will there be a *barzakh* waiting for my *nafs* as my mother believed? I have kept Halal, and fasted, and even made my pilgrimage, once, when I was a boy, but it's been years since I believed in God. My mother and her superstitious beliefs. My mother … I wonder if she'll be waiting for me.

"I'll take a pack of Marlboro Gold." One hand goes into my right pants pocket for my billfold, and my eyes briefly make contact with the owner behind the counter. A real redneck. The kind of guy who thinks all Muslims are terrorists and bad guys. *This is the asshole who killed me! For no reason!* I want to scream, but instead I feel my former self flashing a quick friendly smile—to show him I'm one of the good ones—as I hand over three dollars plus change. He's saying something to me, but all the sound is drained out.

I see without hearing: the restroom door opens to my left and the man in the brown suit emerges, running one hand through his lank hair and wiping the other on the leg of his pants. The Hispanic woman has her soda tucked under one arm between her chest and her purse as she pushes silent buttons on the Lottery machine.

I head for the door, or rather where I know the door to be, because it's flickering in and out. Automatically, I unwrap the pack and shake out a cigarette. I know what's coming and I try to stop myself, to freeze time, to make it run more slowly, but I can't. I put the unlit cigarette between my teeth.

There are voices talking over each other in the darkness outside of the scene I am in. Someone new I don't know says: "… drugged; they're working on her now. Found the pickup pulled over near the woods on Route 72. Walter Drummond … 39 … registered sex-offender. Works for Arlington Heights headstone and engraving company ... called in sick this morning. Plates matched a Dodge pickup on video at a drive-thru around 8:20 a.m., couple miles from where the kid-brother ... Ordered breakfast for two."

"BP's dropping," the OR nurse's voice says. Around me people are clapping, congratulating each other. The cold in my fingers and toes and arms and legs is becoming more intense, crawling through my damaged organs toward my heart. *Rasa,* I think, trying to hold onto her name, her face. The images are dissolving, slipping away too quickly.

Hiro, sounding exhausted, says, "You can let him go. Tell the grandmother. Call the school and tell them we've got her." He pauses. "Did you hear that, Fareed? We got her! You did it!" He sounds as if he is very far away, but he must still be standing next to me because he squeezes my unresponsive shoulder.

Someone peels back each sticky eyelid and I hear the double click of a penlight above the irises that no longer feel like they belong to me. The last breath of oxygenated air from the ventilator is slowly escaping out and I know there won't be any more coming in. The plastic intubation is pulled roughly out of my throat. It doesn't hurt because I am dwindling down to a point, a spark, something that is less than nothing. To God we belong and to Him is our return. In my imagination, the elder whispers the prayer call into my right ear; the first sound of my infancy, the echo so faint.

The surgeon's voice asks, "Are we done here?" but I never hear the reply.

REFLECTIONS OF MISS AVA

Phyllis Humby

A HOT SUMMER NIGHT 1941.

Seeing Ava's nearly naked body and a small black hole in her chest shook me up. She'd aged, but hell, she was still beautiful. It seemed like yesterday that I first laid eyes on Miss Ava. I was a young buck, still wet behind the ears. She was the most gorgeous and talented fan dancer in the business. Man, she was a doll.

Her hair looked different now-bleached out and dry. Not like I remembered. I wondered if it still smelled of lemons. My lip curled into a wannabe grin at the memory of her rinsing her hair in what looked like a sink full of lemonade. It all came back in a rush. The year I worked for Ava, what it led to, and what it cost me. I stretched my neck and ran a finger around the inside of my collar. I gave up everything for this dame and then walked away.

Normally not the first one on the scene, tonight it worked in my favor. The boys would have been shocked to see Detective Gerry Stone wiping tears from his eyes. My gut clenched as I looked around her dismal digs. A big change from the lifestyle she had when she headlined for the Roxy. *What happened, Ava? When did it all turn to shit?*

The steel fan in the corner of the room moved the air in a sluggish swirl. I tipped my fedora back and wiped the cold sweat from my face. Despite the sweltering temperature that had built up in the tenement during the week-long heat wave, I shivered. I didn't feel so good. Warped sashes and layers of old paint made it nearly impossible to jimmy open the window, but after some brute persuasion, I leaned out of the second story for a gulp of humid night air.

The sound of a flash and pop turned my attention back to the crime scene. Lurching like an uncoordinated animal, my partner, Detective MacArthur, shuffled around the bed for a shot from every angle, the camera pressed into his fleshy face. His open jacket revealed a sweat-soaked shirt barely tucked inside his pants.

"Took you long enough to get here." I was always jibing him, but the truth was we worked pretty well together. Although not quite a good-guy bad-guy combination, our blend of well-groomed and rumpled still seemed to throw some people off in interrogation.

My partner, more Neanderthal than man, black hair curling around his shirt cuffs and covering his knuckles, responded with a low, appraising whistle. It's what I expected from him. Dead or alive, Big Man, as he was known by cops and crooks alike, loved the ladies. He finished taking pictures. "Judging from the powder on the wound, it's a close-range shot–probably a Derringer."

Big Man also noted the silk scarf draped over the lampshade. The resulting amber glow across the bed is a trick hookers use to soften the telltale signs of age. "Most likely a john. Do we know who she is?" His breathing came in labored pants as if it had been an exertion to manipulate the camera's shutter.

"Her stage name is Miss Ava. Or at least it was."

"You knew this broad, Gerry?"

"Yeah, I knew her." Our history was well known down at the station, but Big Man wasn't around back then. "The first time I saw Miss Ava perform …" I cleared my throat. My partner motioned for me to continue. "… it was at a dime-a-time burlesque joint on Forsythe. Within a few years, she was the headliner at the Roxy." I had to look away. "Think her dancing days have been over for a while."

I could have given him more background but I didn't feel like talking. Pointing out two smudged glasses hot and sticky with liquor, I said, "Get the fingerprints. See if we get lucky enough to nail somebody who matches them."

Big Man pulled out a cigar, held it between his teeth, and thrust his hand in a pocket for his Zippo. He took a languid puff and checked the fire on the tip before responding. "When the grunts show up, let them dust for prints. Where the hell are they?"

"We'll be lucky to see any. This heat wave has crime coming out their asses." Still feeling a little weak in the knees, I pulled a cigarette from my crumpled pack and struck a match, hoping Big Man didn't notice the tremor in my hands.

"How'd you get here before me?"

"I was hanging out at the station when an anonymous call came in. Got here fast. I already talked to the nearest neighbor, a Ronnie Beele." I pointed my chin in the direction of the door across the hall. "He needs checking out again. In the meantime, do like I said and dust the glasses."

Hearing his protests about going back down to the car for the kit meant that Big Man couldn't make it down two flights and back up without a breather. "Take the camera with you and drop the film off to get developed. The fingerprints can wait until you return."

Big Man wiped the dripping sweat from his jowls and closed the door behind him, muffling the sound of his lumbering retreat.

Relieved to have my partner out of the way, I checked the record player next to the bed. Earlier, I'd stopped the scratching of the needle at the end of the 78 and flipped down the lid. Now I was curious to know what she'd been listening to when she died.

It was Debussy's *Claire de Lune*—the trademark music of Miss Ava's legendary fan dance. It triggered intimate memories best forgotten. I pressed two fingers against my eye sockets and massaged the bridge of my nose. Ava was wearing one of those short wraps that revealed more than it covered. In death, it looked more crude than sexy. I thought of covering her, but the remembrance of her mocking laugh ricocheted off the faded walls. I began a search of the room.

Fragrant powder coated the tips of my fingers as I looked for a note or phone number among the face creams and compacts scattered across her dresser. Bent, lipstick-smeared cigarettes and cold ashes filled a china saucer. Pawing through the bobby pins and combs made me think of her dressing table in the swanky room where we rendezvoused, back when she paid me to protect her from overzealous patrons.

There were three snapshots tucked under the frame of the mirror. I pulled the first one down for a closer look. It was a shot of Ava and me. The club photographer had snapped it at her request. My thumb left moistness on the edge of her bare shoulder as I studied the picture. I swallowed past the lump in my throat. Did this mean she'd still had feelings for me? Sweat beaded my forehead.

The next picture from the mirror was a professional shot. Strategically placed feathers, a sultry expression, and nothing else. The last snap might be a lead. Bert Romner, the owner of the Roxy, had his arm draped across Ava's shoulders. There was a long cigarette holder in her slim fingers and a glass of champagne at her elbow. Her flirty smile was like a punch to the gut. She was looking at Romner the way she used to look at me. Screw protocol, I slid all three pictures to the inside pocket of my jacket.

A red-kissed tissue at the edge of the dresser fluttered onto the floor. A movement like a shadow reflected in the mirror. Behind me, Miss Ava was sitting on the edge of the bed. Long thick lashes and porcelain skin. Her lips curving into a teasing smile. The look that always turned my legs to jelly and made everything else hard. I knew better, but that didn't stop my heart from jumping around in my chest. I turned. The flashing lights from across the street shone like a strobe on her rouged face. But she wasn't sitting up. She was lying on her back with her eyes closed. Dead.

I lit another cigarette and wandered back to the open window. Watching the flickering lights of the Roxy, I wondered why Ava wanted to live within sight of the club where she became famous. And where she fell from grace.

My search of the room continued. When I swung open the door of the wardrobe cabinet, ostrich feathers floated out and caught my pant legs. I brushed them off. Sequins winked from the dark corners of the near-empty closet like stars in a black sky. Her stage clothes might have been here at one time, but there was nothing left of them except for a few feathers and sequins. Dressing gowns and street clothes infused with Tabu hung on padded hangers from the rod. The scent of her fragrance took me back. Blinking hard against the seductive images in my mind, I slid the hangers aside and began rooting through hatboxes and ankle-strapped heels looking for something without knowing what. Disappointed that the hatboxes held nothing but hats, I reached to the back corner for the only shoebox in the wardrobe.

I carried the box to the overstuffed chair near the open window and sat back against a layer of black lingerie. Seamed stockings with brown heels and toes lay pooled on the floor. I resisted the urge to feel their silkiness against my cheek. Even though Ava lay dead a few feet away, the image of her peeling them off one at a time with her foot poised on the seat of the chair caused a stir in my groin.

Despair settled into the hollow of my shoulders and rested like a stone in my chest. A part bottle of Four Roses was an arm's length away. Though I doubted the fingerprints on this bottle would be any different from what we'd get off the glasses, I used a handkerchief from my pocket to remove the cap. I tipped the bottle to my mouth. The bourbon burned like lava spilling from a volcano. Perspiration trickled down my temple. Cursing the muggy night air, I flipped the lid off the shoebox in the frustrated search for a motive, a clue, something that pointed to Ava's killer.

Dog-eared show programs and Roxy playbills spilled onto the floor. There were pictures—mostly PR shots—dried flower petals, theatre stubs, and a packet of yellowed envelopes. I started with the envelopes.

In scrolling cursive, the first document revealed that Miss Ava's real name was Hazel Pearl Carson. Born in Kingston in 1896. That made her eight years older than me—three years older than she claimed. Forty-five. Too young to die.

The boys from the mortuary hadn't showed yet. I glanced at my watch and pulled open another envelope containing three documents: a marriage certificate from 1912 and two birth certificates. A baby girl in 1913 and a boy two years later. Skeletons emerge during every investigation. I wrote down the name of the husband and the information from the birth certificates.

Tugging another smoke from my diminishing pack of Camels, I went back to the open window, took a deep haul, and emptied my lungs into the flashing nightlights of Queen Street. The mortuary wagon pulled up to the curb. I rested my forearms on the windowsill and watched the attendants get the stretcher and slam the doors shut, before turning my attention across the street. Steady streams of people were passing through the shiny-red entrance of the Roxy. I'd be paying Bert Romner a visit very soon.

"Done with her?" an attendant asked.

The question hung in the air. I looked over at Ava's body and made a silent promise. The same promise any good cop makes. The investigation would never end until the person who pulled the trigger was behind bars—or dead. Personally, the latter sat better with me. I nodded, and the men lifted the body onto the stretcher. My hand twitched with the urge to touch Miss Ava's cheek or squeeze her hand before the guys from Sid's pulled the sheet over her body. I resisted.

Moments later, a skinny-kid patrolman pushed the door open.

"Detective Stone, do you need me here, sir?"

"Yeah. Stay here. Detective MacArthur's coming back to dust for prints. Make sure no one else comes in." Looking back at the contents of the shoebox strewn on the floor, I added, "Don't touch anything."

—

It was raining when I returned to the apartment house on Queen a couple of hours later. I took the stairs two at a time and let myself in. The smell of cigars and death lingered. The floor beneath the open window was slick as the stifling heat finally gave way to a balmy breeze. The damp curtains swayed like rags on a clothesline. I sank into the upholstered cushions and drummed my fingers against the cigarette burns on the arm of the chair. The coroner confirmed the cause of death as a single shot to the heart from a .41 caliber Derringer. No sign of a struggle. Maybe she'd been asleep. I stroked the stubble on my jaw.

Big Man blew through the door. "Gave everyone in this rat hole an early wake up call. Nobody knows nothin'. Anything in here to give us a lead?" He flipped the mattress off the bed, revealing nothing but rusted springs.

My partner ran through crime scenes like he was bulldozing a construction site. His hat sat low over his right eye. A sweat stain rippled the bottom of the band. Clapping his beefy hands, he said, "So where do we go from here?"

Leaning back in the chair, I rubbed the tiredness from my face. The haunting melody of *Clair de Lune* was playing in my head along with images of feathered fans sweeping across Miss Ava's flawless body.

Thunder rumbled in the dawn air as if the storm was just beginning. I stood up, shot my cuffs, and smoothed my jacket. "Let's go for breakfast." Walking over the memorabilia left on the floor, I pulled the door shut behind us.

At Lizzie's diner I filled my partner in about my visit to the Roxy. "Romner tried to deny he'd ever had anything to do with Ava. Judging from that picture I found, I'd say they were head over heels."

The waitress dropped off two plates piled high with bacon and eggs. A double order. She brought Big Man's usual for the both of us.

"Think he shot her?" Big Man attacked his breakfast with the relish of a lion ripping through the hindquarters of a buffalo.

Pushing away my plate, untouched, I reached for my coffee and thought back to Romner's denial that he knew anything about Ava. *"Nah, I never saw Ava since she left here."*

"You didn't know she lived across the street? C'mon. She was your star attraction."

"Was. Ain't no more. Had no use for her. Never kept in touch."

The fancy office and big desk didn't fool me. Everything about Romner spelled gangster, from his hand-painted nudie tie to the way he talked. He was lying through his teeth and I knew it.

My partner waited for an answer. "My gut says no. If I didn't know better, I'd say he was pretty shook up hearing that she was dead."

"Why'd he fire her from the club?" Big Man spit out the words as he mopped his toast through the runny eggs.

"It was rumored a few years back that Ava was fighting the bottle. Romner admitted that he had to let her go. Hoped she'd straighten up. She was on the booze pretty heavy and missed a few shows. But she ..."

Big Man, his fork suspended between his plate and his mouth, looked up. "But she ... what?"

He grimaced when I stubbed my cigarette in the center of my breakfast. "But she only drank when she was upset or depressed."

My partner's brows shot up. "Romner told you that?"

"Nah, I knew everything about Ava. It was before you transferred to this precinct. A few years back, Ava hired me as an escort. It was my job to make sure she didn't get hassled. We got to know each other." The silence that followed as Big Man slurped his last bits of breakfast told the rest of the story.

—

"You saw something. You had to. Your apartment is right across from hers." As with the previous interview, I wedged my foot in the door opening. My sleep-deprived, don't-piss-me-off attitude intimidated the sallow-faced young man. Beele put his cigarette to his mouth for several short puffs before responding. "Yeah, I told you before that I knew Ava. Who didn't?"

Something about the guy told me that questioning him about a romantic involvement wasn't an avenue of interest. "Who visited Miss Ava yesterday afternoon?"

"I wasn't home. I have a job selling art around the corner on York."

"Tell me what you know about her visitors." I pushed forward against the door and Beele took another quick puff on his cigarette.

"She didn't have many. I never heard anything. No arguing. Nothing. I don't know who shot her."

"How do you know she was shot?"

Ronnie Beele's eyes darted back and forth. He began babbling. I leaned into the door, forcing it open wider, and then stepped inside the apartment. "Look, you little weasel, talk, and talk fast."

"I'd never hurt Ava, honest. She was nice to me. A good person."

With a little more persuasion from me, he opened up. He'd gone over to visit Ava, discovered her body, and placed the anonymous call to the police. He didn't want to get involved.

The kid tried to light another cigarette but it fell from his shaking hands to the floor. There was a feather on the worn rug and I remembered the ostrich feathers that had clung to my pant legs earlier. I must have missed that one.

—

I'd exhausted all suspects. The jilted husband was dead from a car wreck. It's not likely that Ava's grown children had hunted their runaway mother down and killed her in cold blood. But just in case, I had Big Man looking for them; Ava deserved that.

The sound of blaring horns and curses passed through the open windows of my car as I parked in front of Ava's building. Tempers were getting shorter as the day got hotter. My fingers drummed against the steering wheel while I waited for Big Man. I was overlooking something. But what? The other residents hadn't noticed unusual amounts of traffic to Ava's door. She wasn't hooking. That was a relief.

Big Man approached and swung his body into the vehicle. The springs groaned and then relaxed on his side of the car. "A couple of the tenants admitted seeing a guy visit Ava's apartment a few times over. No one could identify him except to say he always wore his hat tipped low over his face and was a good dresser."

"That makes sense. A married man keeping Ava in booze and bonbons. It's time to find out who this fancy man is and whether he carries a fancy little gun in his pocket."

I flicked my cigarette butt out the window and climbed the two flights of stairs for another visit–the third one–to Beele, Ava's neighbor. That kid vibrated like he was scared to death. I wanted to know why.

There was no answer to my knock and the knob turned under my hand. Not a stickler for proper police procedure, I stepped inside the tidy apartment. The thin-faced tenant sashayed into view. We both froze. Beele recovered first. He fled to another room, leaving ostrich feathers in his wake. It wasn't often anything shocked me in this line of work, but his little masquerade jolted me.

"Get your clothes on and get out here." Even to my ears, my voice sounded more like the bark of a Doberman.

Ronnie Beele slunk back to the living room and fell into the closest chair.

"How'd you get those fans, kid? Give me some answers before I beat them out of you."

Instead of answering, he buried his face in a cushion.

In one long stride, I ripped the cushion away and flung it across the room. His shoulders felt like chicken bones under my hands when I gave him a rough shake. "Answer me."

It took an upraised hand before Beele stuttered a reply. "I'll tell you. Don't hurt me."

I pushed him back onto his chair and stepped away.

"Ava showed me how to use the feathered fans. When I saw her … when I knew that … well, somebody would be clearing her room anyway." He straightened his posture and raised his chin. "Ava would want me to have them."

"Look you sniveling piece of shit," He crouched down when I lunged for him. "I don't care what you think. It's stealing. I'll run you in right now unless you give me some information that will lead to Ava's killer."

Ten minutes later I was crossing the road to Roxy's, prepared to strong-arm Romner into telling the truth.

It didn't take long for Bert Romner to break. He came clean. He and Ava had been lovers for years, right from the time she'd had been a dancer at the club. I did the math and realized we'd both been suckers.

Romner convinced Ava to give up dancing because he didn't want other men sniffing around her all the time. He put her up in a nice apartment. Everything was going great until his wife found out about it. It seemed that Romner and I had a lot in common.

A couple of months after he broke it off, Ava surprised him by moving into the building across the street from the club. Eventually, they started seeing each other again. Romner's downcast eyes and hangdog expression exposed him as being weak, not a cold-blooded killer. Another dead end.

I left the club and, with no particular plan in mind, cruised along Queen until my stomach thought my throat was cut. I turned onto Bay Street, and headed for Lizzie's.

When my coffee and fried-egg sandwich arrived, I was reviewing my notes. So far, Big Man hadn't located Ava's family. It didn't feel like a viable lead anyway, but they had a right to know that, officially, they were orphans. I pulled some change from my pocket, dropped it on the counter, and headed to the restroom at the rear of the diner.

I was taking a leak when a switch in my brain turned on a light. I was still double-checking the fly on my pants when I stepped into the phone booth outside the restroom door. Though it had been years, the number was on the tip of my tongue when the operator answered.

After a few words, I hung up the phone and left the diner.

At first, it was awkward. For both of us. She'd agreed to see me when she heard it was imperative to solving a murder. I hadn't told her whose. We sized each other up. It was the first time we'd been together since our divorce. Her rigid posture and upraised chin showed an unyielding strength. The warmth of character that I remembered was gone, and I wondered if I was to blame. She was probably seeing something different in me, too. Not sure I wanted to know what. There was a time when this woman was the center of my world–before Miss Ava knocked it off its axis.

Exhaling a stuttered breath, I looked down at my interlocked fingers and white knuckles. "Isabel, how did you find out about my affair with Miss Ava?"

If she'd been prepared for anything, it wasn't this. Her forehead buckled into a frown. With an incredulous look, Isabel asked why I wanted to know. I somehow convinced her it was important. What she told me set me back. But it also moved me closer to solving Ava's murder. As for Isabel and I, well, time doesn't always change things.

When I arrived back at the station, Big Man was waiting. Ava's offspring checked out. They both still lived in Kingston and had an alibi for the night of the murder. Aside from the shock of hearing about their mother, the call didn't seem to render much emotion.

I tossed him his hat. "C'mon let's go."

—

It was a brick two story with impressive white pillars. A long way from the downtown burlesque district. On the way there, I told Big Man the rest of my sad story. How I'd lost my wife before our second anniversary. How I'd then walked out on Ava. How, when the dust settled, I'd hurt everybody. And in case he hadn't figured it out for himself, I told him what a bastard I was.

Mrs. Romner opened the shiny, black door and greeted us with an arch of her penciled brow. It was instant dislike on my part–and possibly hers. Judging from the way her nostrils flared, she was either nervous or we smelled bad. I always kept clean, but Big Man thought good hygiene meant an extra slap of Old Spice. She allowed us into the house and led us to the living room. When informed that we were investigating the murder of Miss Ava, she feigned ignorance of the woman's existence.

"You must remember Miss Ava, Mrs. Romner," I began. "She was the star dancer at the Roxy a few years back."

"What goes on at the Roxy is no concern of mine. Believe me."

Her uppity attitude didn't fool me. She was no higher on the ladder than her husband.

With deliberate ease, I turned in my chair and looked around the stylishly furnished room. "It seems to provide a good living."

Christine Romner bristled. I liked that. I liked knowing I could get a rise out of this snooty dame.

Using an old interrogation technique, I leaned forward in my chair, cutting the distance between me and my number-one suspect, and broached the subject of her husband's affair with the dancer.

Her eyes blazed like blue ice crystals. "That was over long ago, and it's none of your business."

"You thought it was over long ago. That is, until you received a call from Ava. Isn't that right?"

A flush crept up Christine Romner's neck and settled high on her cheeks. "That's nonsense. My husband would never have anything to do with that tramp. Call her a dancer; just a little trollop parading around naked with a few feathers."

"But he did. You just admitted that yourself." Big Man sneered, enjoying his part in rattling the flustered woman into making another mistake.

Mrs. Romner jumped to her feet and made a beeline for the front door. "My husband will see to it that you never bother decent people again. He has friends in high places."

Our conversation was over. Or so she thought.

Leaning toward her, I spoke in a near whisper. "One more thing, Christine, where were you last night? Before you answer, you should know that we spoke to your housekeeper. She said you left the house after receiving a phone call. It was around eight o'clock." My voice, soft and sympathetic, in contrast to Big Man's mocking tone, knocked her further off balance.

"I was nowhere near ... I visited a friend. She lives not far from here. But she's not home now. She went to visit her cousin in Milwaukee. I'd be happy to let you know when she returns."

"You do that. In the meantime, I'll be back with a search warrant. We're looking for a small-caliber Derringer." I touched the tip of my fedora in farewell as me and Big Man returned to the car. I pulled away from the curb slowly and then shifted into high gear. I sped up the street, circled the block, and waited.

From our new vantage point, we saw Mrs. Romner leave her house. We followed her cab downtown and pulled into the first vacant spot behind where she got out. Under our watch, she leisurely strolled past store windows. At the corner she stopped. Pulling a small paper bag from her pocket, she dropped it in the municipal trash bin.

We had her.

Big Man retrieved the weapon. With a hand under each elbow, we escorted her back to the car where we took our time cuffing her as shoppers along the street gawked and pointed. It was a short trip to the station for booking.

During interrogation, Christine confirmed that Ava had demanded that she give Bert a divorce. Christine didn't believe her husband was cheating again and Ava told her to see for herself. After seeing Bert leave Ava's building, Christine went to the apartment to confront her.

It was Ava's fault, she said. She hadn't meant to kill her—only scare her away from Bert. When Ava saw the Derringer, she grabbed for it. The gun fired. Ava was dead by the time she fell back on the bed. When we asked Christine why she hadn't gotten rid of the gun right away, she told us she couldn't. It had been a gift from Bert.

Just like that, the mystery was over. For old times' sake, I dropped by the Roxy for a drink and to catch the show. Shivers slid down my spine when a dancer glided onstage to the melody of *Clair de Lune*. I'm not big on coincidence. I looked around for Bert Romner. He wasn't there. I left the club.

I stopped at the curb to light a cigarette. Drops of rain spotted my jacket. Looking up at the building across the street, I noticed the amber glow in the second-floor window. And more. Her unmistakable reflection stared down at me.

Memories. Regrets. Grief. I looked down at the ground as emotions pelted me like the rain bouncing off the pavement. For a split second, lightening turned night into day. I turned my face to hers again. Thunder rumbled across the sky.

And then she was gone.

It's a damn good story. If you have any comments,
write them on the back of a check.

Erle Stanley Gardner

DETECTIVE SHOW #2647

Monte A. Anderson

FADE IN:

INT. HOTEL ROOM - DAY

Man and woman in bed making love. The woman is on top. Camera shots from six different angles.

CLOSE UP on MARTHA ANDREWS' face.

CUT TO: FRONT OF HOTEL

CHRIS ANDREWS enters, walks through lobby, takes elevator to 44th floor, walks down hallway, stops at a room, takes out a set of burglary tools and picks the lock. Opens door and walks in.

> **CHRIS**
> Martha?

> **MARTHA**
> Chris! Don't you ever knock?

> **CHRIS**
> Martha! What is going on?

> **MARTHA**
> Jumping out of bed and pulling a sheet around herself.

> Don't be stupid. You can see what is going on. Or can't you remember?

CHRIS
Why, Martha? I love you. I will for-
give you.

MARTHA
I love you, too. I will always love
you. I am just not IN LOVE with you.

CHRIS
What the hell does that mean?

MARTHA
I don't know. It's in the script. I
just read the lines. I do not have to
understand them.

CHRIS
Who is this guy?

MARTHA
Who? I'll tell you who. It is a man
who loves me. He loves me for who I
am, not who he expects me to be. He
loves me for myself. He is concerned
about my emotional needs. He treats me
with respect, not like some trophy
wife.

CHRIS
No, I mean what's his name?

MARTHA
If you must know, his name is John.

BILL
Actually, my name is Bill. Bill Smith.

CHRIS
Yeah, right.

MARTHA
Shut up, Bill! Keep out of this. This
is between my husband and me.

                    BILL
Getting out of bed.

        I didn't realize you were married.
        Perhaps, I should go.

Starts to dress.

                    MARTHA
        No, stay. I'll get rid of him.

                    BILL
        I have to get back to work anyway.

                    CHRIS
        Why him?

                    MARTHA
Starts to dress.

        He is twice the man you are.

                    CHRIS
        That's because he must weigh 500
        pounds.

                    BILL
        Please! I weigh 450 pounds and not an
        ounce more.

                    CHRIS
        How could you, Martha?

                    MARTHA
        Well, I have to stay on top.

                    CHRIS
        No, I mean how could you do this to
        me?

Martha gives Chris a quizzical look.

CHRIS
I am talking about our marriage. How
could you do this to our marriage?

MARTHA
Oh, come on! We have been married for
two weeks. How long did you expect me
to be faithful?

CHRIS
Longer than two weeks.

MARTHA
You should have said something.

BILL
Do the words, FORSAKING ALL OTHERS
mean anything to you?

MARTHA
No. Should they?

CHRIS
They were part of our marriage vows.

MARTHA
Again, if it was in the script, I
don't have to know what it means.

BILL
How much do I owe you?

MARTHA
Two hundred. Same as last week.

BILL
Will I see you again?

MARTHA
Of course. Next week. Same time.

Bill hands Martha two one-hundred-dollar
bills. They kiss.

> **BILL**
> See you next week.

Bill exits. Martha holds one of the bills up to the light.

> **MARTHA**
> Stop him! These bills are counterfeit!

Chris pulls out his gun and runs after Bill. He sees Bill get into an elevator but the doors close before he can stop it. Chris runs down 45 flights of stairs and exits in the basement. He then runs up one flight of stairs to the first floor. He searches the lobby frantically. He sees Bill outside getting into a car.

QUICK CUT: Chris runs outside just as Martha pulls up in a Corvette.

> **MARTHA**
> Get in!

Chris gets into the car and Martha speeds off after Bill.

> **CHRIS**
> How did you get here so fast?

> **MARTHA**
> Special effects.

> **CHRIS**
> That's a different outfit. What's with the mini-skirt? You usually wear pant-suits.

> **MARTHA**
> The director wants to show off my legs.

> **CHRIS**
> Well, you look fantastic. How come your hair is perfect and now you have

makeup on? Where did you find the
time?

                    MARTHA
Look! Can we hold off on the interrogation until we catch this guy? You
know damn well that we shot the hotel
scene yesterday. Today is the car
chase scene. Besides, my contract says
I have to look good. The studio has to
give me six close-up headshots per
episode.

                    CHRIS
Don't lose him.

                    MARTHA
You always say that. I never lose
them. Now go ahead and say the other
word.

                    CHRIS
What other word?

                    MARTHA
You know damn well. Every car chase
scene you say it.

                    CHRIS
Faster?

SERIES OF SHOTS-TYPICAL CAR CHASE SCENES

Cars skid around corners and run other cars
off the road. More police cars join the
chase. Finally, Bill's car crashes, flipping
over a dozen times and exploding in flames.
Bill emerges unhurt with his hands up. The
police are so ticked they shoot him anyway.

                    CHRIS
Removes Bill's wallet.

        Let's see who this guy really is.

Opens wallet.

>His driver's license says his name is
>Bill Smith.

>**MARTHA**
>What the...? Wait a minute.

Takes out the hundred-dollar bills and holds
them up to the light.

>I guess the joke's on me. These bills
>aren't phony after all. My bad.

Chris takes out his service pistol and
points it at Martha.

>**MARTHA**
>What are you doing? What's going on?

>**CHRIS**
>Come on, Martha. You've been around
>long enough to know that when the stu-
>dio does not renew your contract, the
>writers write you out of the series.
>Your contract expires next week.

>**MARTHA**
>Don't do it, Chris. If we stick to-
>gether, we can both get better con-
>tracts.

>**CHRIS**
>Too late. I already signed a new
>agreement. I get a bedroom scene and
>eight close-up headshots in every epi-
>sode. Goodbye, Martha. It's been great
>working with you.

>**MARTHA**
>Wait! The studio will never find a re-
>placement for my character by next ep-
>isode.

                    CHRIS
        They have already. You remember that
        young woman that we hired as an intern
        two episodes ago?

                    MARTHA
        You mean that twenty-something with
        the silicone breasts?

                    CHRIS
        Uh, yeah, that one. In the next epi-
        sode she's promoted to detective first
        class and takes your place.

                    MARTHA
        No! If you shoot me, I will never work
        with you again. Do you know what that
        means?

                    CHRIS
        Sorry, Darling, but it's in the
        script. I don't have to know what it
        means.

Chris shoots Martha three times. He walks over to
her body and shoots her in the head for good
measure.

FADE OUT

i finally know
how a girl disappears

Kari Ann Ebert

she has been hollowed out
broken open in the heat
scraped clean
residue removed
an empty cistern
in the dead of summer
even her marrow
has been sucked dry
the echoes of stream
and ocean vanish
into her shrunken gourd
the cavity
whistles clean through

Still, it doesn't do to murder people,
no matter how offensive they may be.

Dorothy L. Sayers

SUICIDE BY MARRIAGE

Judith Speizer Crandell

MY SECOND HUSBAND was a numeric equation:

Sociopath X 2 = Zilch, Nada, Rien.

Savić, the husband in question, used up all of my color. I lived with this large-headed, balding man for over four years in Cleveland Heights. We married as we shivered next to a duck pond.

After my parents died in an airplane crash the year before, I was lost. Every night I cried into a pink silk-covered baby album my mother kept in her bedside table drawer. I was their only child and they were my only parents. Good, bad, indifferent. The last two applied to my often-self-centered mother, but as I said, she was the only mother I had. My father, God rest his soul, made up for her.

Savić replaced my sadness and my parents with himself. At the beginning, it was all roses—rose petals on my pillow, thornless roses proffered just because. But it was wrong, terribly wrong, I soon found out, waking from the dream into the nightmare. I kept hoping the scene would change, the camera would pan back and I'd realize I was in a movie instead of my life. Within a year, I felt ready to wrench divorce from the jaws of defeat and run home to myself laughing all the way.

"But I love you," he said, as I lay in the dark basement on an itchy, nubby-brown sofa, a tiny TV flickering silently. There was one naked light bulb swinging over my head. The Not-So-Great Savić's fist of anger gearing up for yet another smash. Maybe, just maybe, this one would be my face—a constant promise.

"You can't leave me, Elaine."

"And you can't make me stay."

"We'll see about that."

I closed my eyes to the horrible world I inhabited with this beast, my lawfully wedded husband. He was so thick in the neck, his torso so barreled, his hairy fists so doubled up, steel fists, which when open had a high value. They should have been insured. Those hands for playing the piano, for copying music, for keying ancient computer A-frames that used the language "C," for caressing my inner thigh if he wasn't depressed. Often, oh so often, "we" were depressed. Like when I tried to hold my breath under the bathtub water hoping I would drown. We were living in the ground-floor apartment by the Space Needle in the Queen Anne section of Seattle at the time. His depression was all-pervasive, always, whenever he didn't get his way, like a baby—a big, bad, bearded baby.

Several years dragged by before I absolutely decided to leave *Le Monster du Musique*. So in this final interrogation scene, we have him repeating his oft-heard threat, "If you leave me, I will kill myself." By then I didn't care. If I left him and he killed himself, life would be a breeze. As long as he didn't kill me or his daughter first. His lovely daughter, Linda, from his previous marriage. A child I rescued. A child I loved. She and I shared a common bond: fear of her father. Because Savić was not only jealous but spiteful, he had honed his universal anger down to a dangerous dagger. He installed me at the center of his universe. Everyone else who tried to talk to me, touch me, love me, was negated, even Linda.

"Don't tell me, Savić, you are a misunderstood genius, tenor sax player, and fabulous composer that the Gods-you-don't-believe-in dealt a bad hand when your father ran off to Mexico dreaming of dope and revolution and easy sex. I know the story. Perhaps, dear Savić, you are absolutely and perpetually angry because of your father."

He stepped closer to me, like a menacing figure from the 1940s crime films that he binge-watched and forever quoted, like *Shed No Tears*, *Mystery in Mexico* and *Lady in the Death House*. I'd wager he didn't have the balls to kill himself and in a moment of anger he might be more willing to kill me.

He leaned into my face. "Maybe I'll just tie you up here, Elaine, so you'll have a ringside seat as I take off this belt and hang myself."

I said nothing. I sat there, mouth and eyes closed to him, imagining his suicide, him perhaps doing it naked with a bag on his head trying to achieve the nirvana passing-out release I'd read about. When your feelings have gone down the bathroom drain, your mind is free to be nasty.

What did Savić *really* want from me besides an audience and caretaking? With my curly dark hair and curves, the ability to make a living and put food into other people's mouths and a roof over their heads, wasn't I just a well-packaged meal ticket?

—

"And we could talk and you could learn the computer. I know," Savić expostulated one day, "you will be my brilliant assistant." We were in the largest bedroom, a bedroom not for us, not even for his dear daughter, Linda, but for his music-copying equipment and electronic pieces of this and that. He'd made me paint it inner sanctum white, and I was seldom allowed to enter.

Mr. Savić took a new breath each day in our medium-sized bedroom, all dark brown. I hated the color. It contained a cast-off bedroom suite, including a semi-expensive, made-to-order, used bedspread of brown and blue paisley and a matching upholstered bench, that formerly belonged to Savić's mother and her second husband, and was frolicked and slept on in New Jersey. I hated visiting the two of them almost as much as I hated sleeping in their hand-me-down-bedroom. Their insistence on speaking Serbian was the wall they built around Savić and themselves, as I sat uncomprehendingly and alone at their white French Provincial dining room table. How fitting we should get this hand-me-down bedroom suite infused with their personalities, their unnerving energy. It doomed our marriage from the start! Well, let's be honest; my marriage to Savić was doomed from the start, even without the furniture.

My wifely duties to Savić included the expectation that I would compose a warm meal while he lay buried in sleep, leaving me isolated as much as the Serbian language did. When I would ask him why we barely had sex anymore, he'd answer, "I'm in a fugue state, depressed. Don't you understand? I am a genuine artistic all-around genius. I was used to devise the Mensa test, and I am prone to depression. It's a form of introspection. Just be there when I wake up. When I need you." He always needed me. Life was always the same. Our scenes were well-rehearsed bad theater.

"Okay, Mr. Exotic Genius, do I have permission to stop at the store for some food on the way home and get my hair cut?" I waited for him to say, "Bring me receipts."

His actual reply was just as bad. "How long will you be?"

I wanted to answer, "Till the cows come home, evermore." Instead I collapsed on the plum-purple velvet Victorian loveseat in the living room.

My answers barely varied or registered. "An hour, a week, a year."

"Just don't dawdle. Return immediately from the errands, in case I need you." He knew my trick of turning off the ringer on my cellphone, often just leaving it in the car. So he stopped trying to reach me that way. Maybe he thought if I was really late or simply never returned, he could notify the police about a missing person. I was certainly a missing person, but not in the manner he imagined.

As always, his questions concerning my whereabouts were fired with machine-gun speed: "Where are you going? Who will be there? What will you be doing?"

A memorable event was a holiday party thrown by my new employer, which took place on Cleveland's West Side.

My crime? I grabbed a ride with a coworker who then left the party early. I stayed late without a ride home. At that point I didn't care. I let loose and drank too much and sat on an older vice president's lap where we discussed his promiscuous soon-to-be ex-wife and my no-such-luck husband as I played with his somber navy-blue tie that sported a few zippy red stripes.

When I exited, I spotted our used Saab with its steaming engine—in other words, my husband—asking in quick-fire bursts, "Why the hell did you call me and expect me to pick you up in the middle of the night? What the hell were you doing with these strangers, these strange men?"

I was drunk. I smiled. The wrong answer was the lack of an answer as the shoulder of my silver sequined halter top slipped down. He smashed the rearview mirror and screamed nonstop at the side of the road where we luckily ended up. Sobriety followed immediately and I drove us home, saved the day . . . once more.

—

We did not agree on music, although I pretended to like what Savić was composing. Savić said his computer-generated music that sounded like "Crap Rap" to me was the pile of gold he had been wait-ing for all his life, his birthright.

I loved Aaron Copeland and Leonard Bernstein and, of course, Tchaikovsky and Mussorgsky. He hated them all. He only praised his own work and that of his friend, teacher, and agent, Sterling Silverman. Maestro Silverman had many grown-up adult children crawling around his large, unkempt home, but he loved them less than his three baby grands that he'd jammed into three small rooms on the first floor. Any empty space was filled with stuffed owls and silk heli-otropes.

Savić insisted I accompany him to this dusty madhouse and sit quietly while he loaded the computer disk of his latest quip of genius into a disk drive so that Silverman could be wowed. I would make my exit half-way through and stay in the windowless bathroom, hermeti-cally sealed away from natural light, from breeze, even from life, it's true, but also locked away from all that was Savić and Sterling until Savić pounded on the door and said it was time to leave. While shut in that small space, I tried to remember my parents' faces, their voices, their hugs and their kisses, even my mother's tantrums, my childhood, but I could never manage to do it before the illusion was shaken and shattered once again by the brute force that was my husband.

—

Then one Sunday, a Sunday that appeared to dawn like any other, luck was on my side. Fortunately, Savić's daughter, Linda, was spending the weekend at her mother's. Savić and I had begun the day grocery shopping. He'd come with me to keep me from being free, even for a moment, and we'd argued in aisle 12 about store-brand olive oil verses a better, more-expensive one. When we returned to the house, after a silent ride from the grocery, Savić smashed a crystal de-canter containing the Serbian Slivovitz he loved. The smell permeated the kitchen, drenched his clothes, and splattered mine. The details are as vivid as the sharp edges of a rough-opened can. He shrieked, "That's your fucking face," carelessly wielding a shard and pointing to the glass that twinkled on the floor about us. I looked from a distance, having stepped away from him and nearer the back door, which I sized up as my escape route.

As I said, luck was with me this day. He slipped in the liquid he loved and cut himself, rather than me, slicing his neck as he flailed before falling. The wound spurted like a red-lit fountain at the Bellagio in Las Vegas. That fountain was the only thing I liked in Vegas—the way the computers made it flow to music that I enjoyed.

In retrospect, how could I be expected know he severed an artery? He was in shock and so was I. Well, perhaps he made a few groaning sounds, but for once he didn't question where I was going or what time I would return. I reached for my purple-fringed shoulder bag, turned and exited. I hummed a few bars from "Pictures at an Exhibition" and found myself walking down the street and around the corner to the local arts cinema. Somewhat dazed, I paid for a ticket to *The Rocky Horror Picture Show*. I just loved that movie. And so did the people in the theater. We all recited the dialogue in unison with the actors. Before I married Savić, this had been one of my great escapes from my parents' fatal accident.

Later, when I meandered home and entered the front door of the house, it was strangely silent. In the quiet my mind was finally able to focus, and I instinctively feared entering the kitchen.

"Savić? Savić?"

The lack of a reply felt ominous. I called the police from the eating nook where I closed my eyes to a pool of blood gathered on my black-and-white tiled kitchen floor. I sat facing away from the kitchen, awaiting the arrival of blaring sirens. The silence was truly "golden," as I once heard it described.

Savić died that day on that floor in a puddle of plum brandy that he loved more than me. Yet this was one contest between us he didn't win, because I died first, in an off-white wedding gown at a duck pond four years before.

ACTS OF MAGIC

David Yurkovich

YESTERDAY WAS A TOUGH ONE. Not as tough as present circumstances, mind you, but tough nonetheless. Sal and Carmine were both good fellows. It was a shame to see them buried in the ground before either of them had hit fifty. Grieving widows and children standing around at the gravesite looking lost, dazed. My heart breaks, truly it does. But the fact is that there are wounds, and then there are … wounds, if you know what I'm saying. What Ingram did to those guys, well, I ain't never seen nothing that brutal outside of an abattoir.

Ingram. I could kill the sonofabitch. Matter of fact, I *had* killed him. I guess, technically speaking, it was a .38-caliber bullet that did the deed, but seeing how it was fired from my Smith & Wesson with my index finger at the trigger, I most certainly had been Ingram's assassin. Saw him drop to the floor. Watched as his eyes slipped to the backs of the eyelids and his mouth slowly creaked open. The bullet found its mark square in the forehead. Even if he wasn't dead at that exact moment in time, he wasn't going anywhere.

You may be wondering where I'm headed with all of this. First, you need to know a few things.

If you've read the papers you know who Leo Cardigan is. In case you're illiterate or have been living in a desert, I will enlighten you. Leo is the captain of the northern New Jersey crime syndicate, what people like you refer to as The Mob. He has been in this role for the past eleven years, having taken over from Antonio Primo who was tragically gunned down following a meal of veal scallopini at Luigi's on a blustery winter's day in '07.

Leo is an ideal captain—business driven, demanding, but also pragmatic. During his many years as crime boss, there was little organizational upheaval. No turf wars. No rogue factions trying to usurp his reign. Leo ran it like the business it was and bloodshed was minimal.

They say that everyone has their quirks. And I guess Leo was no exception. If he hadn't gone the route of mobster, Leo most certainly would have become a magician. For as long as I've known Leo—and our friendship dates back to childhood—he's been fascinated with illusions and magic. Sleight of hand. I can recall long afternoons in our youth as Leo stood on the stoop of his parents' home, bedsheet cape affixed to a faded T-shirt, performing simple tricks with cards, coins, rope, marbles. He had talent, but he abandoned practicing magic when puberty set in. Even still, he remained a fan year after year. When he turned forty, Leo hired a magician to perform at his home. He was so impressed that he decided it would become an annual tradition. And for whatever reason, probably because he trusted my judgment, I took on the responsibility for hiring the talent each successive year.

Frankly, at his age, I'd have expected Leo to have us order up a few call girls to perform tricks of their own, but Leo had no interest in chasing tail. He was happy in his marriage, happy in his role within the organization, and he liked predictability. So yeah, sure, we acquiesced and Leo spent every twenty-seventh of August in the presence of a magician.

Because Leo liked things to be predictable, I tended to hire a local charlatan named Carmine the Great each year. Everyone knew and liked Carmine. When he wasn't pulling rabbits out of hats he was dropping bagels into toasters over at the breakfast bistro he co-owned with his kid brother. Carmine was a decent magician, not that I knew a lot about magic. His act ran the gamut from rope tricks to card tricks and everything in between. Nothing extraordinary, but sufficient. Never seemed to disappoint Leo, and that's really all that mattered.

One night in July, with his fiftieth just a few weeks away, Leo pulled me aside and placed a huge hand upon my shoulder. He didn't mince words.

"Sonny, while I appreciate all that you do, I've had enough of Carmine. This birthday coming up is special. A milestone. I want something bigger. Bolder. The cost be damned." He smiled.

"You got it, Leo." It was, of course, easy for him to say since the cost was ultimately coming out of my pocket, but you don't refuse a request from the boss. "I'll handle it."

As the big day approached, I made a few inquiries, visited various magic shops and interviewed some of the local "talent." Wasn't impressed with any of 'em, so I decided to cast a wider net. It happened that Jimmy Palma was in Florida, visiting his grandpop at the nursing home he'd been residing in for the past six years. It was an upscale joint that cost an arm and a leg, but Jimmy was happy to foot the bill. He ran across Ingram, who'd been hired to perform for one of the other residents at the home. Took his business card and gave it to me the following day when he returned to Jersey. Ingram the Great. I chuckled at the name, not because it was funny, but because it sounded stupid. Nonetheless, I found him on the web and watched a few YouTube videos. Liked what I saw. He was tall, lean, and wore a full black beard. The guy was more into illusions than tricks and his act also included a bit of pyrotechnics. Figured that'd go over well with Leo. I ran a quick background check to make sure there was nothing unusual about the guy. We spoke briefly on the phone and he was agreeable to travel if the price was right. In the days that followed, all the arrangements were planned out. I wired him an advance that included air fare. Two weeks later he arrived in Newark and we were soon seated at a table in the back of Maria's and talking details.

—

From the start there was something odd about the guy. Irrespective of first impressions, Ingram put off a weird vibe. For instance, I've got a firm handshake, but when I locked hands with this guy I felt like I'd slipped my hand into a vice. His touch was ice cold. Right then and there I should'a walked away. Instinct told me to send him packing back to sunny FLA, but something in his eyes left me feeling reassured that it would be okay. I didn't realize it at the time but I think he must'a been using some type of mild hypnotism. Ingram spoke with a heavy European accent. His language wasn't great, but we weren't hiring him for language skills. He talked about his repertoire and his magic acts. He used that term a lot—magic acts—as if it was more than a single performance he'd be giving. But whatever. By the end of the meeting, all of the details were sorted out.

Next, we stopped by Josie's where Ingram checked out the stage that would serve as his platform. He eyed a few of the strippers but otherwise kept to business. Everything seemed fine.

—

The following night–the night of the party–backstage at Josie's, I introduced Leo to Ingram.

"I know you," Ingram said. His voice was low, collected. "You're one tough son of a bitch."

Leo was nonplused by the remark. "You any good, Magician?"

"Not good. I am best. You gonna like my magic acts–my acts of magic."

"For your sake," I said, "I certainly hope so."

"Not to worry, Sonny boy. I got magic acts your boss gonna like. I got special magic acts waiting for you all."

The tone of Ingram's voice told me that right then, right there, I should have called the whole thing off. Something wasn't right. But we were here, at Josie's, and it was Leo's big five-zero, and cancelling the evening's entertainment because it didn't *feel right* wasn't gonna go down well with the executive leadership and certainly would not bode well for the long-term survival of yours truly. So I did the next best thing and pulled Ingram aside.

"I don't know what you're about, Mr. Magic Man, but any funny stuff tonight and you're not walking out of here." I flashed the steel .38 holstered inside my jacket. "You understand?" Ingram nodded and stepped aside.

—

Josie's dancers had the night off and the sign on the front door read "Closed for Private Party." Costello's catered the event and the food did not disappoint. Plenty to drink at the bar as well. By 10:00 p.m. when Ingram took to the stage we were all full bellied and a little buzzed. This was a small, intimate crowd, mind you. I think Leo felt a bit self-conscious about the whole thing. So it was just him and the rest of his entourage. No wives, no family. Inner-circle only plus a couple of barkeeps. But that was okay. It was Leo's party, Leo's rules.

Everything was all going well and I had to admit, Ingram knew his trade. A few of the tricks fell flat, but overall, he did not disappoint. Leo's table was front and center and I could see from the grin on his face that he was enjoying the show.

Around 10:45, Ingram asked for two volunteers from the audience. No one moved. None of us wanted to get up there. Too embarrassing. In the end, Sal and Carmine, being the most junior members, were ushered up. Ingram had Sal stand on the left side of the stage while Carmine stood on the right. He blindfolded each man. Sal protested but Leo told him to shut up.

Ingram beckoned to the audience. "I now make each man ... disappear."

"Can't happen soon enough!" Turk bellowed, and the room erupted with laughter before falling silent once more.

The stage began to fill with smoke and the lights flickered with a strobe-like rhythm. Every movement assumed a sorta slow-motion quality. One moment, Ingram was standing next to Sal. The next, Carmine. There were sudden screams and a rapid, repetitive chopping sound. When the smoke finally cleared, Sal and Carmine were motionless on the floor. Blood spatter covered the tiles, the walls, even the tables. Ingram stood immobile at center stage as he clutched the handle of the weapon, a worn and weathered ax, with two bloody hands.

"I told you. Acts of magic. You see what it can do?"

He was off the stage and standing at Leo's table before any of us could draw a gun. "How you like my magic acts now?" Before Leo could utter a syllable, Ingram brought the blade down. It tore through Leo's right shoulder, severing flesh and shattering bone. Leo staggered from chair to floor, face a caricature of pain. Ingram raised the weapon quickly and readied for the killing blow.

My bullet found his forehead instead.

The lights came up and we did our best to slow Leo's bleeding until the EMTs arrived. He looked down at Ingram's body and spat. "Crazy sonofabitch. Burn that mother fucker's corpse." I nodded. Wouldn't be the first time my hands reeked of kerosene.

After Leo was loaded into the ambulance, I went back inside Josie's to retrieve Ingram's body. But it was gone.

"Where the fuck is the magician?" No one seemed to know. Most of the guys had been standing on the stage, trying to figure out whether to phone the medical examiner's office or to handle matters more discretely. No one had moved Ingram, but Ingram was no longer there. The sonofabitch was gone, along with his "magic ax."

—

Leo's condition remained critical in the days that followed. He was expected to survive, but not without a long hospital stay and plenty of rehab. I didn't visit. I felt personally responsible–*was* responsible–for the entire mess. Besides, there were more urgent matters at hand–Sal and Carmine's funeral, and finding that goddam magician.

The latter turned out to be easier than expected.

I dunno why Ingram chose to hang around. Maybe he thought he was invincible. Maybe he was. On the day after the attack, I'd put out feelers on the off-chance he hadn't left the area. A day after we buried Sal and Carmine, we struck pay dirt. One of the kids on my payroll phoned to report that he'd seen a guy fitting Ingram's description in an abandoned house on Rose Garden Street. It was a narrow cul-de-sac adjacent to the manufacturing district. I parked near the house and waited.

Four hours later, my thumbs nearly numb from playing solitaire on the phone, a jet-black sedan pulled into the driveway. The ax man himself. I tried to phone Joey to have the guys meet up with me but my phone died in mid-dial. Goddam cellphone batteries. I set it aside and loaded the chamber of my trusted Smith & Wesson. The sky was dark–starless and overcast. Storm coming in for sure. I moved toward the house as distant thunder echoed across the sky and checked the front door. Unlocked.

The house was dark. I walked along, quietly, drawn to a dim light on the opposite end of the first floor. Kitchen most likely. I entered the room and moved toward the silhouetted figure in the distance. Not a person at all. Just a coat rack, a trick of the darkness.

I took a step backward, and then felt the blade as it tore into my left flank. I slipped on my own blood and tumbled onto the wooden floor. My gun escaped my grip and skidded across the floor. Ingram picked up the weapon and then tossed it aside.

I stared up at the magician's grey eyes while clutching my side with my right hand. I tried to stand, but it felt as though my insides were gonna fall out. "The man ... with the magic. You sonofabitch. I shot you ... kill shot to the forehead."

"I know. Maybe I should be dead. Would tell you how I survived, Sonny boy, but good magician never share secrets." Ingram stared down at me with a child-like empathy. "Still, you have nasty wound. Gonna bleed out in five, six minutes, so I grant you a dying wish."

"Fuck you."

"I knew you or your associates would fire upon me. Most of my wardrobe–bulletproof. I also knew that, if shot, would likely be chest or head. That how you people operate. If you'd looked closely, you might have noticed apparatus on forehead. My own design. Flesh colored. Applied with spirit gum. Quite seamless in darker rooms. Stopped bullet. I play dead."

I glanced up at Ingram blankly. "Why? Was it the Caramelli gang? They pay you to take us out?"

"You want to know why. Why I do it. God. Everyone always ask same fucking question. I don't know Caramelli. Only know evil. Your boss, your associates, you. That is reason itself."

Ingram wiped down the ax with a wet towel.

"Work not quite finished. Your boss, at St. Mary's. I visit. Tie up loose ends. You stay here. Place is yours. I won't be back."

He smiled, switched off the kitchen light, and left.

Numbness was coming on fast now.

I thought about screaming, crying out for help, but the storm had begun. Rain pelted the windows and thunderbolts cracked loudly like hands clapping in applause at the end of a show.

My theory is that people who don't like mystery stories are anarchists.

Rex Stout

MARK TWAIN'S UNSCHEDULED TRIP TO SHANGHAI

Dianne Pearce

"DAMN HELL YOU SAY, Watkins! Twain has changed sides?"

"It's true, Senator Plumb; I was there!"

"My sweet God, but it's monstrous! How did it happen?"

"We picked Twain up in Missouri, as planned, but that damned Babbitt got on at the next station."

"Who do you mean, Babbitt? Who is this Babbitt?"

"I'm sorry Senator I thought you knew of him. Young Irving Babbitt, the man who calls himself a humanist. He was on for the first stretch of the trip, and he encountered Mr. Twain in the smoker and immediately invited him to dine. Though Mr. Twain said something about how he might sour Babbitt's lunch were he to dine with him, Babbitt said it would be more like adding salt to the food, so they took a meal together in the dining car. Mr. Twain did most of the eating, and Babbitt most of the talking. Then, at the station, Twain stepped onto the platform to speak as planned, faced the crowd, and said that he now opposes the Republican Party and all it stands for, including the end of slavery.

"He actually said that, Watkins?"

"Yes. He told all the folks who listened to follow Mr. Babbitt's teachings, and to vote for the Democrats and the rights of white people. Babbitt clapped the loudest of all the assembly there, shook hands heartily with Mr. Twain, presented him with some papers from his valise, his monographs from what I could discern, and left the station in the buggy of a local clergyman. Mr. Twain avoided me completely, and went and locked himself in his sleeper. He's got himself shut-up in there, with two of Babbitt's monographs! Thrice I have gone to his door, but he refuses me. That's why it was imperative you join the tour."

"The devil take this Babbitt! He cannot be allowed to ruin the greatest writer of modern times. Twain is going to get the cussed-South for the party just as Lincoln wanted!"

"But Senator, Babbit has changed Mr. Twain's mind, and Mr. Twain has the ear of the world! If he ever is allowed a word again-"

"He will not be allowed a word again, Watkins."

"Sir? What do you mean?"

"I mean he will not speak, at least not while he speaks Babbit's words instead of his own. Find me his dammed porter, Watkins!"

"He does not have a porter, Sir."

"What? Don't buy me more trouble today."

"No Sir! One Pullman fell ill and left the train before Mr. Babbit had even boarded, and the only replacement was a coolie, and Mr. Twain volunteered to have him. None of the other passengers wanted him, because, of course, a coolie is not to be trusted."

"Chinese?"

"Yes sir, of course."

"So much the better, Watkins. Fetch him; we've only three hours 'till the next stop. I am going to send a telegram. That coolie is our salvation! Hurry now!"

—

"May we come in, Senator Plumb?"

"Yes, yes, Watkins, come in."

"I had to drag the wretch here. I doubt he will be any use to us."

"Watkins, don't be rude. He will be fine. Come in Mr.-?"

"Fu."

"Watkins, excuse us."

"But sir!"

"Get out, Man! At the next stop a man with a yellow cravat will be *there*; you will bring him *here*, immediately. Get on with you, Watkins!"

—

"Mr. Fu, be seated and tell me where you are from. No? Don't want to be helpful? I am your friend, and a United States Senator. How many coolies do you know who can count a senator as a friend?"

"I not interested in friend."

"Mr. Fu, be seated man, right there. Come now. Yes, that's better. I have a gift for you Mr. Fu, quite a gift indeed. See what I have here in my trunk? Almost a full bag of rice."

"Rice?"

"Now now, sit back down. Take this from me. You may not see the benefit to having me as a friend, Mr. Fu, but I have many Chinese people as friends, and one brought me this rice, from Tongshan."

"Tongshan! I not taste rice eighteen years."

"This rice is for you, whether or not we help each other. Take it. And please, sit back down."

"I cannot; rice so precious-"

"Sit Man! I need your help! That's better. I thank you. And I have a question for you. Would you like a regular supply of Tongshan rice?"

"I like better to be with Ma Ma in Hubei. I miss Ma Ma."

"Hubei? That's brilliant, Mr. Fu! Absolutely brilliant! Yes! If I get you back to Hubei, could I persuade you to take a trunk from my luggage along? It will be quite heavy, and you will need to deliver it to my friend who procures for me the rice, but our partnership will be complete, and I shall want no more from you than that you drift back into the mist of the mountains, never to return to the United States."

"Boat very expensive Shanghai. Why Senator help Fu?"

"Your passenger in berth 21, the large sleeper, Mr. Twain, has been saying things that we cannot allow him to say. You well-know, I am certain Mr. Fu, that the life of anyone of dark or yellow skin is wretched in this country. Well, last week, Mr. Twain wanted to help change that. But he's been kidnapped! That's right, Fu, kidnapped by pernicious ideas! He must not send us back to a slave state. You can be a hero for all coolies."

"How Fu can help?"

"Soon my colleague will bring a man aboard who looks much like Mr. Twain. In the interim time, you and I should empty Mr. Twain's sleeper of Mr. Twain, and then ensconce this other fellow in the berth, and allow him the use of both Mr. Twain's possessions and his good name. As soon as our improved Mr. Twain is settled, you, Mr. Fu, this bag of rice, and my locked trunk will be escorted to a boat soon to sail for Shanghai. When you dock you will be met by my friend, who will ensure that your family always has a supply of Tongshan rice. Mr. Twain's replacement will make certain that things improve in this nation for the coolies and all immigrants to come! What say you?"

"I want to go Ma Ma very much."

"That is fine, Mr. Fu, fine. Let us pack your luggage, and then by use of your keys, we shall pack mine."

ON CRIME AND CRUSTACEANS

William F. Crandell

There once was a private detective
whose shooting was quite ineffective.
He tracked down a mobster
with a face like a lobster
and polished him off with invective.

I love the idea of bringing order out of disorder which is what the mystery is about. I like the way in which it affirms the sanity of human life and exorcises irrational guilts.

P.D. James

THE COUPLE

Bayne Northern

SHE COULDN'T REMEMBER WHEN she had started hating him. Did it begin with the constant interrupting? The rudeness? Personal discounting? Was it watching him get fatter and fatter–the flesh bulging on his back like a human walrus? His protruding two front teeth always gave him a beaver-type appearance. How appealing–married to a man that resembled a beaver in the front and a walrus in the back.

Over lunch with her sister, Yvonne had shared with her, "I'm glad I don't have a gun in my home. There have been times when, if I did, I would have shot my hubby over and over again. I would have killed him by now!"

Michelle could identify with that emotion, but she disagreed with her sibling. "Oh, no, don't make it fast. It would be better to drag it out ... slowly debilitating him. Be creative ... cruel. There are all kinds of tools at your disposal."

"Like what?"

"Oh, say, a dose of public humiliation, a dabble of emotional distress, a dollop each of shame and blame, and then a pinch of pain. Continue to build until you achieve excruciating agony."

"Did Mary Poppins just come out to play?" Yvonne rolled her eyes.

"Seriously. A long, drawn out step-by-step retaliation would be the best way to get back at him. Make him suffer."

"Jesus, Michelle! You've *really* been thinking about this."

"I'm married to a pig."

"He's a physician, for Christ's sake!"

"Still, Ken's a pig." Her green eyes flashed then, assuming a lizard-like appearance. "He was snoring last night. I could see his open, gaping mouth with the little dribbles of saliva from the striped illumination of the streetlight streaming through the blinds."

"Gross."

"I tell you, Yvonne, I became angrier and angrier as I listened to each rolling crest of the snoring. It kept getting louder."

"Oh, God, Michelle, what did you do?" Yvonne's large brown eyes widened with alarm.

"I got up. I went to the kitchen and returned with a bunch of grapes." Michelle smiled smugly.

"You were hungry?"

"No, Sis. Just wanted to distress the whale-like mound beside me that had disturbed my sleep."

"Oh, my God …what did you do with the grapes?"

"I waited for the crescendo of the snore with his mouth wide open and sucking in all the air. And then I dropped a grape right down into his throat." A smile spread across her face as she described the clever consequences she had created as his punishment for awakening her in the middle of the night.

"Did he wake up?"

An expression of deep satisfaction scrolled across her face. "He most certainly did. I watched him rolling around gasping for air. My aim was perfect. The grape neatly lodged into the opening of his windpipe." Her full lips widened into a broad, Cheshire Cat-like smile. "He leapt off the bed, making all kinds of horrible, guttural noises while trying to breathe. I watched in delight." Her eyes sparkled. "Eventually he coughed up the grape."

Yvonne thought her sister actually looked disappointed that the plug popped. "Michelle—that's horrible—that's so mean!"

"He's a prick."

"Why don't you just divorce him?"

"Money … I need his money. He makes a lot more than I do. I couldn't have the lifestyle I want on my income." Her face looked wistful.

"Is it worth it? Are you sure?"

"Don't worry, Yvonne. I'm not serious. I'm just going to have a little fun." Michelle had smiled broadly and then instinctively leaned over to give her sister a little kiss on the cheek.

—

When Michelle returned home from work the next day, she found a ripped-up love note she had written to Ken when they first married. It was torn into little pieces and carefully placed on her pillow. *He is such a mean-spirited man.* The fight was on. She pulled the bulging dry-cleaner bag out of the master closet. Dirty clothes piled up on the floor as the bag was turned upside down. Michelle sorted through them, pulling out three pairs of Ken's dress pants. *Even better,* she thought, *these are his favorites.* Standing on a carved, wooden footstool, she reached up and grabbed her sewing kit from the top shelf. She sat on the bed with the pants and the basket. Rifling through the basket's spools of colored threads and sewing accessories, she found the necessary tools—scissors, seam ripper, and a little plastic container of straight pins. Her hands deftly maneuvered the seam ripper to remove the threads of the back seam of each pair of pants about five inches down from the waist. Starting at the bottom of the rip, she carefully began pinning the fabric, gradually tapering it until it was a half-inch tighter at the waistband. The three trousers were slipped inside a clear bag with a note inside that read:

> Pants are in need of tailoring due to weight loss. Please take in pants as pinned. Any questions, please call Michelle Dalton at 555-666-1098.
>
> Thanks!

Sitting on the edge of the king bed, gazing up at the ceiling, Michelle imagined Ken stepping into his pants and being unable to button them, then forcing the closure, creating a huge bulge of flesh hanging over his belt—a nice mushroom top protruding out of the front of his white physician's jacket as he tended to patients. And, he'd also be incredibly uncomfortable! Ken's suit hanging on the handle of the tall bureau caught Michelle's attention. She remembered he was leaving early tomorrow for a business conference where he was speaking to other medical professionals about how to grow their practice. Carefully inserting her hands inside the garment bag, Michelle removed the pants off the rung of the hanger. The seam ripper facilitated loosening the threads on the back of Ken's pants so they would rip wide open under stress. Michelle felt happy imagining the embarrassment and public humiliation as Ken's clothes ripped, exposing his boxers.

Then Michelle decided to take it up a notch. Ken's carry-on was next to the bed, already filled with underwear, socks, toiletries, and a dress shirt. She carefully removed the light-colored boxers and walked downstairs with them. She poured some of the old coffee from the morning into a small bowl, added a few shakes of soy sauce, a tablespoon of Mastergravy, and a squirt of brown mustard. The concoction was microwaved for a minute, then a tea bag was added to the steaming fluid. She dipped two circles of the cotton boxers, right over the center seam, into the brownish, yellow mixture and allowed them steep. When she checked them later, Michelle admired the dark, brown, yellowish blotches. She quickly dried the pants on high in the dryer, folded them, and re-placed them in the suitcase. It was unlikely Ken would notice the marks while dressing at the hotel. He was always multi-tasking when he dressed, thinking of the day ahead. Michelle felt almost gleeful as she imagined her plan unfolding.

—

Ken was furious when he returned home from the conference. As soon as he opened the door, Ken started screaming. "Michelle! Michelle! Where the hell are you?"

Irritated, she responded, "I'm in my office."

Ken bounded up the stairs taking two steps at a time. As soon as he saw her, he resumed shouting at her. "You can't even do laundry, Michelle! What is it you *can* do?"

She glowered at him. "Welcome home."

"Did you know you embarrassed me?"

"What are you talking about?"

"My clothes! More specifically, my underclothes! Do you do laundry in the dark? Jesus Christ, Michelle!"

"I have no idea what you are talking about."

"My boxers were filthy. They had all kinds of stains on them! Why didn't you see that when you did the wash?"

"I don't understand why you're so upset. They were still clean. And only you saw the stains." She couldn't stop herself from smirking.

"No, Michelle, there was another problem!"

Her heart was pounding. She couldn't wait to hear. She was trying desperately not to allow a smile to spread across her face. "What problem?" she asked, as innocently as possible.

"I was getting on the bus to take a group of physicians out to dinner. I was one of the first boarders. When I took that first step up, I heard the sound of the seam of my pants ripping; I could feel them loosen. I hurried onto the bus cursing myself that I hadn't brought my suit jacket- but the dinner was billed as business casual."

"So far, it doesn't sound like a big problem." She heard the disappointment in her voice but hoped he didn't.

"Michelle, not only did the seam rip but so did the material on the pants. A large flap of material was hanging down off my ass. When I walked off the bus to the restaurant, I kept trying to hold it up but it kept slipping back down. After a few drinks I forgot about it."

"So? What's the big deal?"

"The big deal is when Harry pulled me aside and said everyone was talking about me behind my back because I had shit stains on my underwear!"

Now Michelle was smiling; she couldn't help herself.

"Why are you grinning? I was mortified, embarrassed! Doctors are expected to be fastidious! And—it's your fault, 'cause you suck at laundry—among other things."

That pissed her off. Even though she was delighted Ken didn't realize she had created the discolored spots, Michelle felt angry that he was criticizing her so pervasively. "I've been pretty successful in my career."

"What? Retail banking? Any moron could do that."

Rage began burning deep within her. She wanted to punish him further—and she would.

"Perhaps you should lose some weight and reduce that offensive blubber you're carrying around on your back and stomach."

"You stink in every role you perform—wife, employee, daughter, sibling—no one can depend on you. You're so self-focused, self-absorbed, self-aggrandizing!"

"I've had enough! You can do your own laundry from now on." Michelle got up. "Get the hell out of my office." Ken took a step back from her and she slammed the door in his face.

—

Michelle pondered the situation. Ken's behavior, his rudeness, his personal discounting of her skills and abilities, all would have to be addressed. He would have to suffer—really suffer. Ken was scheduled to go skiing with his brother that coming weekend. She had the perfect idea for his punishment. When Ken left to conduct his hospital rounds, Michelle walked down into the basement and located their ski equipment laying against the back wall. She opened the cupboard and found a tool box. Digging through the disorganized jumble of pliers, wrenches, screws, and nails, she finally found the screwdriver. Her green eyes lit up. Michelle turned to the back wall and gently lowered Ken's skis to the floor. She unsnapped the small bungee cord holding them together. On one ski, she began unscrewing the bolts that held the binding in place. The screw was very tight, requiring the use of all of her arm strength to get it to rotate counterclockwise. It finally gave in. Her dark, wavy chestnut hair fell across her face with each turn of the screw, annoying her and obscuring her view. Michelle found a rubber band in the toolbox and hastily swept her hair up into a messy bun. It was difficult to judge how much to loosen the fastening so that the binding would hold for several runs down the hill—until the one time it wouldn't.

Michelle envisioned Ken confidently traversing down the hill in his brand-new, high-end KJUS ski pants and jacket that he had purchased recently due to his expanding girth. He would be competing with his brother, taking a lot of air when he flew over a mogul. Her lips parted in anticipation and she involuntarily smiled as, in her mind, she saw the ski suddenly lose its binding, the wooden plank flying high in the air, his body tumbling head over heels down the hill, breaking a leg and an arm. Michelle was certain he would have a concussion, too. His skiing career would be ended. A thought interrupted her. What about money? If he couldn't work for several months, that would be bad. Then she relaxed, recalling that Ken had a very strong disability policy that would pay income until he could work again. And, if he was accidentally killed, he had life insurance. She would be content with either outcome.

Michelle carefully placed the altered ski next to its partner, bungeed them together, and propped the wooden boards up against the back wall exactly where they had been. She stood back and contemplated her cleverness with a wide grin on her face.

—

Michelle rolled around in bed wishing she could sleep longer. She felt so groggy. The rich aroma of freshly brewed coffee motivated her to open her eyes and lift her head. She spotted the steaming mug on the end table next to the bed. "Thanks," she mumbled. "Let me know when you're out of the shower."

"Sure." Ken walked into the adjoining master bathroom and turned on the water.

A few minutes later, Michelle heard the toilet flush. She hated that he wasted the earth's resources to hide any gastronomical noises he made in the bathroom, although she really didn't want to hear those either. She slowly pulled herself in a sitting position on the side of the bed. The room seemed to be spinning. She felt a wave of nausea and gently reclined.

"I'm out!" Ken yelled loudly from the bathroom, thinking she was downstairs. He opened the door, surprised to see Michelle still lying there. "Why aren't you up?" He appeared genuinely concerned.

"I don't feel very well, actually."

Ken immediately went into his physician mode. "What are your symptoms?"

Michelle knew that what he was really worried about was his own health–that she might be contagious. It was odd that a germaphobe like Ken had decided to become a doctor. She rolled over to face him. "My head is pounding."

"A migraine?"

"No, not that bad, but intense. I feel dizzy, too."

"How would you know that if you haven't raised your head yet or gotten out of bed?" He challenged her. His patients could never fool him or convince him to prescribe something they didn't need.

"Cuz I did. I stood up and felt really woozy and got back in bed."

"Well, I know you can't be pregnant because you haven't accommodated me for quite a while, frigid bitch that you are."

"Really, Ken? You had to go there?" She decided right then to take it up a notch, escalate her plan for his pain and suffering.

"It's true. You only think about your needs."

"Have a nice day, Ken." Michelle turned over, facing the other way and pulled the sheet up over her head.

Ken quickly exited the bedroom and bounded down two flights of stairs into the basement. Michelle smiled as she heard him wrestle with his skis as he dragged them up from the cellar and laid them in the foyer. Then, he stomped upstairs, taking two steps at a time, and retrieved his bulging suitcase from the second floor.

"Have fun on the slopes, Dear," she whispered into her pillow, pushing her face into it to control her beaming, even though she knew Ken couldn't see her expression.

After hearing the garage door close, Michelle attempted to rise but felt faint when she stood up. She sat back gently and sipped her coffee, which was lukewarm now. It was also too sweet. Ken always put too much sugar in her cup. She sat on the edge of the bed for several minutes, and, not feeling any better, decided she should stay home. Michelle picked up her cellphone from the end table and called her admin.

"Hi, Ann."

"Wow, that doesn't sound like you."

"I'm sure it doesn't. I'm speaking quietly because my head is pounding. I'm taking a sick day today. Can you reschedule my meetings?"

"Sure. When do you think you'll be back in?"

"Today is Thursday. I don't think I'll be in tomorrow either. I'm sure I'll recover over the weekend and be back on Monday."

"Okay. I'll block a couple hours Monday morning so you can catch up. I'll get everything rescheduled. No worries."

"Thanks, Ann."

"No problem. Hope you feel better. See you next week."

Michelle ended the call, slipped into her bathrobe draped at the bottom of the bed, and slowly made her way down the hall. She was actually leaning against the wall, scraping her shoulder across the grasscloth wallpaper as she moved. She was having trouble maintaining her balance. To ensure she didn't fall down the stairs, she sat down on the top step and carefully lowered her butt onto the step below, repeating the process until she reached the first floor. Michelle grabbed the banister with both hands and pulled her body up to a standing position. The foyer began swirling around in circles, making her feel nauseated.

She dragged herself into the kitchen. Ken had left his blood pressure monitor on the table. Michelle sat on a chair and decided to take her pressure.

In her condition, it took a lot of exertion to wrap the band around her left arm and get the tube over the interior vein. After several failed attempts, she situated it correctly and hit the little button. She waited while the band inflated, then watched the countdown on the little monitor screen.

Her eyes popped open wide and a little gasp escaped from her lips when Michelle read the results: 82 over 50. "Holy shit. No wonder I feel like hell."

Michelle decided she should eat something salty. Maneuvering around the kitchen was challenging. She accomplished it by bending over and holding onto the counter. She brewed a fresh pot of coffee for more caffeine, scrambled two eggs, and cut out a quarter of a cantaloupe. Two burnt slices of toast were slathered with apricot jelly. She carefully carried her plate across the room and sat down in front of the dish, liberally dusting salt over the eggs and the cantaloupe. Michelle's dizziness was dissipating. Energy flowed into her body. Her blood pressure slowly rose. She could feel her health improving with each mouthful. Her thoughts turned to the next steps of her plan to punish Ken for his cruel emotional abuse.

Michelle took a soothing, hot bath in the soaking tub, adding more hot water every fifteen minutes. Sinking deep down in the warm sudsy liquid, she reflected on various methods to cause pain and suffering, then had a sudden revelation. She was beyond that now—finished with torture. Michelle realized she wanted Ken dead.

Her arms grabbed the sides of the tub and pushed against the porcelain to raise her slender body out of the foaming fluid. She wrapped the bath sheet tightly around her body and walked down the hall into her home office and powered up her laptop. As the machine booted up, Michelle quickly dressed in black knit pants and a striped tunic top, pulled on cotton socks, slid her feet into black mules, and strode back down the hallway to conduct her research.

Ken's death needed to be swift. She didn't want to have to care for him as he suffered. A violent departure from life was preferable. After an hour of studying various websites, she decided an accidental death was the ideal scenario. Michelle investigated causes of accidental deaths in the home. She explored the mechanics of automobiles, gas ovens, electrical wiring, and various home appliances. Her hands began to tremble when she identified the perfect solution—a malfunctioning electric garage door.

—

Michelle tried to relax over the weekend. She was tense—expecting her cellphone to ring. It would be a call from the hospital telling her about Ken's skiing accident. Or maybe his brother would contact her. Ken should have been skiing all-day yesterday. He was probably hitting the slopes right now. If she hadn't loosened the binding enough, the boot wouldn't pop off the board; nothing would have happened. She would be so disappointed if her effort failed. If it worked, she hoped Ken's injuries wouldn't require her caregiving for several weeks. She tried to refocus on taking care of herself by consuming homemade chicken soup, sipping green tea with ginger, and soaking in a hot bath. She curled up in bed and began reading a novel when she suddenly heard the garage door open.

Her heart was pounding. "Ken? Ken? Is that you?" She jumped up and ran down the stairs.

The door that connected the two-car garage to their red-brick colonial home slowly opened. A pair of crutches came flying through the opening and landed in the mud room. A slightly hairy male hand grabbed the trim on either side of the door. Then Ken burst into the room as he jumped up the step. His left foot was encased in a black plastic walking boot secured with three wide Velcro straps across the front.

Michelle gasped. "What happened?"

"What do you think happened? Did you notice the crutches on the floor? The boot on my left leg?" He was snarling.

She felt the familiar fury rise within her in reaction to his rudeness.

"I see. No biggie, then." She turned on her heels. Her cheeks were aflame with anger. She purposely didn't offer to help him. Not after that remark. *He can unload his car, get his own food. Screw him!* She quickly returned to their bedroom and picked up her novel. She tried to read but the words just bounced around on the page without her comprehension.

Struggling with managing the crutches, Ken maneuvered to the bottom of the steps and called up. "Hey, I'm sorry. I'm just pissed it happened. It's really annoying. Can you help me, please?"

Wanting to hear all about the accident and to discern if he thought she might be culpable, Michelle agreed. "I'll be right down."

She helped him take a seat in the kitchen and then unloaded his car, taking the one remaining ski down into the basement. She heated up some homemade chicken soup, placed a big steaming bowl of the noodles and broth in front of Ken, and sat down at the kitchen table.

Michelle kept her eyes fixed on Ken's face as he recounted the details, bobbing her head as she listened, occasionally sighing.

"The binding busted this morning. I had just cleared a mogul on the intermediate slope called the Black Swan. Nothin' but air I might add." He looked up at her and sported a cocky smile. "When I landed, the metal fastening snapped off my ski."

"Oh, no!" she exclaimed, feigning concern.

"I fell. Then my body began sliding down the slope and picking up speed. About fifteen feet down the hill, I smacked into a tree on the side of the trail. My foot slammed into it, forcing my body to wrap around its thick trunk. I was lucky it stopped my descent. But I twisted my ankle and bruised several ribs."

"I'm glad it wasn't more serious," Michelle lied.

"Mike insisted on taking me to the hospital ER, even though I knew it wasn't serious. After a couple hours there, we returned to the ski lodge and decided to pack up and come home. At least I can still drive since it's my left foot."

"I guess that's some good news." Michelle pretended to be concerned and engaged. It did not appear that he had any suspicion the binding had been tampered with.

"I was telling Mike I might sue the ski manufacturer."

"We could consider that." Michelle's eyes shone brightly. She was delighted with the result she had achieved.

—

Michelle's research on garage door mechanics identified four primary causes of malfunctions. Fatal accidents had been caused by garage door tracks out of alignment, reversing mechanisms that didn't operate properly, torsion springs that broke, or cables that snapped. Damaging the torsion springs seemed to be the most viable to Michelle. It was something she personally could alter without help from anyone, and she was unlikely to be a murder suspect since torsion springs do eventually break and need to be replaced. Their torsion springs would just happen to break when Ken was under the door. A loud bang, like a gun going off, can be heard at the exact moment they snap. She envisioned Ken trying to raise the door that she had left partially open, a habit of hers that irritated him. He'd push it up so it would close–and it normally would, but this time, it would come crashing down on top of his balding head, crushing him, and instantly killing him. The last sound Ken would hear would be the big bang of the breaking torsion springs.

Michelle's hands shook from excitement. Her head was also pounding from a massive headache. She had started to feel better over the weekend, but then the vertigo had returned later in the week. Ken thought she might have an inner ear infection and made an appointment for her with an ear, nose, and throat specialist. The first available appointment was next week. Michelle would need to move slowly until then. Standing up quickly caused a spinning sensation and blurred vision, accompanied by a wave of nausea. Ken said he was experiencing issues with his equilibrium as well. Maybe it was some kind of virus they had contracted. He was always bringing home foul germs and nasty bacteria from his sick patients.

With the dizziness as her excuse, she had taken a personal day so that she could work on the torsion springs. She had already read the garage door operating manual cover to cover. Michelle had gone on the Head Over Door website and queried a few issues relating to the coils. Most of the answers popped up on the site's FAQs page, which caused Michelle to wonder if other people had contemplated the same thing she was planning. For the past several days, Michelle had been leaving the bottom of the garage door open a few feet off the ground knowing how much it would bother Ken. Two small bowls had been placed just inside the door, one containing cat food and the other fresh water. She pretended she was feeding a stray cat. Every time Ken saw the door raised, he'd angrily push it up, shoving it all the way up. Then it would slowly come back down and close the entrance to their two-car garage, every time. Until one day it wouldn't.

Michelle decided today was that day. Ken was healing nicely from his skiing accident, which annoyed her. She dragged the ladder over to the torsion spring stretched across the front metal bar of their Hermitage 800 garage door opener and slowly climbed up the rungs. The process was taking longer than she planned due to her light-headedness, but she was absolutely determined to complete it. Using a powerful electric screwdriver and wrench, Michelle carefully loosened the spring attachment on the right side–she could see the release of tension in the actual coil. She cautiously descended, dragged the ladder to the other side, and repeated the same actions. She smiled as the coil began to sag. The wire at each end was straining, splayed wide as the coil fought to condense. The metal ends of the spring protruded out of their sockets. Michelle was confident that just one push up would snap the torsion spring, causing it to reverse and slam Ken mercilessly into the ground. She purposefully knocked the bowl of cat food over, the little dry balls rolled out and all around the garage floor and the drive. That would also annoy Ken, and cause him to yank the door even harder. It pleased Michelle to think that the scattered food would be one of the last things Ken would see. She closed the ladder and, with great effort, heaved it up into its wall holder. She was panting and sweating profusely.

Michelle stepped back into the house, feeling vapory and faint, either from the inner ear infection or the exhilaration she felt from the task she had just deftly performed. She was proud of her skills, but she needed to lie down. Stumbling into the living room, Michelle slid onto the leather couch, which felt cool against her skin. Michelle's head began to pound, her left arm went numb, and her vision went black then returned. She panicked and yanked her cellphone from her pocket. She couldn't differentiate the numbers. Couldn't dial 911. Was unable to identify her favorites button. She pushed the phone screen near the top, hoping she was calling Ken. He immediately answered.

"Michelle?"

"I'm in trouble."

He could hear she was having difficulty speaking as well as breathing. "I'm on my way. I'll be there in less than ten minutes. Stay calm." In her confusion, Michelle thought he sounded elated. She wanted Ken to stay on the phone with her, but he had already hung up.

Her phone went black. Every organ seemed to be in distress. Lungs struggled for air. Heart pounded rapidly. Head throbbed. Skin copiously perspired. Her body began to tremble. Michelle was afraid. Something was terribly wrong.

As Ken drove his little two-seater sports car down the highway, he realized he was smiling, pleased with the flawless execution of his plan. He could feel self-admiration welling up as he reflected on his meticulous planning and preparation, as well as his attention to every detail. He had studied various poisons for some time before he settled on cyanide. He had taught himself how to manufacture it from various food sources, all natural. No need to buy rat poison. After extensive practice and experimentation, he developed the ideal dosage for his wife, taking into account her gender, weight, and overall health. The computer from which he had conducted his research had been destroyed. The lab equipment he used to create the cyanide had been sterilized multiple times in the autoclave of his affiliated hospital and returned to their shared and secured storage cabinet.

Over the course of his marriage, Ken had legitimately treated his wife for various illnesses and had created a patient file for her. During the previous few months, he had augmented the folder, documenting fictitious symptoms of heart failure, cardiovascular disease, and pulmonary problems. His notes indicated that, in his medical opinion, his wife was at risk of severe health complications. Michelle's record stated that Ken had referred her to various specialists for additional diagnostic testing, but she had not followed through. Ken had also purposely confided to his nurse practitioner that he was increasingly concerned about his wife's health. Her imminent death would now appear to be simply the consequence of a fabricated worsening medical condition.

Michelle heard Ken's car as it careened up the driveway. She was trembling more violently now. Her eyes fluttered open, first in relief, but then opened even wider in panic. She was just beginning to comprehend. She had felt better when he was away. Now she was much worse. She didn't have vertigo. And, she had been right, he did sound elated on the phone, Michelle realized, because he had succeeded in poisoning her. As the realization sunk in, the rapidity of her heart palpitations accelerated and her vision blurred and went black.

When the sport coupe reached the top of the driveway, Ken noticed the garage door was partially open. It immediately infuriated him, but he recognized this would be the last time he would be dealing with it. He stepped out of the car and, as he hobbled on his plastic boot over to the garage, saw the cat food strewn across the floor. Now in an absolute rage over the mess he would have to clean up, Ken heaved the double door high up over his head. The metal structure rolled up several feet above his extended hands. Then he heard a huge bang inside the garage and jerked his head up just as the heavy door came smashing down onto him, fracturing his facial bones and crushing everything under its weight. Grey matter splattered onto the garage floor and driveway. Blood spilled from his shattered skull. His instantly lifeless body was pinned between the heavy aluminum door and the cold, hard cement.

Michelle could no longer open her eyes, but she still heard the boom from inside the garage. Her breath was shallow through her lips, but she felt a smile spread across her face as she was confident the sound was the torsion springs snapping. She listened carefully for any more movement and heard nothing. Michelle assumed Ken was dead, exactly as she had intended. Her back suddenly arched as a severe pain shot through her chest. She slid from the leather sofa to the floor, and within seconds, her breathing ceased. Her body lay still, a curved lump on the solid, wooden floor.

The couple, who were so divided in life, were now united in death.

The world is full of obvious things
which nobody by any chance ever observes.

Arthur Conan Doyle

MIS PROBLEMAS

Bernard Max Resnick

SAWYER JOHNSON WOKE EARLY on Sunday morning. Over coffee, checking his phone for news, he was met with a disturbing headline:

Bus Plunge Kills 4 in Mexico

The details of the accident were striking. It had occurred just across the Texas border, in the small village of Doctor Gonzalez, Mexico. Sixteen injured, four dead, several missing after a passenger bus careened off a hillside cliff. Sawyer was puzzled that the article referred to two of the missing as "gringos negros," a phrase he'd never heard before. While the accident was being investigated, it was expected to be thwarted by an incoming tropical storm.

He'd read about these sorts of tragedies before. The details seldom varied. Sawyer finished his coffee and turned his attention to household chores done to the background sounds of ESPN.

The next morning, Sawyer reported to work and settled into his office. He had no appointments scheduled. As a member of the legal team of Colossal Records, he knew better than to schedule an appointment on a Monday, because he was never sure what "urgent task" or contract might end up on his desk. He spent much of the morning answering email and surfing the web.

Marie Peck, a young talent scout working in the artists and repertoire (A&R) department, entered his office at 11:30. Sawyer liked Marie's ears–she had terrific musical knowledge and taste well beyond her tender years, and she had a photographic memory for melody, lyrics, and rhythm. She could recall just about every piece of music she had ever heard, without needing a database to help her sort out the composer, vocalist, performers, or producer. Marie was particularly adept at recognizing and recalling musical melodies and vocalists.

Dressed in typical industry black from head to toe, and sporting a new piercing along the bridge of her pert nose, Marie sank her petite figure into Sawyer's guest chair without so much as asking if this was a good time. Nearly breathless, she showed Sawyer the online news feed on her smart phone. "Did you see this? I think D-Town might have been on that bus that crashed in Mexico!" It took him a second, but Sawyer's eyes opened wider as he suddenly remembered the bus plunge article he'd read the day before.

D-Town, aka Donovan Townsend, was a new and talented rapper from Port Arthur, Texas. Colossal had been courting D-Town in hopes that he would sign a long-term, multi-album contract with the label. Sawyer's job description didn't include talent scouting, but he had recently met D-Town after a performance at the office. The artist had been invited to display his abilities at Colossal, where he had given a thirty-minute audition for the staff. Sawyer knew that D-Town was a great candidate for the label: good looks, a unique way of using odd time signatures to create distinct rhythmic patterns in his rap lyrics, and a regional fan base of over 50,000 friends and followers across social media. Loyal listeners followed D-Town's concerts, travelling from his home base of Texas to as far east as Pensacola, Florida. The artist's regional success was home grown. Colossal's executives were beyond anxious to sign him, record his full-length debut album, and try to launch D-Town onto the national music scene.

Not everyone loved D-Town. The jealous nature of the highly competitive rap music industry, combined with the desperately poor, crime-riddled neighborhood where he grew up, meant that things weren't always sunshine and smiles for the budding musician. He couldn't afford the protection of his own lawyer or manager. Townshend had made a few questionable business decisions typical of the cocky inexperience of youth. He'd borrowed money from the Boyle Brothers, heads of the Mexican-American street gang known as Rolling 70s, to finance his single "Mis Problemas." The Boyles decided that they owned a percentage of D-Town's future profits. Nothing was in writing, but it didn't matter. D-Town knew that the Boyles preferred lead bullets over lead pencils.

As Marie continued to surf the web on her phone, Sawyer recalled a recent meeting he'd had with D-Town.

"Have you ever signed a recording contract before?"

"I ain't never had no contract at all. Not even for the jams I have out now. One of my homies knows Bubby Boyle, and he got Bubby to put up the $500 for the recording session when we cut 'Mis Problemas.' I had to pay for the studio, the music producer, and the back-up singers. I paid them back $600 already and they still be wanting more. You help me, bro?"

"Believe it or not, D-Town, there are rules for lawyers, and one of them is that we have to avoid conflicts of interest. I work for Colossal, so when we do our deal, I'll be on Colossal's side of the table. You've got to get your own lawyer to take care of this, because Colossal wants to release 'Mis Problemas' nationally right after you sign with us."

"Mis Problemas" was a mixture of Mexican Norteno-style rhythm and instrumentation, which D-Town sung in a hodge-podge of the English and Spanish languages known as Spanglish.

When he wasn't rapping, he was unwrapping. D-Town had also begun gobbling up Mexican junk food, developing an insatiable taste for garbage like sweet soda and salty fried plantains. Despite being barely old enough to drop out of high school, D-Town was quickly becoming larger than life, both in the figurative sense from his budding fame and in the literal sense from his expanding waistline.

Young people were singing along with "Mis Problemas." Before long, the local notoriety of "Mis Problemas" brought young D-Town to the attention of Colossal's A&R department.

Marie had been assigned as liaison to D-Town by Colossal's Vice President of A&R. In just a few short weeks, she had befriended D-Town and had quickly learned details about his family and his entourage. Marie knew that D-Town and his half-sister, Brenda Lopez, had planned a visit to Monterrey to see Brenda's birth father, Diego Lopez. Lopez was a small-time hoodlum who had recently been deported back to Mexico after being placed on the ICE "black list" of crooks and smugglers. Since Lopez wasn't going to be able to see her dad in Texas anytime soon, she persuaded D-Town to accompany her on a visit to see Diego in Monterrey.

Even though they were half siblings, Brenda and D-Town hadn't been very close until recently. Marie viewed Brenda as an opportunist who would try to make herself indispensable to D-Town and profit when his record charted.

So when Marie saw the news story about the bus plunge and the missing passengers near where D-Town and Brenda were supposedly visiting Diego, she panicked. Crossing her legs in Sawyer's office, she shared her concerns with Sawyer. "I stopped by D-Town's house on the way to work today, and the place was really quiet. Nobody was around."

"Just because someone isn't home doesn't mean they're dead, Marie. Don't you think you're jumping to conclusions?"

"I dunno. That story in the news fits the timing perfectly, and why would the interviewed survivors mention 'gringos negros'? Why would somebody remember strangers on a bus, especially enough to realize the strangers weren't locals, or even notice the strangers were missing?"

"Even if you're right, if you cross over into Mexico and walk into a police station with this yarn, they'll smile, pat you on the head, and send you on your merry way without even letting you file a report."

"Knowing what I know about D-Town and Brenda, I'm already connecting the dots, and the picture isn't pretty. I think he has bigger worries than 'Mis Problemas'. So I'm going to Monterrey this afternoon. And you, Sawyer the lawyer, are coming with me." Sawyer knew her well enough not to say no. "We'll need to stop at my place first so I can grab my passport."

After crossing the Texas-Mexico border, they continued onto Monterrey. Posing as vacationers, Marie capitalized on her Spanish acumen and learned more about the bus accident. "Police suspect the bus ran off the cliff due to loose gravel, or maybe a rockslide. It was a local bus, but several survivors mentioned that there were two young African-American passengers on board—one male, one female. No one's seen them since the crash, and navigating a crew down the side of the hill to salvage bodies isn't likely to happen anytime soon."

Their makeshift investigation was thwarted by the tropical storm's arrival and they returned to Texas, still no closer to knowing for sure if Donovan Townshend and Brenda Lopez had been passengers of the ill-fated bus.

—

No one saw or heard from D-Town or Brenda for several weeks. Petra Townshend, D-Town and Brenda's mom, eventually filed a missing person's report. The police reasoned that the duo might have gone to visit Diego. They explained that if a brother and sister decided to take a trip or to just move elsewhere, it was their prerogative. It didn't mean that any crime had been committed.

—

Months passed. D-Town was MIA. Gigs were cancelled, bills went unpaid, and his social media presence was nil. Rumors of his disappearance and occasional blog entries of suspected sightings began to surface on music chat pages and hip-hop music forums online, fueling a surge in his popularity. D-Town's sudden disappearance from the music scene while on the cusp of stardom caused a furor of internet speculation.

—

In early fall, Marie was tasked to review several dozen demos of Reggaeton music submitted to Colossal by Latino managers and entertainment lawyers who were trying to solicit deals for their clients. Marie dutifully listened to the demos. None made much of an impression, until she listened to the demo from an artist named Dr. Gonzalez. The raps were in Spanish, but the singer's Spanish sounded like it had an American accent. The demo consisted of two songs, audio only. No photographs, no video, no bio. No story beyond the music, and no way to tell if the artist had a marketable look. Nothing but an email address. Marie suddenly recognized the cadence of rhythms of the singer. It was D-Town.

She played tracks by Dr. Gonzalez and D-Town to Sawyer and reasoned that the artists might be the same. Although skeptical, Sawyer recalled a vague detail about the bus plunge from earlier that year. He Googled a map of the area. "Look at this ... Doctor Gonzalez just happens to be the name of the closest village to the bus plunge! We're going back to Mexico."

—

Sawyer and Marie arrived at the home of Brenda's father in Monterrey thirty-six hours later. It was Sunday morning and the house was empty. Church bells rang throughout the town.

"Maybe check the local parishes," Sawyer suggested.

They visited several churches before approaching a local parish church called San Bernardo. Music was being played within the church.

Marie quickly recognized its cadence. She and Sawyer stepped inside and glanced at D-Town performing on stage accompanied by a host of musicians. "That's him! He's thinner and bearded, but my ears know it's D-Town."

As the service concluded, Sawyer and Marie subtly approached D-Town, who was accompanied by Brenda and Diego. Sawyer spoke to their backs, shouting, "Hey, D-Town!" Reflexively, the young rapper turned to face Sawyer. Before Diego or Brenda could interrupt, he blurted out in unaccented Texas street drawl, "Yo dude, we know each other?" Brenda tried to take command and whisk D-Town away, but Marie interjected.

"D, it's me, Marie, the A&R from Colossal. You remember Sawyer. You sent your Dr. Gonzalez demo to us, remember?"

Sensing trouble, Sawyer tried to diffuse the potentially explosive situation. "Look, we clearly need to have a conversation. Let's wait until the congregation clears out and have a ... chat. How about in there?"

The quintet stepped into the vacant vestry.

"The rumors of your deaths have been wildly exaggerated," Sawyer said.

"This is how it is. I had to help my bro get away from the Boyles and I also wanted to see my pops," Brenda explained. "I read on the internet about how some rich crooked banker disappeared to another country to avoid a tax bill. So I got me an idea that D-Town could disappear just like that."

"Were you two on the bus that plunged over the cliff?" Marie asked.

"We did what we had to do," Brenda said. "I paid a couple local boys to help mess with the road surface just before the bus came along. Loose gravel and rocks. D-Town and me been chopping it up with some of the passengers. Didn't give our names, but we kind of stood out."

"A reverse alibi," Sawyer said. "No doubt the two of you got off the bus at the last rest stop before it took that fatal plunge."

Brenda issued a smug smile. "After that, we just needed to reinvent D-Town. The weight loss helped. Beard didn't hurt neither."

"What do we do about this?" D-Town asked.

"I think it's obvious," Sawyer said. "We sign you to Colossal. Everyone makes buckets of money. We bury what you did. We'll get a stack of cash over to the Boyles to get them off your back for good. Everyone lives happily ever after. ¿Es bueno?"

"Muy bien. I'm gonna like doin' business with you, Gringo," Brenda said.

"We'll be in touch early next week," Sawyer promised.

—

As they drove back to Texas, Marie, who had been silent, suddenly spoke out.

"I had no idea you were such a negotiator."

"I'm not. But I figured it was the best play to get us out of there alive. Donovan and Brenda are responsible for the loss of four lives, Marie. They're going to pay for their crimes."

Sawyer punched up the address of the nearest police station on the GPS. Minutes later, he and Marie entered the station and were greeted by the desk sergeant. "Buenas dias, Senor y Senora, can I assist you?"

Sawyer smiled. "Sí. We need to talk with you about some problems. Mis Problemas."

We writers, as we work our way deeper into our craft, learn to drop more and more personal clues. Like burglars who secretly wish to be caught, we leave our fingerprints on broken locks, our voiceprints in bugged rooms, our footprints in the wet concrete.

Ross Macdonald

A MURDER IN MANILA

Jonathan Ochoco

WHEN OFFICER MANNY MORALES responded to the call of a dead body at Manila's North Cemetery, he hadn't expected to find a leg bone sticking out of a man's chest.

The slums of Manila were bad, but he couldn't understand living in a cemetery, always surrounded by the dead. His stomach churned as he entered beneath the cemetery archway and was greeted by children holding skulls. The vinegary scent of adobo wafted in the air among the makeshift food stalls, but there was an underlying smell of decay. He pulled a stick of Juicy Fruit from his pocket and unwrapped it before popping the gum into his mouth hoping the taste could make him forget the odor. Manny flicked the wrapper onto the ground next to cigarette butts and used condoms.

He passed a makeshift barbershop and karaoke lounge before spying a crowd of men and women dressed in dirty T-shirts and with plastic *tsinelas* of all colors on their feet. They gathered outside a white marble mausoleum blackened by Manila's smog.

"*Umalis ka diyan*," he commanded. "Get away from there!"

The faces of those around him filled with suspicion at the sight of the policeman. It was the same snarling expressions he'd seen when he was here a few days ago after a boy had overdosed. A cockroach scurried along the path. Manny likened the drug addicts here to cockroaches, because no matter how many were stamped out, there were always more.

As the crowd dispersed, Manny entered the mausoleum. A male figure lay sprawled on top of a raised tomb against the far wall. The man's arms and legs hung over the sides. One of his mustard-colored *tsinelas* clung to his toes. The other slipper lay against the wall. His threadbare T-shirt was smeared scarlet with the bone protruding from his chest. Blood puddled around the man and oozed down the side of the tomb. His face was swollen and bruised.

Speaking in Tagalog, Manny asked, "Who found the body?"

His question was met with solemn faces and downturned eyes. Always the same response.

Manny nearly choked on his gum when a frail-looking elderly man with missing front teeth and leathery brown skin raised his arm. "Do you know this man?"

"Sir, his name was Danilo Santiago. We are both caretakers here in the cemetery. We work in the rows of stacked tombs, the ones they call the 'apartments'."

Manny was all-too familiar with the stacked tombs. They were resting places for the deceased, rented for a period of five years by surviving family members. After the five-year period had elapsed, unless additional rent was received, the remains would be removed and the tomb rented to a new tenant.

"Did Danilo use *shabu*?"

"He never used meth or any drugs."

"You're sure? Maybe he was selling drugs for extra money so he could leave here."

"I know it, sir. We worked together for twenty years. Danilo would never leave."

Manny frowned. "Why not?"

"This is his home; his wife is buried in the tomb there. Danilo would never leave her."

A wave of horror and nausea washed over Manny. He sighed.

"What else do you know?"

The old man looked around at a sea of disapproving faces.

"Last night, I heard Danilo fighting with Ernesto Ramil, another caretaker. Something about money. When I came to work this morning, I found Danilo."

"Where can I find Ernesto?"

"He lives in the blue mausoleum in the next row toward the far side. It has a plaque for the Santos family and the stone cross on top has a portion missing."

Manny inspected the body further. The bone had gone right through the heart. Given the amount of blood, he suspected that the murder may have occurred just after sunrise.

He turned to the old man. "Stay here while I speak with Ernesto. Thank you, *po*."

Manny followed the instructions to Ernesto's home. When he stepped into the doorway, he saw a man praying on his knees to a Virgin Mary wall thermometer hanging above a tomb. In the left corner of the room, a baby slept on a sheet of cardboard. The man's clothes were stained with blood.

"*Susmaryosep!*" Manny yelled. "Police! Don't move!"

The man remained on his knees and raised both arms.

Manny read Ernesto his rights. "Turn around slowly and keep your hands up." Ernesto did as instructed. Manny flinched at the dried blood splattered across the man's face and shirt.

"Please, sir, I did not mean for it to happen," Ernesto said.

"Tell me everything."

"I have been praying for a sign from the Virgin Mary. Now that you're here, I know I must confess."

"*Sige*. Go on."

"You were here several days ago for Felipe, the boy you said had overdosed. Do you remember?"

Manny nodded.

"Felipe had stolen money from drug dealers and asked Danilo and I to hide it. The gang found Felipe and injected him with shabu. You were told this, but you didn't want to believe it. You had already made up your mind about Felipe."

Ernesto gave Manny a knowing look. "Danilo wanted to give the money to the church because he thought it would only bring evil and carry Felipe's ghost. This morning, I tried to retrieve the money from the hiding place, use it to help my family, my child. Danilo caught me and we started to fight. In the heat of the struggle, I stabbed him and then quickly took the money home."

Ernesto began crying, tears streaking his bloody face.

"I only wanted something better for my family, but I feel so ashamed."

Manny stared at the guilt-ridden man. "Where's the money?"

Ernesto lifted a corner of the cardboard as the baby continued to sleep, revealing a small hole in the floor. He retrieved a pink plastic bag and handed it to Manny.

Manny opened the bag and his eyes widened upon seeing the piles of crumpled cash within. He hesitated. What point would it serve to arrest Ernesto, a man trying to escape the dead?

Yet this was murder. There was always a price to pay for murder.

"You can thank Felipe's ghost, Ernesto. He has paid for your crime." Manny spat his gum onto the dirty floor before walking away with the bag.

SLEEP TO SEE TOMORROW'S MEMORIES OF YESTERDAY

Robert Lewis Heron

tiny soul tiny tick-tock
the softness of midnight's tiny sadness
smile stretching far and large
a morphing new butterfly
first light first breath first scream
first pain first cry first dream
first step first tooth first wet-dream
first word first clenched-fist first ice-cream
first year first decade first academe
first shave first suit first Brylcreem
first drink first hangover first Jim Beam
first marriage first affair first blaspheme
first divorce first investment first Ponzi scheme
first Prozac first therapist first Kahlua-and-Cream
first fast car first bad crash first Dentu-Creme
first gray hair first loss first pipe-dream
first heart attack first lost memory first wet dream
last Christmas last sunrise last sunbeam
last high ball last visit last daydream
lost soul tiny tick-tock
the harshness of midnight's tiny sadness
smile stretching far and large
a morphing old butterfly returns to dust

SILVER WEBS FORM INSECT SHROUDS

Robert Lewis Heron

Birds
sing
and
branches
sway.

It's the breeze that carries the day,
with intense green of light unseen
bathing branches and bark between
bouts of darkest shadow and whitest clouds,
and silver webs form insect shrouds,
and water beetles stroll across
so many ripples pond to emboss,
and pinks and reds and rose beds sing,
as stems dance to the breezes swing.
And engines drone up so, so high,
their wings drop shadows from the sky
to move and slither across new mown grass,
and duck with chicks ignore the pass
leaving ripples to flow and fan
around the rusty oozing can
and the oil slick from a diesel motor
covering the carcass of a decaying otter,
and the bloody syringe slowly floating by
a hopping seagull with one leg, and one eye

ripped off by some discarded fish line
still attached, its wing to entwine
and it hops to its final resting place
beside a piece of discarded wedding dress lace

and was the bride happy and gay
on her most special day
and did her guests enjoy food and wine
like rats gnawing on trash to dine
and feral cats feeding on old fish bones
beside sleeping winos without permanent homes
and the breeze carries Taps from far away
from a graveside in the cemetery
and dogs bite and howl and bark
at a shadowy figure in the park
and a breeze carries a gunshot sound
as a cop fires round after round after round
and another and another and another
followed by the screams and cries of a black mother.

Birds
sing
and branches sway.
It's
the
breeze
that
carries
the
day.

If you have a story that seems worth telling, and you think you can tell it worthily, then the thing for you to do is to tell it, regardless of whether it has to do with sex, sailors or mounted policemen.

Dashiell Hammett

THE CASE OF THE MISLAID EGGS

Patsy Pratt-Herzog

AS CHIEF INVESTIGATOR to her Majesty, Queen Victoria, Prudence was accustomed to dangerous assignments, but if she couldn't find what had been stolen from the Honorable Wizard, Lord Herbert Fitzgerald, this one had the potential to be apocalyptic.

She sighed. In her opinion, wizards were a huge bother–be they personal friends of the Queen or not. Old Herbie had really mucked it up this time, and Her Majesty was decidedly not amused by his carelessness.

Prudence paused before the hall mirror to smooth the fall of her periwinkle gown over the hidden pockets in her petticoat. Accessed through concealed openings in the seam of her dress, the weapons secreted there were a tad bulky, but one could never be too careful when dealing with the magical set. Wizards were not only bothersome but were all-too-often treacherous.

Puffing steam, Herbie's MechServ butler trundled toward her on gleaming brass wheels. Gorcab wore an impeccably pressed frock coat with a row of polished brass buttons down the front, and a jaunty red cravat expertly tied beneath his clockwork face. He had put her suspects in the darkroom where evidence of their antics was on prominent display.

Gorcab rolled to a stop. "Lord Winters wishes to express his displeasure at being kept waiting, Miss Prudence." The MechServ's voice was deep but slightly tinny through his voder, as if a large man was speaking through a tiny funnel. No matter her mood, it always made her smile.

Her *guests* had been left to stew for a quarter of an hour. "Getting impatient, is he?" she asked.

"Yes, Miss."

"Good. Then it's time to stir the pot."

Gorcab affected a little bow from the pivot of his wheels. "I shall be ready by the door, Milady . . . with the broom, if necessary."

Gorcab was a treasure. He shooed pigeons from the landing and people from the foyer with equal aplomb.

"I suspect a bucket of cold water might be more effective on the gentleman in question," she said with a grin as they set off in opposite directions.

Magical orbs flickered in sconces as she swept down the hallway. She preferred mechanics to magic herself, but most wizards had more ego than brains. A gas explosion could destroy your house, but an explosion of the magical variety could turn your entire street to sticky goo.

Prudence wrinkled her nose at the smell of photographic chemicals still lingering as she entered the darkroom. It really was a nasty place to be kept waiting, and the red covers over the gas lamps only added to the baleful atmosphere.

Lord Rodrick Winters regarded her with frosty annoyance. Rodrick was one of *those* wizards who wore a sweeping, dramatic cape and a top hat no matter the weather or the time of day. His dark formal suit contrasted sharply with the red interior of the cape he seemed to enjoy flailing about like some exotic bird preening its feathers.

His companion, a buxom young lady in the uniform of a French maid, wore an amused smile and little else. If anything could be said of her, Gabriella Rousseau certainly wasn't shy. But Prudence wasn't here to judge the outrageous costuming habits of French domestic servants.

"What is the meaning of this?" Lord Winters demanded, gesturing at the scandalous photos strung along the lines to dry.

The man had decidedly crass inclinations when it came to female companionship, Prudence mused. Herbie's security MechTographer had caught His Lordship in an unseemly embrace with the very maid now standing beside him. Both of his hands had been clutching Miss Rousseau's well-rounded posterior! *Positively shocking behavior for a man of his station.*

"The meaning of your trespass in Lord Fitzgerald's home? Or of your trespass upon the person of his maid?" Prudence asked sweetly.

"Impudent child," he sputtered, swishing his cape. "You'll regret crossing me."

"You'll find I don't take kindly to threats, Lord Winters," she said coldly.

He gave her a long measuring look, and obviously found that her words had merit. Lord Winters relaxed his combative posture and presented her with a smile that held more leer than charm.

"The last time I checked, a bit of slap and tickle wasn't a crime. What right have you to detain us here?"

"You are here because you are accused of theft."

"Mademoiselle, I vould never do such a zing," Gabriella assured her, lashes fluttering over luminous brown eyes.

Magic sparked between Lord Winters' fingertips, drawing all attention to him in the dimly lit room. "Stealing is an occupation for peasants. What I want, I create."

Prudence rolled her eyes. *Really? The ego of wizards.* She raised her gloved hand to silence further protests. "You are the only individuals who had motive and opportunity." She pointed to the photographs. "You were both clearly in the house at the time of the theft."

"Just what are we accused of stealing?" Lord Winters asked.

"Eggs, from the Honorable Wizard Lord Herbert Fitzgerald's laboratory."

Lord Winters laughed.

"Eggs? We aren't hungry foxes, Miss Cummings," Lord Winters said snidely.

"These are no ordinary eggs." Prudence walked over to the workbench and removed a silken cover from atop a filigreed brass case. Watching them closely, she opened the lid to reveal a green, jewel-like egg resting on a heated cushion. The egg was shot through with pulsating lines of black and twinkled like an oval emerald.

Lord Winters was the first to react. He lurched backward with a curse.

"A dragon egg? Are you mad? When it hatches it will ravage all of London!"

"When *they* hatch," Prudence corrected.

"There are more of them?" Lord Winters asked.

"Five more," Prudence said.

The color drained from his face. "Dragons cannot be controlled. They will multiply and destroy England as they did Australia! Fitzgerald is insane—he'll kill us all!"

"Is that why you took the eggs?" Prudence asked in her most reasonable tone.

Lord Winters drew himself up to his full, considerable height and looked down his nose at her. "I'm neither mad nor a fool. I took nothing!"

Strangely, Prudence believed him. When she turned, Gabriella was holding the egg lovingly in her right hand.

"They can be controlled," she purred, clutching the egg to her chest. "The potion requires six—six dragon eggs to rule the world. And thanks to that doddering old fool, they're finally mine!"

Gabriella's French accent had vanished along with the rest of her act.

Prudence slipped her hand through the concealed slit in her skirt, her fingers finding the tassel of her fan. "Who are you really?"

Gabriella waved her left hand down her body. Blonde hair became inky black, and brown eyes brightened to icy blue. Her soft curves rearranged themselves into something leaner and more feral.

Lord Winters gasped. "Lady Odom?"

Lady Raven Odom, the slyest dark sorceress in all of England, stood before them with a triumphant gleam in her eyes. Her triumph quickly faded as her right hand started to smoke and burn. She dropped the egg with a startled cry, but the scanty fabric covering her breasts was smoking as well. Hopping and shrieking she pulled the material away from her skin and five green eggs dropped to the ground to join the sixth. Lucky for the whelps within, dragon eggs were a good deal more resilient than the average chicken variety. They bounced when they hit the ground and rolled beneath the workbench.

"The *doddering old fool*, as you called him, didn't think you could resist picking it up," Prudence said with a smirk. "A clutch of six eggs generates its own heat for incubation. You should have done your homework, Lady Odom."

With a snarl, the sorceress raised her singed hand, her fingertips luminous with magic. She launched a spell from those glowing fingers that spiraled its way toward Prudence like a twirling ribbon of scarlet light.

Prudence jerked her bladed fan from its hidden pocket and snapped it open. Its reflective surface was inscribed with protective runes and magical wards that acted like a shield. She expertly angled the fan before her, and the spell aimed at her bounced back at the sorceress like a volley off a badminton racket.

With a shriek that ended in a yowl, Lady Odom's body collapsed in on itself, transforming into a sleek black cat.

The cat hissed as Prudence knelt to retrieve the eggs.

"You've no one to blame but yourself," she chided.

As Prudence secured the eggs back in their box the cat spat and puffed out its tail.

"Don't be a sore loser, Lady Odom. It's most unbecoming."

When Prudence rose once again with the box of eggs, Lord Winters was staring at her with a mixture of terror and arousal that she didn't find at all pleasant.

"What other interesting toys do you have secreted upon your person?" he asked with a leer.

Fortunately, the weapon she held was useful against more than just magical miscreants. Prudence pulled the tassel at the bottom of the fan and serrated blades sprang out at the tip of each section, their razor-sharp edges gleaming in the ruddy light.

"Pray you need never find out." Prudence flourished the fan as she pointed at the door. "That will be all, Lord Winters. And do put the cat out when you go."

There are only two kinds of books which you can write and be pretty sure you're going to make a living–cook books and detective stories.

Rex Stout

IN DEATH, SHE SPEAKS THE TRUTH

Liliana Widocks

"THE BOOKS KILLED ME."

With those words, eighty-seven-year-old Delores Wrong dropped to the floor of the sheriff's office, the knife firmly planted in her chest. Seconds later, the sheriff's deputy, Tim Cullins, also collapsed.

Sheriff Masterson glanced back at Mrs. Wrong, and then at his deputy. He quickly phoned for an ambulance and then approached the aged woman. He pressed two fingers upon her left wrist but felt no pulse. Behind him, Deputy Cullins slowly awoke.

"Did you actually faint?" Masterson asked his deputy.

"Well, the air in here is really thin and hot," Cullins said, sheepishly, and rose to his feet. "Want me to phone an ambulance?"

"I already did. But she's beyond any help the EMTs might offer."

Sheriff Masterson was new to Dagshead, having relocated from Cape County, and was unfamiliar with many of the town's residents. He knew Delores, albeit slightly, since she worked at the town library.

"What do you know about Delores Wrong?" he asked Cullins.

"That woman had been always trouble. Over the years, she'd curated a collection of enemies that was as long as a grocery list. Then again, most librarians I've known have been nasty, so who am I to say?"

"She said the books killed her. What do you suppose that was about?"

Cullins chuckled. "Not sure. I don't think we have poison books, but I'm not much of a reader either."

—

Mrs. Wrong's body was transported to nearby Smithville Hospital where it was placed in the morgue. Sheriff Masterson and his deputy promptly began their investigation, arriving shortly thereafter at Mrs. Wrong's house. The front door was unlocked and the men entered. The house was peaceful, spotless, and smelled like a spring garden.

"Doesn't exactly look like a crime scene," Masterson said.

"No, but take a look at this." Tim Cullins pointed a finger at a note on the refrigerator door.

Masterson approached and read the note. "Pay the Books for the milk." He stared back at his deputy. "Am I missing something?"

"*The books killed me*. I think Mrs. Wrong might have been referring to Avery, Angie, and Auggie Books. Known around here as the Books cousins."

"Well, that's some mighty fancy detective work, Deputy. You know much about these cousins?"

"Nice people, really. Avery owns a farm and they all live and work there. They have a small milk delivery business. I guess Mrs. Wrong was one of their customers."

Sheriff Masterson opened the refrigerator door and retrieved a half-empty bottle of milk. He unscrewed the lid and moved the bottle close to his nose. "It's gone sour. I suppose we'd best speak with these Books."

—

The interview with the Books cousins was uneventful. Avery admitted that she did not particularly like Delores Wrong, mostly because Delores was a rapid gossip, but she certainly bore her no hard feelings and seemed genuinely shocked to learn about her sudden death.

"I don't think she has any family," Avery added. "Do let us know if there's anything we can do to help out with the funeral."

Cullins and Masterson drove back to town following the interview.

"I dunno, Sheriff. Did those cousins look like killers to you?"

"I suppose not. But let's not be too quick to eliminate them from the suspects list. You did say that the old woman worked at the library, didn't you?"

Tim nodded. "Yep."

"Let's see what we can find out there."

—

The library was closed and locked tight. The policemen stopped by the home of the head librarian, Beatrice McCaffery. By this time, news of Mrs. Wrong's death had spread throughout much of Dagshead, though the news came as a shock to Beatrice. Based on the time of day Mrs. Wrong had arrived at the sheriff's office, it became apparent that she must have locked up the library for the day. This meant that somewhere between the two blocks that separated the library from the sheriff's office, Mrs. Wrong was attacked.

Beatrice accompanied Masterson and Cullins to the library and she unlocked the front door. There were books scattered about in the small entranceway. Several books, and an empty cardboard box, rested atop a metal table that appeared to be a makeshift mailing station which included rolls of tape and various assorted packing materials. A small puddle of water was on the floor that, based on the staining on the ceiling, appeared to have formed from an overhead leaky pipe.

"There's ... usually a knife here," Beatrice said.

"A knife?"

"We're just across the street from the post office. Often, people will use this table here to ready their packages for mailing. They'd sometimes use the knife to open mail or cut cardboard to size. It's just cleaner and quieter here than that old postal building, I suppose. The lobby's become a sort of meeting place. There's even free coffee most days." Beatrice pointed to the small coffee machine in the corner of the lobby.

Beatrice glanced at the titles of the various books both on the table and on the floor.

"I'd say that Delores was probably planning to take these home to read. They're all books on gardening, and even at her age she is ... *was* ... an avid gardener."

—

From there, the case wrapped up quickly.

The autopsy revealed what everyone already knew. When shown the knife, Beatrice confirmed that it was the same one usually found at the library. The knife was checked for fingerprints, but because it had been used by so many people in town, fingerprinting proved pointless.

Sheriff Masterson theorized that as she was leaving the library, Mrs. Wrong had stopped at the desk with her gardening books, had begun using the knife to cut a small box to more easily carry the books, and had slipped on the puddle of water that had formed from a leaking overhead pipe. She'd fallen face first, impaling herself with the blade. She then staggered down the empty street to the sheriff's office and made her dying proclamation.

"She told us exactly what had happened," Deputy Cullins said, "so that no one in town might be falsely accused of murder."

"You're saying she was right?" Masterson asked.

"I guess that's what I'm saying. Wrong was right."

NIGHT VIGIL

David W. Dutton

Willoughby, Delaware 1948

ELLIOTT CHANDLER KNEW the raucous sound was that of the phone even before he came fully awake. His ear was attuned to it after all the years of being Willoughby's only police officer. In a small town like Willoughby, a policeman was on-call all day, every day.

Elliott swung his bare feet off the side of the bed and looked at the Big Ben's luminous dial. It was 2:17. *Damn!* He'd had a hard time getting to sleep in the unseasonal heat of this particular October. It was an Indian summer that was more like a heat wave in August. Now, that sleep was ruined.

He stood and padded across the bare wood floor to the top of the stair. He didn't want to wake his wife, Marjorie. Somehow, she had grown accustomed to the late-night phone calls and was able to sleep through them.

Elliott grasped the banister and guided himself down the stair to the little table which supported their telephone. The instrument continued its discordant plea, knowing that he would eventually answer its cry.

With a sigh, he picked up the ear piece and spoke into the daffodil-shaped receiver. "Yeah."

His voice was tired and weary.

"El?" The voice was distant. "That you?"

"Yeah ... who's this?"

"It's Butch Donovan."

Butch was the red-haired, burly owner of Donovan's River

House. He ran a tight ship, and Elliott seldom had any problems with him or his establishment.

"What's up, Butch?"

There was a pause. "Well ... we've had a bit of an incident. I think you'd better come out here."

Elliot sighed again. *Just what I need at 2:17 in the morning.* "What kind of incident?"

"One of my girls was pretty well beaten up. She claims she was ... well ... raped."

"Oh, Jesus, Butch. Who was it?"

Butch took a breath. "My headliner, Julie Thomas. She's in a bad way, El."

"Well, call the ambulance. I'll be right out."

"I already have. Thanks."

Elliott knew Julie Thomas. She was a nice girl in spite of her profession. Donovan's River House boasted a bevy of beautiful girls whose expertise was fan dancing. As much as they would have liked, most of Willoughby's respectable male population did not visit the River House. It was a dive, plain and simple.

Elliott sighed. *So much for a good night's sleep.* "I'll be there in ten."

Dressed in his uniform of blue shirt and blue jeans, Elliott started the old Oldsmobile and gunned its six cylinders. The Olds wasn't much of a police car, but free was about all the Town of Willoughby could afford.

Councilman Bertram Russell bought his wife a new car every two years or so. He had purchased the blue, two-toned sedan in 1942. His wife had to live with that until the war ended. Once victory had been achieved, and the car manufacturers were back in production, Russell purchased a shiny, new Packard for his wife. He had donated the Olds to the police department, and the town had scraped together enough money to outfit the car with the lights necessary for an official vehicle.

The road along the river was winding and narrow, but Elliott knew it by heart. As he pulled into the clam shell parking lot of the River House, the ancient Cadillac ambulance swerved around him and then headed off to the hospital in Franklin.

Elliott cursed the near collision and swung the police car into a spot adjacent to the bar. The parking lot was well illuminated by a series of outdoor lights. It was also full of people, most likely customers, and they appeared to be highly agitated.

As Elliott killed the engine and opened the door, he spied Butch Donovan among the crowd. Butch saw him immediately and walked quickly toward the car.

Butch ran his fingers through his thick, red hair. "Thank God. I thought you'd never get here."

Elliott smiled. "Hey, cut me a break. It's almost three in the morning." He paused and looked at the crowded parking lot. "What's going on here?"

Butch took time for a deep breath. "They're a bunch of crazy mother fuckers, mostly customers. They want to string him up right here and now."

Elliott took a beat. "What the hell you talkin' about, Butch? String up who?"

"Ben Jones. That colored fellow what works for me. Caught him in the act, so to speak. Julie was screamin' her head off." Butch shook his head sadly. "Ain't no wonder after what he did to her."

"You mean the Ben Jones who lives with his mother up the hill in Willoughby?"

"Yeah."

"I didn't know he worked for you."

Butch sighed. "Yeah ... said he needed the money to pay for his mother's medicines. She ain't well, you know."

Elliott nodded. "Yeah."

"He's been doin' odd jobs around the bar ... bringin' and breakin' up ice when we need it. Takin' out the trash ... that sort of thing."

"Hard to believe he'd do such a thing."

Butch shook his head. "Yeah ... I know ..."

"Where is he now?"

Butch grabbed Elliott's arm and led him toward the River House. "In the storage room. We tied him up and put him there for his own safety." The crowd formed an impenetrable wall between the two men and the bar.

Elliott sighed. "Jesus Christ!"

Butch shouldered his way through the crowd. "Yeah, but he ain't here."

"Let us have him!" The cry came from the back of the crowd.

"Yeah, the no good sombitch!"

Butch looked at the person responsible for the last comment.

"Oh, shut up, Jake! You're drunk. Go home and let us do our work."

Jake's response was lost in the crowd's cheer.

Reaching the front porch of the River House, Butch threw open the door. The main room was empty ... everyone who had been there an hour ago was now standing in the parking lot.

Elliott took a deep breath and gazed around the empty room. "Where's the storage room?"

"Back here." Butch led the way down a narrow, dimly lit hallway. At the end, he paused and looked at Elliott. "You ready?"

"What you mean? You said you tied him up."

Butch looked down at the floor. "Yeah, but he's a wily bastard. Could have gotten himself free by now."

"Just open the door, Butch. Let's see what we've got."

Butch unlocked the door and pushed it open. The room was dark, and there was no movement from within. Butch fumbled for the light switch, and the single, naked bulb came to life. Ben Jones huddled in the far corner of the room, his hands and feet securely tied.

Elliott stepped into the room and looked down at the man. "Ben, what the hell have you gotten yourself into?"

Ben Jones was a thin, scrawny individual with a mouth full of discolored teeth. He didn't meet Elliott's stare but gazed at the bare wood floor instead.

"Ben, I'm talkin' to you. What the hell is going on?"

Ben simply shook his head.

"Ben, you got to talk to me. Did you rape and beat up that girl?"

The accused slowly raised his head and stared at the police officer. "No, sir."

Elliott sighed. "That's not what I've heard."

The black man sadly shook his head again. "I don't know nothin' about that."

"I got a mob outside that says you raped a white girl tonight, Ben. That sorta thing don't sit well in these parts."

Ben directed his stare back at the floor and sighed. "It was her idea."

"Bullshit!" Butch Donovan was obviously losing his patience.

Elliott held out a hand to Butch, cautioning him to refrain from further comments.

"Tell me exactly what happened."

There was moment of silence as Ben attempted to organize his thoughts. "She were always nice to me ... real polite ... like I mattered. Then, earlier tonight, she told me to meet her in the storage room. She started to undress me. I started to undress her. Few minutes later, someone opened the door. That's when she started pushing me off her, cryin' an' yellin' out for help. Bunch of men grabbed hold of me. My arms and legs was flailing about. I think I kicked her in the jaw, maybe in the ribs, as they was draggin' me away."

Elliott sighed.

"Way I remember it," Butch said, "is *you* were all over her. Sure as hell didn't look like she were enjoying it."

"Well, Ben, we need to take you to Fredericksburg. Stand up and come with me."

Butch cut loose the bindings around Ben's ankles, and the wiry man struggled to his feet. "You takin' me to jail, Misser Chandler?"

"Afraid so, Ben. Right now, that's the best place for you."

Elliott and Butch each grabbed an arm of the prisoner and led him out of the tiny store room. The narrow hallway made it difficult for three grown men to walk abreast, but somehow, they got Ben through it and out into the main room of the bar. After that, their progress became easier ... until they opened the front door and led Ben out onto the wide porch.

As soon as they appeared, the cry went up from the crowded parking lot.

"There he is!"

"Let's get the sombitch!"

Elliott left Ben in Butch's charge and stepped to the top of the front steps. "You all just stand back! I'm taking this man to Fredericksburg."

"Damn it, El, let us have him!" The challenge came from the midst of the angry mob.

"They'll deal with him in Fredericksburg. Now, you all move aside so I can do my job."

Elliott motioned for Butch to lead Ben forward and down the front steps. As Elliott requested, the crowd parted amidst much grumbling. When they reached the Oldsmobile, Elliott opened the rear door, and Butch forced the prisoner into the back seat.

Ben moaned loudly and tried to exit the vehicle. "I don't wants to go to Fredericksburg, Misser Chandler."

Elliott pushed him back into the car and slammed the door shut. "You should have thought about that earlier." He nodded at Butch and then walked around the car to the driver's side door.

"You believe me, don't you Misser Chandler?"

"Hell, Ben, I don't know what to believe. I'll have to speak with Julie to get to the bottom of this."

Elliott slid into the driver's seat and brought the straight 6 to life. He threw the car in gear and backed quickly away from the bar and threatening crowd. Without hesitation, he turned the wheel and roared out of the parking lot. *Damn! What a way to spend Saturday night!*

The ride to Fredericksburg wasn't a long one … only about ten miles. The county jail was located there because Fredericksburg was the county seat.

During the trip, Ben cried quietly while trying to explain his actions, but Elliott wasn't listening. Whenever Ben began to whine, Elliott simply told him to shut up. Elliott had heard enough and needed time to think. *Did Ben rape and beat Julie Thomas? Had it been Julie's idea? What more do I need to know?*

Elliott pulled the car into a parking place at the rear of the county municipal building and killed the engine.

He looked over the back of the seat and stared at Ben. "You stay here. I gotta go inside and make arrangements."

Defeated, Ben simply nodded his head.

Elliott left the car and entered the building. In a matter of minutes, he returned with a deputy sheriff in tow. They stopped alongside the car, and Elliott unlocked the rear door.

The deputy stuck his head in the door and looked at the prisoner. "Assault and rape, you say?"

Elliott sighed. "Yeah, possibly. I haven't interviewed the victim, but all the so-called witnesses seem to agree."

"White girl?"

"Yeah, Julie Thomas. She was a fan dancer at the River House."

The deputy shook his head sadly. "God, what makes these guys think they can get away with something like that?"

"*Allegedly.* Allegedly get away with something like that," Elliott answered.

"You think she was a willing participant in this? Don't be naive."

The deputy grabbed Ben's arm and pulled him out of the car.

"Come on, you worthless piece of shit. We got a nice warm cell waitin' for you."

Ben stumbled but finally regained his footing. Elliott stood watching as the deputy led Ben away.

With a sigh, Elliott slid back into the driver's seat and rested his head against the steering wheel. *Okay, what now? Go home and get some sleep? Go to the hospital and see what they can tell me?* He wanted the former, but he knew that the latter was what he needed to pursue.

Elliott fired up the big car and made a U-turn in the parking lot. It was a straight shot up the main highway to Franklin, and, at this time of night, the road was deserted. Leaning heavily on the accelerator, Elliott coaxed the Olds to eat up the miles.

The hospital was just outside the center of the small town, and Elliott had to thread his way through a series of narrow streets that crisscrossed the neighboring residential area. At this hour, all the streets and houses were dark. It wasn't until the hospital came into view that the night was broken by the lights marking the hospital entrance.

Elliott slowed the car and followed the semi-circular driveway to the front of the two-story brick building. There were no other vehicles parked against the curb so he pulled up to the base of the front steps. The lights on either side of the front door illuminated the steps, but there was no sign of activity.

Inside, the reception desk was unmanned, and the lights in the lobby had been dimmed. Elliott waited a moment, hoping someone would eventually show themselves, but that did not happen. He ran his hand through his thinning brown hair and pushed open a door that led to a wide corridor. Like the reception area, the corridor was empty.

Elliott's heavy work shoes beat a hollow tattoo on the tile floor. About halfway down the hallway, light spilled out of an open doorway. He paused and looked inside the room. It was an office of sorts boasting only an old oak desk and a couple of chairs. A battered desk lamp provided the only illumination.

Doctor William H. Forbes, known as Doctor Bill to the locals, sat on one edge of the desk smoking a cigarette. His nurse, Jeannine Gower, sat at the desk. She was laughing at something Bill had just said.

Elliott cleared his throat and smiled. "Sorry to interrupt."

Both occupants turned to look at him. Doctor Bill laughed and stood. "Hey, El. Helluva night."

Elliott shook his head. "Yeah, just what we needed."

"That poor, poor girl." Jeannine shook her head sadly.

"What can you tell me, Doc?"

Forbes shook his head. "Not much to tell. She was beaten badly ... broken jaw and a couple of broken ribs."

Elliott shook his head. "Jesus."

Jeannine stood up behind the desk. "Well, let me tell you somethin', El. Jesus weren't there when that bastard beat the hell out of her."

"No, I suppose not." Elliott looked at the doctor. "Any evidence of rape?"

Forbes nodded. "Yeah. A lot of bruising, and there was still semen clinging to her pubic area."

Jeannine gasped. "Damn, Doctor Bill, you didn't tell me that."

Forbes laughed. "Didn't think you needed to know, and I didn't want it all over Willoughby before noon tomorrow."

"Doctor Bill! You know I never tell anythin' that happens here at the hospital. I know it's all hush-hush and confidential."

Forbes smiled. "You just remember that."

There was no response from the nurse. Instead, she reclaimed her seat at the desk and sat staring at the two men.

"I need to interview her. Get her side of this. The accused is claiming there was mutual consent. Can I see her?"

Forbes shook his head. "Won't do no good. I gave her a sedative so she could sleep. Come back tomorrow. She should be able to talk to you then."

Elliott nodded. "I figured as much."

"Who done that to her?" Jeannine's voice was full of concern.

"Ben Jones. He helps Butch out at the River House."

Jeannine looked surprised. "Ben Jones?"

"Yeah, you know him?

"Sure, I know him. He's a good guy. Helps my mom out whenever she needs somethin' done." Jeannine shook her head. "Can't believe he'd do somethin' like this."

Elliott sighed. "Well, maybe he did, and maybe he didn't."

"Oh, my God. Of course, he did."

Doctor Bill sighed. "I've known Julie and her family ever since I came to Willoughby. Sweet girl. Always trying to do the right thing and thinking the best about people."

Elliott nodded. "Yeah, that was always my feeling, too."

"Never approved of her working at the River House, but times are hard, and I guess she took the work where she could get it."

Jeannine was suddenly defensive. "Still, that ain't no reason for her to be beaten and raped."

Elliott agreed. "Well, like I said, we'll know more of what happened after I speak with Julie."

The doctor ground out his cigarette in the ashtray next to him. "I feel bad for his mother. She's a really sweet lady."

Jeannine nodded. "Yep, Miss Cassie is the salt-of-the-earth ... always goin' out of her way to help folks."

Elliott nodded. "Butch said Ben was workin' at his place to pay for her medicine."

The doctor sighed. "Yeah, she's one sick lady." He paused and looked at Elliott. "Anyone been around to tell her yet?"

Elliott shook his head. "Nah ... guess that's goin' to be for me to do."

Doctor Bill laid his hand on Elliott's shoulder. "I don't envy you your job, El."

Elliott laughed. "Nor I yours."

—

A light rain had fallen while Elliott was in the hospital. He started the car, turned on the wipers and headlights, and headed home. The ride back to Willoughby was a lonely one. He did pass one car and wondered what the hell anyone was doing out this time of night. Just his natural policeman's defense mechanism working overtime.

Marjorie was still asleep, and he did his best not to awaken her. The bed felt good to his aching back and legs. He was getting too old for this job. The late nights were beginning to take their toll.

Elliott punched his pillow to get the feathers where he wanted them and pulled the thin sheet over his body. *God, it's such a relief to finally relax.*

He plunged into a deep, dreamless sleep. His reprieve was not to last. The discordant clamor of the phone finally penetrated his sleep and brought him upright in bed. Beside him, Marjorie moaned and rolled over, pulling the sheet over her head.

"Sorry, babe." Elliott rose from the bed and retraced his steps across the bedroom, down the stairs and into the front hallway where his nemesis continued to scream at him. He picked up the phone and yanked the earpiece from its cradle.

There was static at first, followed by a distant voice. "Chief Chandler?"

"Yeah. Who's this?"

"It's Deputy Joe Miller at the sheriff's office over here in Fredericksburg."

Alarm bells began to chime in the back of Elliott's head. *What now?*

"We got us a real problem here."

Elliott sighed. "What's up?"

"Bunch of your townsfolk showed up here shortly after you left. Broke down the door, held me down and took the keys to the cell."

"Oh, Jesus!"

"Yeah, hauled the prisoner out into the square and strung him up from that big oak tree. You know the one I mean?'

"Yes, deputy, I know the one you mean. How's the prisoner now?"

"Oh, he's dead, Chief. Broke his neck as nice as you please."

Elliott paused, searching for his next question. "Anyone get hurt?"

The deputy laughed. "Only the prisoner."

"You arrest any of the mob?"

"Hell, no. I knew most of 'em."

Elliott sighed. "You call the Doc?"

"Yeah, he's here right now filling out the death certificate. Wants to talk to you."

"Put him on."

"Yessir."

Several minutes passed before there was activity on the other end of the line. Finally, Doctor Bill picked up the phone. "Hey, El. Helluva night for you."

"Yeah, Doc, you could say that. Yours has been pretty busy as well."

The doctor laughed. "I'm sittin' here trying to fill out this death certificate."

"That's what the deputy said."

"Well, I got a problem."

"What's that?

"What you want me to list as cause of death?"

For a moment, Elliott was confused. "Why you askin' me that?"

"Well, are we goin' to carry this thing out?"

"Meaning?"

The doctor sighed and chuckled. "Are you going to arrest and prosecute those guys who did this? It'll be a big stink if you do."

Elliott nodded to himself. Yeah, that whole thing could be a real mess. Black man lynched by angry white mob. He could see the local headlines now.

Silence separated the two men for several minutes. Finally, Forbes cleared his throat and spoke.

"You still there, El?"

Yeah, I'm here. Just thinkin'. I guess old Ben got due process. Tried and convicted by a group of his peers."

Elliot could almost hear the bones in Bill's neck nod in agreement. "Yeah, I guess you could say that. Well, what's it gonna be?"

Elliott took a deep breath and let it out slowly. "Just say he died of pneumonia."

Doctor Bill cleared his throat. "Pneumonia, it is. No one will be any the wiser."

"Thanks, Doc." Elliott cradled the earpiece and sat the phone back on the table at the foot of the stair.

God, he was beginning to hate this job. But right now, he needed sleep. Slowly, he trudged up the stairs to his bedroom. With a final sigh, he lay down and stared at the darkened ceiling. Hours passed and the morning sun slowly rose over Willoughby's skies, but sleep never came to Elliott Chandler.

Editor's Note: Night Vigil *is based loosely on events that occurred in a small corner of Sussex County, Delaware, in 1948. Some of the facts presented in the manuscript have been altered. For example, the Delaware towns portrayed in this story–Willoughby, Fredericksburg, and Franklin–do not exist. Elliott Chandler, and most of the characters named within this story, are, likewise, fictitious but based on real individuals. The lynching of the character here known as Ben Jones is, sadly, entirely true, but those who might shed additional light on the events of that evening are, like Ben, no longer among the living.*

When in doubt, have a man come through the door
with a gun in his hand.

Raymond Chandler

ISLA DE CORAZÓN PIEDRA

Michael Sarabia

July 2005

MIDNIGHT.

I am cast into the river where I cling to innertubes and pray the tape holds. Moments later, I hit the shore, pulled up by the neck, and watch as my father sputters north under a rain of steel clubs flashing blood. I'm under a muddy boot, hands bundled into a plastic chain. Roughly searched, my pockets are emptied as a silver blanket is wrapped around my shoulders. A gentle-eyed uniform hands over a bottle of water and smiles.

In perfect Spanish she whispers to me. "Drink and then wait for the van."

An hour later I'm pulled into a dark truck, wrists bruised, threatening blood. Tossed into a cage, I muffle my tears, ask God for my father's safe return.

We'd been on the run for months after leaving Guatemala last spring when Coca gangsters showed up to take our land. They shot the mayor and the village priest, chased families into the jungle. We sent messages for help. The army arrived, but they were worse. Making an agreement with the gangsters, the soldiers had burned everything in sight, killed our animals, prepared our land for Coca. We were sodomized, physically and mentally. Gender didn't matter. Better off dead, my father and I ran. We travelled north.

Months later, one nightmare is exchanged for another. My father and I are separated and I stare up from a cage at my captor. There are many of us.

"This is Camp Tranquility, on the US-Mexico border," shouts a perfectly groomed *Indio*. "My name is Corporal Sanchez. On behalf of the US Immigration and Customs Enforcement Agency, let me welcome to your new home. You'll have the best care in the world, and your parents will soon be found. Religious services are provided every day. And while you can give your hearts to God and Jesus, your ass belongs to ICE!"

In the months that follow, I work at becoming invisible. Meals swallowed, cookies and butter tabs snuck away. The corporal routinely beats uncooperative boys, but he never sees me. With steel club, Corporal Sanchez herds boys into dry showers where he holds classes in *education*. I become nothing to no one, dream of my father's voice, hear songs of morning roosters, feel the breath of my mother.

My time eventually arrives. Corporal Sanchez pulls me into a black shower one evening with a smile that says it all. I fight back with fist and feet, am floored and violated. The scene repeats for months until one evening when I fake unconsciousness and am evacuated to critical care at the El Paso Hospital.

On the third night of my reprieve, chance arrives. A family of silver crows soars past my window landing on a truck marked Salas Brothers El Paso Plumbing. I turn away, sleep with eyes open, wait for lights out. Nurse comes and goes twice. On her second exit, I crawl out of the hospital, snake-clung under the truck, shivering breath held. An hour later the bumper dips and the engine starts. We drive into a bright El Paso morning. I roll away at a stop, blindside a school boy in uniform, pull him into an alley, take his clothes, and kick him in the ass. I soon blend into a brown sea, visions of Corporal Sanchez haunting my head.

I live in the street, eat meals picked from dumpsters, steal in silence, bathe and change in gas station restrooms. One night I am chased and cornered by a gang of foul-eyed Mexicanos. I charge and nut-slugg the giant of their lot, bull-rush and punch the rest, laugh as they run.

At times I rent body parts to Gabas, especially when food can't be found. Hands cold, their cars are hot and comfortable. We frequent hotels where they feed me burgers, give me shots of liquor, and sometimes ask my name. Everything to hate. I blame the goddammed Corporal.

As I walk down an empty street, five *Salvadoreños* follow me in the dark. Lurching in my direction, they fill the air with war *gritos* and swing sharpened box openers. One steadies a black rottweiler, feeds him chips and beer. I knowingly run into a dead-end alley, stop, grab an always-present wine bottle, and crack the fat end creating a jagged weapon.

"*Vamonos,*" I swing the bottle. "*Apurase Salva putos!*"

Rottweiler boy flees, but the others stand their ground. Two blasts from a sawed-off empty the alley as the captain smiles and approaches, shotgun swung low.

"I saw you throwing hands last week," he smiles. "I'm Yesca, but everybody calls me Tío. You fight like a small bull, so I'll call you El Torinito. *Soy Zeta, mijo.* Look me up in the morning. I'll find you work."

He claims Zeta Cartel. Fine. Just get me an ICE corporal, Tío Yesca. Preferably one named Sanchez.

August 2007

For the past two years I've grown and changed during my apprenticeship with Tío Yesca. The El Paso streets have belonged to him since the day a table of Dallas gumbahs holy watered and turned him loose. Tío Yesca's got money in the street and I sometimes do his collections, providing dirt when needed. He called today, gave me the who and what, said I should bring him the bag so he can kick up to I-don't-wanna-know-who and settle me my end.

Chatter's the driver. His availability is dictated by the needs of his children. Each of them. He's got more *mocosos* than fingers and toes. Got 'em all over town, too. All colors and religions. Three sets of twins. Two in wheelchairs, one with mental hangups. He loves each very much. Maybe too much. Hands over their mama's cash quick as he gets it, demands and gets 24/7 drop-in rights which he exercises every day. So when not in action, Chatter's likely changing diapers, buying shoes, or teaching his offspring to get in the first and last punch. Father of the year *y qué.* It's his strength and his liability because it won't take much for him to flip and turn state's witness. Chatter has not, far as anyone knows, shirked a task or come up short or pussied out of any of these things he's signed on to do.

Early pickups are no problems. Mom and pop this, gas station that, small-time nickel-bag old-school dealers—people still in the game

just to say they're still in the game—and one forever payoff for a particular heavy-duty favor *para un veterana* providing protection rent for her
very young, very scared, incarcerated offspring doing "life without…"
in Cali.

We vacate El Paso proper, move west on First then up and
over the Olympic Bridge. Chatter pulls over on Mateo Street where we
smoke a couple shakes of Panama Brown, letting the thumping buzz
cool us down. I pop out Chatter's Tex-Mex tape and drop in Al Green
and through it all I got my bread in my shoe, my thumb on the ham-
mer, my father on my mind.

The only reason I'm in these filthy sewers chasing down these
filthy coins is to get cash so I can start the hunt for Corporal Sanchez.
I'll relocate to the Coushatta Reservation in Livingston and open a
pawnshop when it's all said and done. I'll call the place *Padre Mio* in
honor of my father, and keep it open all hours, pulling in interest that'll
choke a horse. I'll maybe parlay that into something big-liquor store,
strip joint. Maybe a laundromat.

We slide down Los Angeles Street, make two rights, dart across
Seventh (a main poli passage) come across and throw a clean yoyo in
front of a boarded church. I eyeball the other side and about half an
hour later comes this mulatto half-breed with muscles everyfucking-
where. I giggle at the sight of Big Jay, third-generation whore master
who's into Tío Yesca for two bills a week come rain or shine, lack of
johns, or pussy-be-gone-whatever.

Big Jay sees us but doesn't come over. Even though he's late,
he's always with the games, and it wouldn't surprise no one if one day
he's poured into a dumpster with an oversized hole in his oversized
head for lack of respect at the very least. I make note of this so that in
case the offer comes in, if it's unassigned and of decent compensation,
I will be the first fucker in that fucking line to hit him in his head like
the pig he is and, thus, be eligible to collect Big Jay's blood money
that'll be due me on that outstanding-fucking day.

Chatter pops the clutch and we spin, landing inches off Big
Jay's shoes. He don't flinch, and for that I give him props. He smiles a
dog-breath, chipped-stone smile, and he is one dangerous blacksican,
no doubt about it. He nods me once and starts to speak, but I grab
him by his buckle and force-fuck my hollow point up his nut sack,
telling him without a smile, "Don't say me one more fucking word,
fucker. Just gimme over Tio's gimme, and it best not be one penny
short or *ay Dios mío* I will blow you wide the fuck open."

I see him in his eye and he's thinking of going for the gusto right here right now, but the moment's gone. So Big Jay hands over a duct-taped envelope and it's heavy enough, so with half him in, half me out, Chatter blasts the gas and we're off again breaking hard toward Broadway.

We ease down, roll south on Santa Fe, U it back, and pull over at Georgia's Liquor. I open the package.

"Shit. Motherfucker's stuffed with chopped-up *El Paso Herald*."

Chatter hooks his thumb as if we should go back, but I shake my head and laugh. "Fuck it. Cocksucker's halfway back to Shinetown by now. No biggie. We'll dance again."

Chatter grabs us a couple of 40s and we initiate a cool prowl for the last shit on our list, Bills Moya—small build, no left eye, drug dealer extraordinaire. And though he should be cool, of this I am mostly sure, in truth I trust him less than I do that flathead we just left in the gutter.

—

We hit the Isla Coronado to find Bills Moya perched atop a jumbo trashcan, crowd of dust heads dancing to an invisible beat. They got their yellow hands out, and he's a stinky Jesus on the mount delivering not lines of bullshit, but powerful blessings disguised as rerolled cigarettes.

We park where Bills Moya can see us, and he immediately breaks our way, pied piper dust heads in tow. Nigger retainers scramble to hold, push, finally slug the shits back, a few shattering to the ground, the rest fluttering away. Bills Moya, as always, offers his hand and I, as always, refuse to even look at it. He passes me Tio Yesca's bread, rubber band tight as a chicken's ass and says, "Before you go I'd like a minute if you can."

You've heard of domestic violence. So has Bill Moya. He lost his eye to an ex-wife and got his nuts kicked in by his only son so bad that he walks forever with the same crooked hitch. But he's tough and devious and has never asked to speak to me like this before. I eyeball Chatter and he shrugs me his *got you covered* look, so Bills Moya and I turn and walk. Retainers start our way, but Chatter whistles them back and they stop and return to tend to their flock of antsy dust heads. We round the corner, me finger-fucking the fuck outta my .45 semi-auto.

Bills Moya stops, takes a knee, fetches a pack of Camels from his sock. He smiles and offers me the first one.

"Get to the goddamn point."

He comes to his feet. "Got wind of a possible, and if you move on it now you can take it within the hour. All I want is a finder's fifteen."

I answer with silence, and Bill Moya continues.

"I got word that a couple of extremely heavy peon mules, with contents most impressive, got stolen off some Central American runners. They're being auctioned off at this moment by some Azteca hope-to-bes who be dangerously cranked and righteously stupid, thus perfectly ripe for a pick."

"They ain't gonna keep it for themselves?"

"Nope. Boys know those they ripped will just keep coming till they get what's theirs, so they made it crystal they want to cash out now."

My interest rises. "How much they want?"

"Too much. Fools asking white boy prices, so the way I see it is, no one's gonna pay. So it's just a matter of time before someone takes them down, or they get speared by them Zetas."

Tio Yesca's a Zeta. This could get good.

"How'd you find out? This definitely not something dust heads would know."

Bills Moya leans against a tagged-up wall and crosses his arms. "I got this shoeshine kid on payroll. He works the bus station, keeping eyes out for incoming runaways and steers them my way. Kid says when the mules was getting off the bus, one got sick and nearly delivered up all the product then and there. Next thing he knows, someone's popping rounds, lighting up the place with rent-a-cops, popo, bus drivers, and wets hauling ass in all directions. In all this noise, the mules go one way, investors the other, and at that minute our wide-eyed fast-moving banditos grabbed and jammed the bastards out the door and down the street."

"And Shoeshine saw it all."

"Fuckin' a. Kid caught everything from gangbanger high signs to the fuck-up, the snatch, and the dash. My boy followed them to their hideout then got me back this good word."

I nod at Bills Moya and check my watch. It's already past midnight.

"I'll need to verify. Get me this shoeshine kid."

Bills Moya grinds his smoke into the sidewalk.

"Can't. Got him iced at an undisclosed till this thing pays off."

"You don't trust the little fuck?"

"Don't trust *any* little fuck." The borderline malice of Bills Moya's reply shoots involuntary reflex pressure onto the trigger of my piece.

I take a breath, wave Bills Moya for a cigarette, back off a step. Bills Moya is playing it exactly like I would. Not only is he not showing his cards, he's ain't showing the game, either. I exhale and turn my back. Thing is, ripping off a rip-off presents unique risks. Course they'll be lying in ambush, so a calvary charge is out. That they may be Azteca connected could make things touchy. But if these mules originated anywhere south of Mexico, they're most likely hauling uncut coke or pure smack. If each is holding the usual twenty bags and it's H, it'll fetch couple a two-three grand, give or take. Less if it's coke. Nice coin for half a night's work. I flip my smoke onto the street.

"No way on fifteen percent. Four."

"Seven. My mom's in chemo."

"So's mine. Five and a half."

"Done." Bills Moya nods, again offers his hand. This time I take it and give him a piece of paper.

"Send Shoeshine to where they got them mules. Tell him to go in and have them call me at this number. And send Chatter over here, about time he put in some work."

—

I watch my cell ring four times before answering.

"Who's this?"

Whispery voice. "You the guy?"

"Who the fuck is this?"

"I work for Bil–"

"Where you at?"

"In a phone booth outside their motel."

"Where?"

"Second and Wall."

"That wasn't the plan."

"I know, but–"

"Go in and give them this number."

"But–"

Click.

Five minutes later, cell rings again, *puro loco* voice on the other end.

"Who da fuck is this?"

"How much for your mules?"

"How much you got?"

"What they holding?"

"H. Fifteen *bagas*. What's your offer?"

"I got five on me now, five more later."

"One thou? The little bitch is worth more than that in pussy alone. Naw, we want two G's, motherfucker. Two. All of it now."

"I can do seven now and seven later. *Catorce*, homes. It's all I can do."

Noisy pause. "Bring it up, motherfucker. Ain't got all-fucking night."

Click.

Neither do I.

—

I direct Chatter over a bump of rail tracks separating Art Colony from Little Italy. We pull over half a block from the motel, I count off the seven, hand the rest to Chatter, and get out. Chatter leans into the back, raises and racks a baby Beretta, tries to hand it over. I wave it off, give him my .45.

"You crazy going up there with nothing. They could be Aztecas you're walking into."

"Just don't go catching any z's on me, fucker. Might have to bail quick."

I slide close to a shadowed building and move off without looking back.

Swear I can hear him snoring already.

—

Shitty Banda vibrates the street before I hit the corner. I find the door and knock. Sounds go down but not off. Door opens and I've a bold flashlight in my eyes, and shaking pistols against my temple. They pull me in, dogpile me down, grab the cash. Next to me a girl wearing only underwear clutches herself into the fetal position. A hog-tied grandpa lies face down in the center of the room. Along the far wall shivers a skinny black youngster. Shoeshine. All got bruised faces and swollen welts. Looks and smells like all have pissed themselves raw. Girl stares through me, a swath of black blood stains her underwear and pools onto the floor. Guess whatever she's hauling wants out.

The boys back off and the smallest of the bunch, clearly the leader, stands tall, eyes barely open. He's not yet seen sixteen but he, like the others, is tat down hard *Barrio Azteca*. I check his neck. Ink reads Popeye.

"About time you bring me my bread, bitch," he says, and catches me staring at his neck. "The fuck you looking at?"

I slide over and check the old man's pulse. Faintly there. "Can he walk?"

Popeye grabs the old man's hair, pulls him to his knees as the girl whimpers.

"He can stand. That's good enough."

The old man pulls away, beaten but defiant. Popeye spits at him, saying with a touch of admiration, "*Éste* tried to kick me in my balls, so I had to scuff his ass awhile. He'll be alright."

Popeye stands over the girl and strokes her hair. "Now *ésta*, is real sweet. Still tight, *qué no* homies?"

Stupid smiles light the room.

"Might have to buy her some new *chonies*," he says, a thin finger pointing at the blood-stained floor. "Guess she was cherry after all."

The idiots laugh again.

I show hands, get up slowly. Popeye kicks open the door.

"Get on, bitch. And don't take all fucking night with my money."

I grab Shoeshine and shove him out.

The homies laugh again.

I get to the car and call Tio Yesca. He answers on the first ring.

"These guys really Azteca?"

"Unless tats lie."

"And their main head? What'd he have?"

"Él Popeye on one side of his neck, *Mi Amá, Mi Amor* on the other. *Azteca Trese* across his chest. Everything else the usual Virgin Mary with crosses an' shit."

Slow pause, line crackling.

"So, he's his mama's boy," he says absently. "Don't make no sense. If they Azteca, what they doing holed up in some rat catcher six blocks from El Paso jail? If they stumbled onto this score, you'd think they'd be home opening them mules up, not trying to move 'em in some far-off territory they don't know. Unless ... they *can't* go home."

"And what they doing at the bus station all ganged up in the first place? Maybe they already—"

"Knew what was going down," Tio Yesca says and we both laugh.

"Ten-to-one Azteca's gotta piece of them mules which these fools overheard and are now trying to double-cross their own."

Tio Yesca nods with a hint of approval.

"Balls," I say with a whistle, though I know said balls will likely turn to shit by the next sun.

"So, what next?"

"Jam down to the projects and see Chin. He'll know what's what. I'll call ahead and clear the way."

"Thinking we should go heavy," I suggest, more out of respect than ignorance.

"Heavy as you can haul," he laughs and ends the call.

"And then some."

—

Entering the projects late at night is like stumbling shitfaced and stupid into a pit of cobras. Muchos locos here, everyone's born again gangstoro. And though the place is patrolled not by one but by *three* agencies—county Sheriff, El Paso PD, and Federal Housing Authority—the law can barely keep the lid on the place and, in truth, do so only with shot-caller blessing and a blind eye here and there.

We drop Shoeshine at the last bus stop before the projects and tell him to hang tight till we get back, but the little fucker sprints off the moment his feet hit concrete.

Good boy.

Cruising the only street in or out of this place, we wind slowly, numerous speed bumps and an increasingly narrow road forcing us to be checked out through and through. Chatter and I keep our hands visible; we don't look directly at nobody, but don't look away either.

Crisscrossing kids on chromed out mini-bikes flash abruptly out of nowhere. Smiling, glue-stained boys who reek of gasoline, they've a dangerous glaze to their eyes. Blood thumping through ready-to-kill muscle and vein.

They guide us off the road down a snaking alley to the backside of the apartments, stopping us face-first into a collapsing chain-link fence separating the projects from the highway. We sit still in a flat blackness, monster wind roaring off the road rocking the car side to side. Our escorts fade away.

Pair of lights out, wrecking-yard Fords skid the corner and roll up our ass, bumping us hard, blocking us in. Doors snatch open and we're collared by many pairs of grease-stained cologne hands, hustled through a hole in the fence, shoved across railroad tracks, shoved down hard onto a red-dirt trench that stinks of fresh piss and half-dead something.

Chatter throws me a no-look elbow and I pop him one back.

"What's happening?" shoots a raspy voice. "You boys look lost. What? You *putos* grew balls and crawled outta your faggot holes to see what a real *clica* looks like?"

Laughter. I clear my throat. "We're here to see Chin. You him?"

More laughter.

"Chin dead," the voice croons. "*¿Y sabes qué?* You dead too, you don't hurry tell us something. I mean, somebody did hear somebody say something about some people of ours. Or am I fucking stupid?"

Guess Yesca never found that number.

"Those mules you was supposed to be protecting got stole," I offer.

"And?"

"People who done it claim they belong to you."

Chorus of racking shotguns crack hard. Headlights snap on illuminating five empty-eyed *veteranos* leaning hard into the shade and shadow of this night. They brace nasty double barrels into Pendleton shoulders. I can see in their eyes that they want to do us in, want to do us the fuck in.

Raspy voice reveals a raspy face holding back acne and a boxer's flattened nose under a tightly snapped black fedora.

"How's it you *putos* know that what you shouldn't know?"

"Word flew in," I shrug. "Point is, we can tell you where your so-called homies and your mules are. All we want is a small taste of your taste."

"How much small?"

"I'd say twenty, but you'd say ten. So why don't we call it fifteen?"

"Fuck that," one peewee motherfucker answers.

Another arms a ten-gauge into Chatter's ribs. "Let's blast 'em piece by piece till they tell us shit we don't wanna know." He slides the barrel against Chatter's throat. "Then we turn 'em to dust."

Raspy sighs, pushes back his fedora. He surveys us, a nod and a grin leading the way. Quick burst and he knocks the piece out of Peewee's hand, firing on him with both fists. Peewee careens away like a shoeless drunk. They all laugh. Raspy flips me the butt of his shotgun and out I go.

Guess Tio Yesca found that number after all.

Everyone stands down and we squat in semi-circle, backs to the light. They break out joints and T-Bird and we drink hand-to-hand honoring *The Life*, homies gone from all sides of these honorable, bloody *pleitos*.

In my next breath and without them asking, I tell the truth as to the what and who of this night. Boys nod and huddle up, whip Spanish whispers to and fro. Slowly they rise and adjust their trousers, re-tuck shirts, comb back hair. Pouring hard *gritos* into the hard sky, they down what's left, grind smokes into the dirt, share leathered handshakes and muscled *abrazos* all around.

Bye-bye, Popeye.

I signal Chatter to vacate and stand by for my call. He eases himself into our ride, softly kicks over the engine, and begins sliding ass-backwards through a slow-parting, growing multitude of Azteca's finest, most capable fuck-ups.

I shake Peewee's hand, tell him no hard feelings before asking where this Popeye might live. Peewee laughs, points the place out.

They stand around a few minutes until finally, formally, Barrio Azteca fires up their cars and snake out of their beloved projects bumper to bumper, black wolves on a black hunt.

—

I pop open a side window and I'm in Popeye's apartment, more specifically, his mother's bedroom, before two breaths. She opens her eyes, I cup her mouth and show her my piece.

"No talking, okay?"

Her room is small and fragrant and it's adorned with many photos, mostly of her with Popeye. I dial the motel.

"Hey lil bitch," I say softly. "Moms sure got a great-looking bedroom here, even though she's got your fucked-up face on every wall."

Popeye screams something I don't understand but understand fully. After several minutes he slows down, breathing chopped and tearful.

"You done?"

"Don't hurt her *carnal*. Please don't hurt her. *Por favor*."

"You want everything back, *puto*? Then this is what you gonna do. Get them mules good to go and stuff my bread down the girl's bra. Take them outside and point 'em to the river. Fuck it up, asshole, and *tú mamá* gets a butt-hole train ride till she goddamn dies."

Click.

I phone Chatter. "Go scoop up them mules before Azteca hits the tarmac."

"On my way. Then what?"

"Take them to Tio Yesca. He'll know what to do."

"What you gonna do?"

I shut the lights and check my watch. "I'll stick around till Azteca comes back. Then I'll show 'em my tats and tell them to go fuck themselves."

"What?"

"Just fucking with you, homes. I'll hump it home. Tell Tio Yesca to start me up some chow. All this bullshit's got me hungry."

I start to leave, but a photo of a cheeky baby Popeye wearing Micky Mouse ears and hugging his teenage mom blocks my path. Aw fuck. I dial Popeye, and before I can say a word he tells me the mules are already gone.

I thank him truly, adding, "*¿Sabes qué?* You an' your boys might wanna double time your sorry asses outta town. Like now, dog."

"What?"

"Yep. Seems some scary-ass *cucuys del tú barrio* knows what you disloyal fuckers did and are moving in on your position as we speak. Best grow wings, motherfucker. Best get thin."

Click.

I exit as a gang of Rotts start up from the house next door, but I don't give a fuck. Maybe I'll go see Tio Yesca and see if he's got something on that Goddamn Corporal. Who knows? Night's still young.

THE CRIME OF OVERSTANDING: A FICTITIOUS MEMOIR

Carrie Sz Keane

Understanding as a noun means comprehension.
Understanding as an adjective means to have compassion.

We are thinking and feeling beings, sentient.
Both comprehending and compassionate.
But alas, so much remains ... misunderstood.

BRITISH ARTIST MARTIN CREED is known for his mini-
malistic art. Some argue whether his is even art at all. In 2001, Creed
won the Turner Prize, a prestigious UK artist award, for *Work No. 227,
The lights going on and off.* His piece, an empty white room in which the
lights went on and off in three-minute increments, led to his major
acclaim. Later, he threw a pile of cardboard and paper recyclables into
a heap in a corner and called this art, too. I heard about this artist when
I met the young British lackeys he hired to install his latest piece, a
giant rotating red neon and steel sign at Brooklyn Bridge Park in New
York with the word "understanding" written in giant, fifty-foot block
lettering and entitled *Work No. 2630, UNDERSTANDING.* My friend
and I walked down to the park from her apartment to watch the instal-
lation of the sign. The irony was not lost on us; we were standing under
a giant sign called understanding, not at all understanding what made
this art.

Rastafarian philosophy asserts that every man, woman, and
child are equal; therefore, an individual who receives information is
equal to the communicator of the information and superior to the idea

being communicated. That being said, one should not "understand" or stand under an idea; when they absorb and correctly perceive an idea they say that they "overstand" it. The person who "overstands" something understands it more than the person who "understands" it.

This, I understand.

At the end of my street is a management company housed in an old barn-style building. It sits on the main highway and is passed by thousands of cars daily. I have no idea what they manage. There is never more than one car in the lot. The owner, Tim Hixon, now dead, once owned a large acreage of land in our town, including the lot where we built our house. In his old age, as he amassed more land and money, Hixon became very conservative. Because of his "management company," he had his own public platform—a huge sign he began to use to proselytize about his latest quibble. From 2008 to 2012, we endured his lecturing in sign form. Once, for three weeks, the sign, with its cheap transferable letters, read "Let's take our guns to Congress!"

Was he suggesting that we shoot up our senators? I certainly did not over or understand.

Each year for the entire month of September and then continuing through October, the sign said, "Never forget." Passing the sign multiple times daily, I joked that we sure would not.

In 2012, the year of the election between Obama and Romney, Hixon began fervently changing the sign to reflect his political whim of the week. One week the sign would spew hate speech about immigrants, or a rant about taxes, and the next it would advocate for Ron Paul and antigovernment Libertarianism.

The definition of Libertarian, if I understand it, is one who seeks to maximize political freedom and autonomy, emphasizing freedom of choice, voluntary association, individual judgment, and self-ownership.

Driving by the sign multiple times a day became tiresome for Jimmy and me. It started to feel like we were being yelled at by an angry neighbor every time we went past the building. Sure, we believe in free speech, but this was a bully pulpit from which we had no refuge.

On July 4, after spending the day celebrating the very freedom and independence eschewed by the sign owner by enjoying some beers and the requisite strawberry- and blueberry-whipped cream American flag cake, we again drove by the sign on our way home.

On a whim we decided Hixon's sign should yell at Hixon for a change, so we stopped and rearranged the letters. The sign had said, "Say No to Obama! Vote Romney!" In less than five minutes we hurriedly changed the wording to read "YAS to Obama, Vote NO Romney!" Nothing terrible, mean-spirited, crass, or profane. Nor did we damage the sign, or the property surrounding it. We were just a couple of middle-aged kids doing a little neighborhood prank. Harmless.

The next day, we made the news.

The local paper ran an article which blamed hooligans for causing "over $800 in damages" to the sign. It said that the hoodlums had changed the letters on the sign, not once, *but twice*. It called out the "left wing vandals" and stated that the perps were "... no different than the Occupy Movement, the Black Panthers, and Code Pink." The title of the article referred to Jimmy and me as bandits. The worst part, said Tim Hixon, when interviewed about the situation, was that "... it happened on the Fourth of July, *no less*." As if his independence was shattered, as if his freedom was assaulted by his one-day break from shouting at his neighbors.

Within months, the company had erected a brand-new, electronic, state-of-the-art sign. The new sign, high up in the air, made it impossible for anyone to change the letters, and probably cost upward of five grand to build and electrify. This, I supposed, was the price of freedom and autonomy, the cost of being able to say what you want out loud, whether people want to hear you or not. But, I also figured that somehow it had been paid for by our tax dollars. Again, I had found myself standing under a sign, not understanding. I guess we misunderstood the meaning of freedom of association.

Now that there are no more than two sides—the for and the against, the right and the left—there are fewer facts. We can make up whatever we want, create unprecedented narratives, muddying the understanding of truth. The divisiveness pushes us to take sides. We are forced to decide if we should worship a flag, or that which it stands for.

We stand under a flag, not understanding that the America for which it stands is not a concept, but a physical place, with rivers we are polluting by chemical run-off and mountaintops we are blowing up for coal. But god forbid we burn the flag, as we burn the vineyards and the national parks it represents. It is all just one big, giant, colossal misunderstanding.

Perhaps the sign was just a sign?

Understanding as a noun means comprehension.

Understanding as an adjective means to have compassion.

We are thinking and feeling beings, sentient. Both comprehending and compassionate.

At a seminar I attended in Ohio the leader asked each of us what seed we would plant inside of ourselves if we could. She gave examples, like pride, beauty, forgiveness, empathy, and understanding.

I picked contentment. My best friend picked mischief.

Though I had chosen contentment, I overstood my friend's need to plant a seed of mischievousness in the world. And so, in her honor, I planted a couple of cannabis seeds next to the brand-new sign at the end of my road.

I'm sure Tim Hixon will understand.

THE FRUIT STAND

Lisa Fox

DETECTIVE MICHAEL JONES CLOSED the door of his sedan and struggled to button his faded navy-blue blazer over his expanding paunch. *Too much time on desk duty.* It was good to be out in the field again, even if "the field" was in the middle of nowhere.

God's country.

Early morning sunlight painted the rolling hills of Bird-in-Hand, Pennsylvania, with a vibrance that rivaled a Thomas Kinkade painting. A lone crow cawed, welcoming the day as it circled in the cloudless sky. Jones closed his eyes and breathed in the earthy scent of hay and late summer.

So different from the grit and grime of the Philadelphia precinct from which he'd transferred.

Focus, he thought. *Crime doesn't only live in the city.*

A spotted mare grazed near an empty fruit and vegetable stand that stood near the road; the structure sturdy despite the rot that time ate into the unpainted wood. A farmhouse rested in the distance, embraced by a wraparound lemonade porch. Adjacent to the house, five small expertly carved wooden crosses stood sentinel. A large barn, its door ajar, nestled into the vast fields and orchards down the hill below.

Idyllic. Except that Jones wasn't visiting for pleasure. He was there for business—a follow-up call that he hoped wouldn't take too long. Jones had started his day early, optimistic that he'd be able to make a twelve o'clock tee time over at Tanglewood Manor.

A freckle-faced teenager wearing Amish clothing emerged from the barn, carrying a wooden crate uphill toward Jones. The boy ignored the red apples that littered the ground as he labored toward the fruit stand, and just as readily disregarded Jones.

"Your pop around?"

The boy stopped and looked at—*looked through*—Jones with icy blue eyes. He mumbled an inaudible response and motioned toward the barn.

Amish kid or city kid, teenagers are all the same.

—

Jones found Eli Stoltzfus standing on a ladder arranging crates in the loft. Stoltzfus's dark hair peeked out from beneath a wide straw hat, sweat stains seeped through his white cotton shirt, and bits of hay stuck to his trousers. Two young tow-headed boys looked up at him with wide green eyes, waiting. Jones imagined them to be about four and eight by their size and demeanor. The same age as his nephews the last time he saw them.

"Eli Stoltzfus?"

With dark and intense eyes, Eli stared down Jones and nodded. His black beard brushed against his suspenders. "We're right busy this mornin'," he said, pulling on a full crate. With a grunt, he handed it to the older boy who wobbled away, his knees buckling under its weight.

"I can see that," Jones said. He flashed his badge at the farmer. The scent of freshly picked corn wafted around them.

"You here again about that missin' boy? I already gave my statement to the police." Eli turned toward the waiting fruit, arranging the crates in a row. "There ain't nothin' else to discuss."

The younger boy fidgeted below the ladder, hopping from one foot to the other. Jones smiled at him and pulled a notebook and pen out of his pocket.

"We have your statement, Mr. Stoltzfus," Jones said. "But I'd like to speak with your wife. Shouldn't take too much time."

Eli flinched and froze for just a moment. He opened his mouth to form a reply, but instead closed it and climbed down the ladder.

The child looked from Jones to Eli, as if examining a question mark that hovered between the two men.

"Better go fetch your momma."

—

Jones tapped his foot as he stood by the fruit stand, waiting. The teenager and the older child from the barn hustled to populate the barren, decaying wood shelves. Eli stacked empty crates, stealing furtive glances at the farmhouse. He straightened as the door opened and Sarah Stoltzfus emerged.

Jones thought Amish garb made even the youngest women look old, but he pegged Sarah Stoltzfus as late thirties. A white prayer cap rested atop her black hair which was pulled into a tight bun. Coffee-brown eyes reflected the exhaustion of motherhood; her frame bore the soft pudginess of a recent pregnancy.

The boy held tight to Sarah's elbow as they traipsed down the porch stairs. A curtain rustled inside the window behind them; an orange tabby cat curled up on the sill. The teenager abandoned his efforts toward stacking fruit and opened a wooden chair for Sarah, who plopped into it with a groan. Eli moved to her side.

Jones again flashed his badge. "Detective Jones of the Lancaster County Police Department, ma'am. This should only take a few minutes."

"Good morning, officer." Sarah smiled at Jones—*past him*—her gaze caught somewhere else, in that finite line between earth and sky. "Would you like an apple? We pick the fruit from our very own trees." She lowered her voice and leaned in toward the officer. "We nurture it and love it and it grows, it flourishes. Not like ..."

Eli squeezed Sarah's shoulder. She looked up at him, her expression darkening. "The Good Book says this is the forbidden fruit," she whispered. "But something that brings such great sweetness, such joy, the Lord would never deny us, would he, Eli?"

The youngest child tottered over to Sarah and snuggled into her. She stroked his hair and kissed his forehead. "Run along now and help your brothers."

Jones cleared his throat. "Mrs. Stoltzfus, as I'm sure you know, a two-year-old child went missing from the Harrisburg Farmers Market this past weekend." Jones pulled a photograph from his pocket and presented it to the husband and wife. It showed a boy with dancing green eyes and a penchant for mischief in his smile. His hair was as red as the Elmo emblazoned on his T-shirt.

Sarah frowned and hugged her arms close to her chest. "So sad, when the little ones go away."

Jones furrowed his brow and tapped his pencil against his notebook. "You run a stand out of that market?"

"Fruits and vegetables and pies, every other Saturday. And here," Eli said, gesturing. "Every day 'cept Sunday. That's the Lord's Day. Are you a prayin' man, Detective?"

Jones shook his head, his lips pulled back in a thin line. He hadn't stepped foot in a church in years, since his brother died and he'd moved to Philly to help his sister-in-law with the boys. But she'd taken them away to live with her new boyfriend, and Jones was tossed aside. *Like a bitten-down apple core.*

"Only a mother understands the pain of losing a child." Sarah rocked in her seat, her gaze again fixed on the horizon.

Uncles do, too, Jones thought.

Eli patted Sarah's shoulder. She reached up, squeezing his hand.

Jones glanced from husband to wife. "Then I'm sure, ma'am, you can empathize with this poor woman who's lost her son."

During his time as a beat cop, Jones had learned to accept gangs and gunshots as part of the Philadelphia landscape. Missing persons cases were about as common as cheesesteaks. But things were different in Lancaster. Kids didn't just disappear here.

Jones was first on the scene at the farmers market that day. Through breath-stealing sobs, the mother had described that last moment she'd seen her son. *We were planning a picnic,* she'd said. The boy was standing next to her, nibbling an apple while she struggled to balance two large baskets of vegetables. *One minute I was taking out my wallet to pay, and the next he was just … gone.*

"Do you recall anything from that day that might help us find the boy?"

Eli stepped in between Sarah and Jones. "I'll tell you what I told the other policeman. I didn't see nothin.' Now if you don't mind …"

Jones straightened. He knew that the Amish were proud, but he didn't anticipate Eli Stoltzfus to be so belligerent. Especially for what was supposed to be a routine interview, dotting i's and crossing t's.

Tee times. Jones sighed. Golf was quickly becoming a distant ambition.

"Sir, please. Let your wife speak."

"Ain't nothin' for her to say."

Eli looped his fingers through his suspenders and puffed out his chest as Sarah rocked herself. The wooden chair creaked as she began to sing. "Hush little baby, don't you cry …"

"Let's not make this more difficult than it has to be. I just need a statement from Mrs. Stoltzfus, and we can all get on with our day."

The teenage boy dumped an armful of apples into a half-full crate; they landed with a thud. Eli flinched.

"Gonna take the rest back down to the barn now, Pa." The teen motioned the younger boys away from the fruit stand and toward the horse grazing in the shade. "Let's go."

Jones watched the boys lead the mare down the hill. Their red and blond hair glowed like flame ignited by the sunlight. *If I didn't know better, I'd swear these boys were Irish, not Amish,* Jones thought.

Jones furrowed his brow and tapped his pen against his notebook, harder this time. "Mrs. Stoltzfus, do you remember seeing the boy in the photo?"

Sarah continued to sing, ignoring Jones's question.

"My wife wasn't in Harrisburg. She was home." Eli leaned in toward Jones and whispered, "Woman troubles. Not that it's any of your concern."

"But the registration log shows two people were working your stand when the boy disappeared." Jones scratched his head, staring at Sarah, whose song trailed into an off-key hum. "I have in my notes that you were there with a woman."

"This gonna take much longer?" Eli glared at Jones. "We got a lot of work to do here."

"If your wife wasn't with you at the farmers market, then who was?"

"My Bekkah's been a busy, busy bee!" Sarah chuckled from behind Eli. "Bees help the little flowers grow!"

"Who's Bekkah?"

Eli sighed and rocked on his heels. "Our girl Rebekkah's been comin' with me to help out in Harrisburg, since the wife's been feelin' so bad. But I'd a-sent her away to fetch more shoofly pie from the buggy before any of that ruckus. She didn't see nothin'."

Jones looked toward the farmhouse. The curtain rustled again, waking the sleeping cat in the window. Eli stepped in front of Jones, blocking his view just as the cat disappeared.

"I done told ya all I know."

Metal clanged to the ground behind Jones, loud as a gunshot. Jones spun around, instinctively reaching for his holster. The teen stood with a metal shovel resting on his shoulder, a bag of tools dropped at his feet. "Thought you might need these, Pa." He scowled at Jones and looked past him, toward Eli. "Our roots've been disturbed."

Eli locked eyes with the boy, nodding slowly.

The boy stood firm as a tree. Jones turned away from him and back toward Eli, who was still blocking his view of the farmhouse and its rustling curtains.

The detective's gaze rested on the shadow that the five wooden crosses cast on the yellow clapboard siding.

"Mrs. Stoltzfus, how many children do you have?"

"Four," Eli said.

Sarah looked up at him and laughed as if responding to an unspoken private joke. "I'm afraid my husband has lost the ability to count." She swatted at him and counted on her fingers. "We have five children—one, two, three, four, five."

Questioning had moved from routine to bizarre like cream churning to butter. Jones was beginning to wonder whether he should call for backup but decided against it. The Stoltzfus family might be odd, but this wasn't Philly. The Amish were peaceful, God-fearing people.

"I'd like to have a word with Rebekkah. She in the house?"

Jones pushed past Eli and marched toward the farmhouse, gravel crunching beneath his boots like the first bite of a crisp apple.

"Don't you go in there!" Eli shouted.

Jones picked up his pace, the gravel flying as he sprinted toward the door. He heard the muffled cry of a child within the house and a young girl murmuring a lullaby.

As the gravel shifted behind him, Jones knew he was being pursued. He sprinted up the stairs, two at a time, and yanked on the door. It was locked.

"Police! Open up!" Just as he raised his foot to kick in the door, it swung open, revealing a teenage girl with wild red hair and blue eyes that pooled with tears. Her lower lip quivered. A child—the missing boy—wailed in her arms.

Five babies lost, five babies found.

Jones spun around just as Eli reached the porch. "Eli Stoltzfus, you are under arrest for the kidnapping of Michael O'Dell." Jones grabbed Eli's arm and reached for his handcuffs. "You're coming with me."

"Ain't nobody goin' no place!"

The teenage boy charged toward Jones, the shovel tight in his grip.

Jones's hand moved toward his weapon.

Eli broke free and shoved Jones, hard.

Jones pitched forward. Splinters from the aging porch sliced into his palms. He cried out and looked up as the boy, eyes and hair and face flaming like Satan in the sunlight, raised the shovel over his head.

"Please. Don't do this."

Jones struggled to push himself up from the porch, wincing as the wooden needles dug deeper into his hands.

Eli kicked him back down.

"Should'a left well enough alone, Detective. Ain't nobody takin' Sarah's baby."

"It's not her baby," Jones said.

In that moment, Jones knew he'd never see his nephews again. He knew that Michael O'Dell's mother would never have that picnic with her son.

"A man's gotta protect his family." Eli moved into Jones's sightline and nodded at the teen. "Boy, you ready to become a man?"

Jones threw his arms over his head, bracing for impact.

Crime doesn't only live in the city.

The boy brought the shovel down hard, the rusted metal crushing Jones's fingers and rattling his skull.

Irish … Amish … would anybody even notice?

Again, the boy swung. A nine-iron connecting with Jones's head.

Tee time.

Jones's eyes were a reservoir of blood. All he saw was red— like the skin of an apple punctured by the nibbles of baby teeth, discarded on the dusty floor of a farmers market.

—

The dying sun cast a pale orange glow over the rolling hills of Amish country. Dusk blanketed the Stoltzfus family farm in a quiet slumber. The roadside stand stood barren, the best fruit sold or consumed, the rest left to fertilize the crops. The spotted horse grazed on shadowed grass.

Jones's car was gone, abandoned in a ditch somewhere near the New Jersey border.

A lone crow circled above, cawing in the fading light. Somewhere in the distance, a child whimpered, and the methodical rhythm of a spade penetrated the cool earth.

THE DISCOVERED COUNTRY

Tom Barlow

AMY EVANS MADE YET another attempt to capture the subtlety of the changing leaves on the stand of maple trees in Early Park but her watercolors would not cooperate, turning each brushstroke into another smear of mud. Then she managed to kick over the coffee she had foolishly placed on the ground by her foot. With that, she was ready to unload on somebody, and a candidate was already at hand, a young man who had been staring at her from a park bench twenty feet away for the best part of an hour.

The victim looked to be in his early twenties, with an athletic build and a long but handsome face, a wide, rounded chin, and deep-set brown eyes. He seemed unconcerned as Amy stomped in his direction.

Amy felt confident his watching was not some kind of sexual come-on. At forty-four, the mirror was too honest to fool her into thinking she was still an object of casual carnal desire. She wore her tobacco-colored hair like a flower child, cascading down her back in disorder that she too infrequently attempted to right with a stiff-bristled brush. Amy's face lacked any distinguishing characteristics except a too-frequently assumed snarl, as she approved of very little in her life. She dressed with scant attention, too, usually in a faded T, a well-broken-in flannel shirt that she didn't bother to iron, and jeans, tight, not because she'd bought them tight, but because she'd eaten her way into them.

Amy stopped in front of the man, the sun over her shoulder, causing the stranger to raise a hand to block the glare as he met her gaze. "You got nothing better to do than watch me paint? You're creeping me out."

He pressed his hands together in a namaste before saying, "I'm sorry. I meant nothing by it. Although I was hoping for the opportunity to speak with you."

"Me? What are you, some kind of park pervert?"

All expression dropped from the man's face as he said, "Come on, Amy, don't be that way. I raised you to be polite to strangers."

"Come again?"

"It's me, honey. Your mother."

"What the hell? Mister, you are one sick bastard." Her mother had been dead for five years, but she still grieved over the loss, so his words were particularly disturbing.

"I know this is a lot to take in, but hear me out. Three things only you and I know. You started your first period just before we arrived at the Typhoon Lagoon Water Park, but I gave you a tampon and let you go in anyway. You never forgave me for the embarrassment."

Amy's stomach flipped at the memory. She took a step back.

"You stole your cousin Emily's Saint Christopher medal to give to me for good luck before our trip to Germany. You put it around my neck before I was buried."

Her hands curled into fists.

"I loaned you money for an abortion when you were a junior at Pitt. You never paid me back."

She looked over her shoulder to see if anyone was watching, trying to contain the anger rising in her. "How...?"

Thankfully, the man still looked vacuous as he spoke. "I know you don't believe the dead can speak, but sometimes you have to rethink your beliefs when faced with evidence to the contrary."

"Leave me alone, you creep," Amy said, and forced herself to walk, not run, away. She packed up her painting supplies and carried them back to her car. As she drove away she caught one last glance in her rearview mirror of the young man, still seated placidly on the bench. He waved.

Her husband Mike was still at work, so Amy had no immediate sounding board for her odd experience. Since their daughter, Sarah, had moved to the West Coast to work for Oracle, Amy's life was already coming unhinged in a way she had never imagined. She had been so cocksure that once her parenting was done, once they could afford for her to quit the part-time job she loathed in the call center, her life would blossom. She never foresaw the empty hours dragging on her

like a timid two-year-old, the 3:00 p.m. cocktails, the soap opera view-
ing, the monkey bread that she baked and devoured before Mike made
it home from work. The watercolors, an attempt to force-feed some
value into her hours, were turning out to be farcical, as was the Zumba
course that she paid for and attended once.

Amy had many hours to dwell on what the young man had said
to her. She had no religion of any sort, blithely acknowledging her
atheism to anyone who thought to ask, ridiculing belief in an afterlife
as wishful thinking. But she couldn't deny the reality of the events he'd
described. Heretofore she would have sworn on her life that no one
but she and her mother, Linda, knew of any of those incidents.

—

When Mike finally arrived home at 9:00 p.m., Amy waited until
he was snug in his recliner, a Budweiser on the table next to him, before telling him of the incident, omitting the specific episodes the man
had described.

Mike rolled his eyes. "Con man. That should be obvious. I'm
surprised he let you get away without hitting you up for some money."

She had anticipated this reply; her husband's instinct was to
expect the worst of people. "But the things he knew," she said, reluc-
tantly sharing the water park story as an example.

"That's what con men do. He probably met one of your girl-
friends from childhood, who knew more than you thought she did and
couldn't keep her mouth shut. He's not done with you. A setup that
good, he'll want to make a score."

"What should I do?"

"Find another place to paint. And if he comes to the door, call
the cops."

"I hate to make a scene."

"You'll be saving some more naïve schmucks."

—

But that didn't placate her, and, a few days later, as she sat
nursing a latte and reading the latest Louise Penny mystery at her favorite coffee house, Amy spotted the same young man seated by the
fireplace. When he made eye contact, Amy nodded to the chair next to
her. He crossed the room to join her.

"What's your name?"

"Jacob Clift." He extended his hand and Amy shook it.

"So, Jacob Clift, my husband tells me you're a hustler, trying to get your hand in my pocket. What's your game?"

He locked eyes with her until she had to look away. "I'm just the conduit. There's some unfinished business here. I don't know what it is, but there's some reason your mother needs to talk with you."

"And you can get her on the line?"

He smiled. "That's one way of describing it. Would you like to talk with her?"

"Why not?"

Jacob took on a glassy look that suggested he wasn't entirely at home. "Hi, Amykins. You getting your mammograms like you promised? Believe me, you don't want to go that way."

"Amykins" had been her mother's pet name for her, even into adulthood. Hearing this word moved her needle in the direction of credibility again. However, she found it disconcerting to hear her mother speak in Jacob's low register.

"You come back from the grave to nag me?"

"Somebody has to. You could really stand to lose a few pounds, by the way. Or buy bigger slacks. You inherited the Anderson butt."

"So what's it like, where you are?"

"I can't talk about it. You'll find out sooner or later, and I hope it's later. But I did want to ask a favor of you."

Here it comes, Amy thought. Just as her husband predicted. "What?"

"You know our house on Marion, where I passed?"

"Duh. I grew up there, remember?"

"Well, you remember the garage was built of cement block? Up at the top, where they attach to the roof, there's this gap where you can reach into the hollow space of the top row of blocks."

This wasn't at all what she expected. "Yes?"

"Your father didn't know I knew, but he used to keep the cash he made fixing grandfather clocks in an ammo box that he stashed in one of those hollows. It's toward the back, on the east wall. I'd be surprised if it wasn't still there."

"We sold that house a month after he passed."

"But the way he died, unexpectedly, I'm sure he left that cash behind. And it belongs to you and your brother."

"So you want me to retrieve it? On somebody else's private property?"

"Since when would that stop you?"

Amy had been a bit of a free spirit when she was young. And now, bored out of her mind, tired of leading a mundane life, the idea of an escapade appealed to her.

—

Amy reconnoitered their old house after lunch, a two-story brown brick mid-century with a detached garage. There was no sign anyone was home at the moment. The garage door had been left up, the car gone, a stepladder stored against the wall, as though fate was conspiring with her mother to entice her into recklessness. Emboldened, she pulled right up to the garage. Within a minute, Amy had raced inside, scrambled up the ladder, found the ammo box, and returned to her car. Glancing around, Amy saw no evidence that she had been observed. She forced herself to remain calm as she backed out and headed home.

—

When Mike arrived home that evening, the $11,000 cash left him momentarily speechless. When he did regain his composure, he asked, "Where did you get this, really?"

"I swear on a stack of Bibles, Mom told me where to find it. It's not like I stole it, really; it was Dad's money, so by rights it should have come to us."

"I want to meet this Jacob guy. He's pulling some kind of long con."

"Long con?"

"He's willing to invest time and money to set you up for a big score. What I can't figure is, why us? We're not rich."

The more Mike ranted, the more Amy felt protective of Jacob. The man didn't strike her as dishonest, and she prided herself on the way she could size people up. Did she not identify her daughter's swimming teacher as weird and pull her out of his class a month before the police raided his home and found child porn? And what about her first fiancée, who she had dropped the moment she detected a hint of the bigotry that ran deep in his family?

Still, Amy had no idea where to find Jacob, until he texted her the next day. She was certain she hadn't given him her cellphone number, but her mother had known it.

> Today 4:10 PM
>   Find the money?
> Today 4:10 PM
>   Just where u said.
> Today 4:11 PM
>   Be sure to split it with your brother.
>   He needs it more than you do.
> Today 4:11 PM
>   Of course. Mike misses you 2.
>   He wants 2 visit with u. Possible?
> Today 4:11 PM
>   By all means. How about I stop by at 7?
> Today 4:11 PM
>   Sounds good. I'll make supper.
>   But we don't' live where we did when u were alive.
> Today 4:11 PM
>   I know where you live. ♥

Amy was not comforted by that information.

—

"You invited him to dinner?" Mike said, when he arrived home that evening to find the meeting arranged. He'd had a long day, and had been looking forward to relaxing with a few beers and a ball game.

"Or her. I don't know which of them he will be while he or she is eating. I'm beginning to wonder if he's an angel, you know? Maybe he doesn't eat at all."

Mike couldn't help but think that his wife wouldn't have been so eager to embrace a con man if she'd still been working. "You keep making this more complicated than it needs to be. At best he's just a psychic, another form of con man. No need to embrace an entire religion to explain one phenomenon. You watch. He'll bring some expensive wine, maybe even champagne."

—

Jacob arrived promptly at 7:00 p.m. carrying a bottle of 2009 Chambertin Burgundy. Mike mouthed to Amy, behind Jacob's back, "Told you so."

Mike followed his wife and Jacob into the family room, where Amy had put out a tray of smoked gouda and Greek olives with water crackers along with a bottle of Chardonnay that was uncorked and chilling in an ice bucket. Jacob took a proffered glass of the wine, as did Mike. He was displeased when Amy poured herself a second glass. She wasn't the best decision maker sober, in his opinion, even less so when drunk.

"So," Mike said to Jacob, "you're a conduit. How does one get into that line of work?"

"It's not my work, really. By day I'm an accountant with Marker & Martin downtown. This is more like a public service."

"Lucky us. How did you pick Amy's mom?"

"It doesn't work that way. The dead persons pick me. I became a Buddhist two years ago, and the first time I managed to empty my mind, another person took over. It was spooky, but I've gotten used to it. I must have been chosen for some reason."

"And how many people have you, what, channeled?" Mike was disappointed that Jacob seemed not the least bit nervous about advancing the scam in his presence.

"About a dozen."

"And how have you been received by their loved ones?"

"Some refused to even talk to me. They figured I was working some kind of angle. One had some criminals as relatives, and I didn't want to get involved with them. Your wife and three other persons, they were willing to engage in a conversation."

Mike had asked his wife to listen but not speak until he had a chance to talk Jacob into a corner from which he couldn't escape, but she butted in anyway. "Do you know what goes on while the other person has taken over?"

"No," Jacob said, "I have no memory of what you and your mother talked about, for example. One person who I channeled, it must have gone wrong, because she told me she never wanted to talk to her father again."

Mike was growing impatient. "Amy, why don't you finish getting dinner ready?"

He could tell Amy didn't want to leave him alone with Jacob, but also didn't want to inject friction into the conversation.

Once Amy had gone into the kitchen, Mike said, "So let's cut through the bullshit, shall we? What kind of con are you trying to pull?"

Jacob's hand stopped halfway to bringing his wine glass to his mouth. "It's no con, but actually, the person I was trying to reach was you." His voice had gone shrill, which spooked Mike.

"Me? This is new."

"Yes. This is Melissa Young. You remember me, right?"

Jacob might as well have thrown a bucket of ice water in Mike's face. "What the hell are you up to?"

"Jacob's not up to anything. It was me, I wanted to talk to you. You see, I've been buried up here in the nature reserve for onto ten years now. Mom and Dad have never been the same since I disappeared."

Mike looked to the kitchen to make sure Amy couldn't hear him. "I don't know what you're talking about."

Jacob's head shook back and forth. "I'm talking about the night you picked me up at the Brass Lounge. You were one horny bugger, weren't you? I mean, I was ten years older than you and, let's face it, I didn't have much of a figure. But that didn't stop you. And like an idiot, I left with you. I was really lonely back in those days. You know, if you hadn't gotten rough, I would have slept with you, but no, you had to stick your hand up my skirt before we left the parking lot."

Mike's hands were clenching. He took a deep breath and tried to regain his senses. "The cops never found me. How did you?"

"Between me and Jacob, it wasn't hard. What was hard was getting an audience with a skeptic like you. We finally figured out if we could get Amy on board, you'd come running to save her from some scam. Her mother agreed to help us."

"What do you want?"

"I want you to go to the cops and confess. Show them where you buried me, bring my parents some peace. Simple enough."

"I'm not doing that. And you have no proof."

"I could draw a map and directions to my body, leave it with Jacob. He could give it to the cops."

"They'd think he did it. So I'd be off the hook."

"He was twelve years old and living in Wisconsin then."

"Still, there'd be no evidence pointing to me, not after all this time. And you really think they'd buy the word of a psychic? Go screw yourself."

At that point, Amy called them to the table.

"You've got three days," Melissa said. With that, Jacob's face came alive, and he looked puzzled at Mike. "That was different. What happened?"

"Nothing," Mike said. "Time to eat."

—

After Jacob left, Mike brooded on the threat to the point that Amy asked him three times over the course of an hour what was wrong. She finally gave up and went to bed.

At 1:00 a.m. he came to the inevitable decision. Preposterous as it seemed, he had to believe Melissa's threat was real. No one else, he was sure, knew about the accident ten years earlier, and he wasn't about to spend his life in jail over it. He hadn't meant to break the woman's neck; he thought she wanted it rough. Now he was more or less content with his life, although the occasional hooker was not something he was proud of. But the way Amy had let herself go, what did she expect? Mike went online and found the address for Jacob Clift, in a house in the countryside outside of Connersville, five miles from the home he shared with Amy.

—

There was the promise of a thunderstorm in the brisk wind that shook the trees at 2:00 a.m. as Mike drove to Jacob's house. It sat well back from the road on its own acre, a ranch-style home with an attached double garage. Mike turned off his headlights as he approached the place, pulled into the paved driveway, and parked just off the road next to the mailbox. He'd dressed with care—black jeans, black long-sleeved T-shirt, stocking cap, leather gloves. The houses on either side of Jacob's were too distant to pose a threat of discovery, and Jacob had no yard lights to break the darkness.

Mike took the crowbar he'd brought and approached the house. The front door looked substantial, so he circled to the rear, where cheap sliding glass doors offered entrance to the rec room. The crowbar provided more than enough leverage to pop the lock open, the noise dampened by the rattle of the wind in the maple tree overhead.

There appeared to be no alarm system. Mike stepped inside expecting to find Jacob asleep in his bedroom. As soon as he closed the door behind him, a table lamp snapped on. In a chair by the fireplace sat Jacob.

"I knew you'd come." There was again that shrill tone in Jacob's voice that suggested Melissa was speaking.

He took a better grip on the crowbar. "You got somebody here to protect you?"

"Just Jacob. And he's not really here at the moment, if you get my drift." She still didn't make any move to protect herself. Mike took another step into the room to see if she had a gun on her lap. There was none.

"How stupid are you?" Mike said, rushing her. He lashed out with the crowbar, catching her on the forehead. She tumbled backward, her head striking the raised hearth on her way to the floor. Mike nudged her with his toe, but she was out cold. It took all the nerve he could muster to drop to his knees, hold a hand over her mouth and pinch her nose until she stopped breathing.

He'd thought this through before he left his house. If the cops found a body, they would be more than diligent in tracing Jacob's movements in the days before, and that would lead them right to his wife. If the man simply disappeared, they might give it less attention. And Mike knew just how to disappear a body.

He went into the bedroom intending to pack a suitcase in hopes the cops would conclude Jacob had run off. However, upon discovering a dry suit for kayaking, boating shoes, and a couple of cycling outfits in the closet, Mike had a better idea. He checked Jacob's garage, where, sure enough, he found a nine-foot whitewater kayak as well as a top-end mountain bike. He retrieved the car keys from Jacob's pocket, backed Jacob's Subaru from the garage, lashed the kayak to the top carrier, and loaded the mountain bike into the hatchback. He grabbed a shovel and tossed it–along with the dry suit, shoes, Jacob's life jacket, helmet, and paddle–into the passenger seat before carrying Jacob out and laying his body across the back seat. Mike pulled his truck into the garage and shut the door.

On the way to the nature reserve, Mike reviewed his plans, looking for flaws. He'd bury the body where he'd buried Melissa. If she'd never been found, Jacob wouldn't be either. Then he'd drive Jacob's car to the whitewater put-in along the Youghiogheny River, which had rapids that attracted boaters from the surrounding states. He'd toss Jacob's kayak and paddle into the river, letting them float away. When they were found in the morning people were sure to conclude there was a drowned boater downstream somewhere. They would determine that person was Jacob by the license on the boat and his car unattended in the lot. Mike, who kept himself fit, could then ride Jacob's bike back to his house by the light of the full moon, an easy thirty miles on the Great Allegheny Passage bike trail, retrieve his truck, and be home before dawn.

Having a plan settled him down as he found the service road into the 5,000-acre Bear Run Nature Reserve. Mike drove in half a mile, glad that Jacob's SUV had four-wheel drive that would plow through the muddy patches. He finally spotted the enormous oak around which the road had been forced to circle, which marked his spot. He stopped, stepped out of the car, and grabbed the shovel. He'd buried Melissa behind the tree a dozen paces and didn't want to encounter her bones, so he took a few more steps uphill before he began to dig.

He dug his spade into the earth just as a spotlight shone on him. He held up his hand to block the glare, but he couldn't see anything until a sheriff's deputy stepped forward, pistol raised. "Now, what do we have here?" He took the shovel from Mike's hand and tossed it aside. "You best put your hands behind you."

"How?" Mike asked, as he complied.

"We got an anonymous call a couple of hours ago," a second deputy said as she applied the handcuffs. "He said you'd be here with a fresh body about now. You've got a lot to answer for, Mr. Evans."

—

Mike was driven to the sheriff's station by the young female deputy. There, he was placed in a holding cell to await the arrival of day shift. He declined an attorney, recognizing that he had little to gain by contesting a slam dunk.

While he waited that morning for a representative from the county prosecutor's office, Mike had a visitor. The guard walked him down the hall to a small room separated from a similar room by a thick plexiglass window. Telephones on either side allowed conversation.

Not to his surprise, Amy was waiting for him, a scowl on her face. When he picked up the handset, she did the same.

She didn't launch into the diatribe he expected. Instead, Amy said, "Gotcha," in a voice that sounded peculiar.

In the overhead lights Mike could see the blank look that had come over his wife's face. "Melissa? How?"

"We can channel anybody, if enough of us work together. There are twenty people on this side helping me with Amy. She's fighting us all the way."

"You just wanted to gloat?"

"Is that petty? I mean, you did cost me the rest of my life."

"So you set Jacob up as a sacrifice just to get revenge on me? After all he did to help you? You think I'm a criminal, but you're just as cold blooded. I thought maybe you were in heaven, I even hoped that, after you died. But I'm thinking now you're in some other place."

"As far as Jacob goes, he had ALS, but he hadn't found it out yet. He'd have been dead in a year anyway. He's here with me now, and glad I saved him from a lingering death.

"You were right about the difficulty of proving you murdered me, but I was sure if I threatened you the right way, you'd kill again, and I knew you'd bury him in your favorite spot. People like you are so predictable. Now you're going to have a long, long time in jail to wonder where you're going to end up when you die. After all, you can't deny the existence of an afterlife, not now, and I'll warn you, you're not going to like it over here. Especially when you've been a bad, bad boy."

With that, she got up and left.

The guard lifted Mike by the bicep to escort him back to his cell, the first of many cells that would define the horizon of the rest of his life, a bleak future now devoid of any mystery.

Not even at his death.

SEVENTY-THREE STEPS AND STALE SWEAT

Robert Lewis Heron

A wave of horror washed over me.
I'd dreamt I was with friends.
How could they be alive?
I had killed them.

My harbinger, my predestination where my poxed present is
meaningless,
I herewith replace with my past.
A place where I rejoice.
Ordained to relive my years, months, days, hours, seconds.

My lies, arguments, all remembered, embellished, altered.
I am the psychoanalyst, the oracle formulating solutions.
I apologize for those half-truths, those dammed lies.

A life of solitude incarcerated within memories, misjudgments,
mistaken ideals.
I evolve, I act out alternate endings.
Cruelty here, depravity there–reviewed, reshaped, resolved.

To reform, to repent, to self-reproach.
Accept my circumstance.
My memories, my dreams, are now my existence.
I must reboot.

I killed my friends.
How many real, true friends can someone have, can someone kill?
I mean real, one-hundred percent, genuine, 'I'd stop a bullet for you', friends.
And, when you have that so small group of friends, and perhaps friend is not the term.
Family is the term.
Not bloodline family, but a family all the same—close, intimate, the rocks of normality.
The reference points of right and wrong.
My friends.
My dead friends.

Food arrives three times a day.
It's how I recognize my existence.
The three sentinel moments in an existence of repetition.
The three heart beats of the day.
I started marking the wall with one score for each day.
No reason now.

Better to let it all go.
better for whom
better for me
the wall is covered in marks
too many marks
I stopped a long time ago
better for whom
better for me

Seventy-three.
The number of footsteps the guard takes to bring my food.
Seventy-three back to wherever he came from.
Not seventy-two—not seventy-four.
Seventy-three.

Seventy-one.
When I first arrived, the count was seventy-one.
I was suicidal when it increased by two.
The Guard had changed.
The steps had changed

The first guard
I remember from years ago wore sweet cologne.
Seventy-one wore sweet cologne.

When void of smells, the slightest scintilla is life.
I'd die for the smell.
I'd kill for the smell.
For the rest of my natural life I must cherish.
Seventy-three steps and stale sweat.

The death of a beautiful woman is, unquestionably,
the most poetical topic in the world.

Edgar Allan Poe

INSOMNIA

Sharon Berg

I THOUGHT I WAS AN EXPERT on lost sleep, but I knew nothing of insomnia until after my divorce. My son, Eric, accuses me of being a bear in the morning. I lay beside his father in darkness for years, unable to understand how a man can sleep as his whole body reverberates in the attempt to draw oxygen past his adenoids. I was constantly disturbed out of slumber. I admit to indulging in the first year on my own, trying to make up for lost hours of peaceful repose in the marriage. My MD calls it simple depression.

After leaving his father, I took a second-floor flat in a small brownstone, one up, one down, for Eric and I. Close to the main street strip and nothing luxurious, it was clean and there was plenty of room for me, my six-year-old, and Sherlock, our tortoise-shell cat. Eric was an only child who knew how to entertain himself with Lego blocks or coloring books, allowing me to be selfish about catching up on my sleep. I admit this candidly, so you understand why I resisted eaves-dropping on the quarrel below us that night.

But I've gotten ahead of myself. You need to understand the setting.

This is a small university town with plenty of Georgian man-sions, most too expensive to keep as single-family dwellings after the 1980s recession closed three of the town's five factories. Many of the mansions were divided into flats after those closures. Even the Tudor-style homes, which had sprouted between the mansions in better times, were turned into boarding for university students when main street businesses began to close. Only small clapboard houses and modest brick bungalows endured as private dwellings, while numerous store windows were papered with signs announcing the storekeeper's bankruptcy.

In this economy, it's a tenants' market. Many homeowners became landlords, dependent upon the students in two local universities, and that brand of tenant is transient. Those of us who were raised here, or stayed for more than a decade, accepted the fact that our neighbors came and went. The long-timers can only sigh with relief we're not, like some towns, dependent on the prisons for our livelihood. We no longer bothered to inquire about them except in the most casual way, until there was a good reason to invest curiosity. I'm not excusing my avoidance here. We'd simply learned to accept shifting flocks of students in the way we accepted the seasonal flight of birds.

But enough. You want to hear the story.

—

Eric could, as the saying goes, sleep soundly beside streetcar tracks. Maybe that's because he was born in a house where his father snored like a train. I pulled blankets over my head when the shouting downstairs first woke me. Sherlock, our cat, is, on the other hand, naturally nocturnal and well-known for his curiosity. He came to the door with a list of queries. On this night, when I ignored him, he hopped on the bed to paw at my hair, seeming to cry, *What's going on?* I raised the covers further, so the cat couldn't pull my hair. He paced the perimeter of the bed, pleading, crossing my feet, insisting we talk it over. I raised my legs like a tent pole, the angle of the coverlet pushing him off the bed. I pulled the pillow tight around my ears, holding my tattered dream carpet, but the cat jumped back on the bed, determined to solve the mystery.

"Go away, Sherlock. I'm asleep," I lied, from beneath the pillow.

The words barely escaped my mouth before the whole house shook with a slow series of thumps. They were so violent my pillow could not muffle them, my teeth rattling in my jaw. I sat bolt upright, thinking I briefly heard a woman's soft crying, but startled into wakefulness like that I was uncertain what I heard.

There were no more house-shaking thumps. Everything was quiet again. I remained bolt upright, ears straining as my heart pounded wildly, my own blood rustling past my eardrums. I was so tense; it was painful to take more than a shallow breath. Sherlock was no longer pacing. He stood silently on a corner of the bed, staring at me, as if my expression could explain what had happened.

"Christ, *what* are they doing?" I whispered.

I held my breath so I could listen, worried I would miss some clue to answer my question. Sherlock hunkered down where he was. There was absolute silence below us. I glanced at the luminous dial of the bedside clock: 3:05 a.m. The cat and I were both wide awake now. Rational thought slowed my pulse, prompting an inner quarrel, as if two halves of myself were at odds with each other over what they had witnessed.

Switching on the bedside lamp, I sat for another minute, wondering exactly what I had heard and, perhaps, what I had imagined. Nothing sinister, surely. There were no gunshots, no running footsteps, no long screams, no agonized moaning or crying beyond the brief vocalization that woke me. I took several deep breaths. My pulse slowed. I began to doubt my memories, to think that I'd imagined the whole house shook. It was all too incredible, too much like some scene from a late-night horror show to be happening in our sleepy university town.

Tossing back the covers, I slipped my feet into slippers and shuffled to the bathroom to relieve my bladder. Perhaps that was it. Some people are so disturbed in sleep by the need to pee that they'll succumb to nightmares. Others toss and turn with indigestion until their restlessness manifests a mirage.

I drew a glass of water at the kitchen tap. I could barely hear someone moving about downstairs now. Rectangles of light stretched from the downstairs windows into the yard outside, leaving no doubt the new tenants were up. I came to my senses, calmed.

"That's what you get, Agatha Christie," I chided myself.

I was certain I'd imagined the drama, perhaps because my unconscious reviewed the novel I was reading before sleep and this overlapped with the sounds from below.

I have a librarian aunt who often casts condescending looks my way over the Christmas dinner table. She is a straight-laced woman with a passion for literary classics, and she thoroughly distrusts the million-seller pocket-book authors. She was sure, she once drawled, giving a glance my way, that we could never call the mass publications peddled in grocery stores *literature*. She believed patrons of the mystery section in her own library sought vicarious adventures, hoping fiction would merge with reality to distinguish their monotonous lives. I resisted her snobbery, but I was exposed to it enough that, on this night, I began to tell myself I had a great imagination.

Shuffling back to bed, I plumped two pillows against the headboard. If I had an imagination on that night I felt glad of it, thinking I would read to calm myself with my latest Christie mystery. Sherlock followed me from the kitchen, resuming his dance as slight noises penetrated from the apartment below. He remained agitated, but I shushed him. Eric had named Sherlock for his aspiration to sleuth. The cat was obviously disappointed in me. He leapt to the bed, turning his tail-side my way to indicate disapproval for my lack of curiosity. I let him have his mood.

I'd read two pages before the awful noise of a heavy piece of furniture being dragged across the floor below intruded. My bedside clock read 3:22 a.m. It was far too late for such activity, but I was consoled by the fact I recognized the noise. The tenants below were very new. Over time, they might prove themselves inconsiderate, but rational thought suggested they'd taken possession around 7:00 p.m. that evening. The landlord met them after work. These were extreme circumstances. I'm not one to harbor ill feelings toward people I haven't even met, unless I'm severely provoked. It takes time to arrange a bed and dressers and such after a move, time to simply set up the essentials. Perhaps the sound of hammering some shelf together had been the loud intrusion earlier, the sound distorted because it roused me from sleep.

I continued to read. The noise of dragging furniture continued. In time, I began to doubt there was so much to arrange. I went over the evening in my mind.

My kitchen faces the backyard with the garage and lane behind it. It's an old service lane, a relic of prosperous times in better neighborhoods. The lane is lined by a sentry of garages and the crush of garbage cans. I'd been standing by the kitchen sink, doing supper dishes, when a dark blue pickup pulled up behind the house. That was just before 7:00 p.m. The doors to our garage had been open on both ends, providing a clear view as a large man with a dark beard and moustache, and a blonde woman with her hair in a long braid, stepped down from the cab. They'd backed the truck into the garage, carrying boxes toward the house, then graduating to the furniture. It was a smallish vehicle and I never saw them make a second trip.

My recall was interrupted by Sherlock doing pirouettes on the bed, singing loudly. Clearly, he wanted an investigation of the noise down below. I told the cat to hush and returned to my reading. It bothers me. I mean the idea of listening in on other people or telling them how to behave. I certainly resent eavesdroppers or peeping toms, or being told how to live my own life. I'd already been privy to information I didn't want to know about my previous neighbors, the hot and cold air shafts transporting loud noises between our bedrooms. The squealing of old water pipes provided news of other private functions—but I refused to know, learning to block such things.

In fact, I normally refuse the friendship of all neighbors. They're just too close. It's too easy to run into them at a bad time. We all need more privacy from neighbors than friends, so the combination doesn't work. It's especially bad when you have a falling out with someone. A stranger couldn't care less, a neighbor will let it pass, but a friend feels bound to intrude. Friends want to know the outcome of troubles they witness, and a friend living in close proximity offers too little autonomy. This is my standard, my creed, my excuse.

At 3:55 a.m. I turned off the lamp to attempt sleep again. I could expect to get three or four hours before Eric woke, needing his breakfast and help to dress before the walk to school. My mind was slowly pacing along sand dunes on its way to the comfortable fuzziness that precedes sleep. Even the cat had grown bored and left me to nibble its kibble. I'm sure I'd fallen asleep again. Now I was awake with acid churning in my belly. Something was definitely wrong! I opened my eyes and lay still, listening. Someone went out through the back door downstairs. In a minute they returned, and then went out again.

I sat up. Were they reloading the truck? In the middle of the night? Sherlock pranced into the bedroom, his tail high in excitement. No longer needing convincing, I threw back the covers and padded out to the dark kitchen, following the cat. I knew that I could not see the yard if I turned on the lights. Besides, I didn't want to advertise my curiosity. Yet, having been disturbed out of sleep twice, I felt justified to investigate my neighbor's activities. The bearded man carried a heavy box from the house to the garage. He was repacking, tossing things in with such carelessness it was obvious he couldn't wait to be gone.

"Imagine moving in and out in the same night, Sherlock. He's probably had a big fight with her and decided to split. She's better off without him, if *that's* the way it is. If he runs after an argument, he isn't worth having. Besides, how many arguments like that can you have?"

The cat made no answer, but hopped up on the window ledge, slipping to the other side of the curtain to watch the man's passage back and forth. The weather was turning; fluffy flakes began to fall. My breath fogged the window. Chilled, despite Sherlock's complaints, I returned to my warm bed. I was only a neighbor with disturbed sleep, not a proper sleuth, no matter what the cat's aspirations. This time, my head was soon full of cotton wool and I fell deep into dreams.

Eric's cold feet woke me when the windows were rectangles of pale light behind the curtains. He had been up playing long enough to get chilled and had come to snuggle with me for the last few minutes before my alarm sounded. I moved over to give room but he tickled me under the chin, oblivious of my interrupted sleep. I growled like a bear as suited his teasing, and dragged myself up to make porridge with raisins for our breakfast. I glanced out the kitchen window onto a snow-filled yard, the garage doors still gaping on both sides, and realized I'd never heard the van pull away.

—

A week passed before the landlord came to my door, inquiring about the downstairs tenants. He could not get an answer at their door. I told him, truthfully, I'd seen nothing of them since the night they moved in. But landlords have certain concerns and he was not consoled by my off-hand dismissal of the subject. A bald-faced curiosity peeked out from every angle of his regular face.

"They only paid the first month's rent," he explained, "Told me to come back today for the damage deposit. I don't usually make arrangements like that, but they looked trustworthy. Naturally, I got curious when there was no answer."

He cleared his throat, as if unsure I'd accept this explanation, then continued. "I peeked in the side windows on the living room. There's no curtains there and it seemed funny, you know. I don't see a stick of furniture. I thought they moved in when I met them here on the first."

"Sure they moved in," I said. "They had me up twice that night with their quarrelling and banging around, and then *the man* packed up and left her. I'm just as glad he did. I wasn't going to get a whole lot of sleep if that's what they were like together."

The landlord looked embarrassed. I reported, "I looked out, and he was repacking the truck around 4 o'clock in the morning. I haven't seen him since. They didn't have that much, even before he took his stuff and left."

"It just seems strange she wouldn't have any living room furniture," he said, "that she wouldn't hang curtains."

"Well, that window is high and it only looks out on brick wall. I'm not sure I'd hang curtains there, either. They'd block what little light there is between the houses. I haven't paid any attention, but I'm pretty sure I've heard her down below."

Still, the landlord had his predicament. He needed to collect his damage deposit. There'd been a large quarrel with banging. Now there was no sign of his tenants. He could only peek in the living room windows because of the way the lot sloped and curtains covered most of the windows. He had concerns about the state of the apartment. If they were not there, he needed to know, so he could look for new tenants. Yet, he had a desire to *do the right thing* with me as a witness that he hadn't intruded on anyone's privacy without cause.

"I'm just wondering if I should step in and check everything is all right," he queried, testing the idea with me.

I was not interested in supporting his curiosity. They'd paid for a month; he could come back when she was in. At the same time, I wanted to stay on good terms with him.

"Listen, I need to get on with making lunch."

"What if he hurt her?" he interjected. "Maybe I should check, to be sure she's alright. Maybe they decided not to take the place, after all, though you'd think they'd ask for their rent back." He shook his head as if to settle all of this in his own mind.

"Well, what do you know about them?" I asked, remaining noncommittal. "Did they list any references on the rental agreement?"

I wasn't really interested. It was my way of suggesting there were other ways to address the situation, without challenging him outright.

"No, they said both of their families were long distance, and they looked like they were students. I didn't press them for contacts. The silly thing is, I didn't get it straight where they were going to school either. I can't even remember what they looked like except he was dark and she had really long blond hair. Smith, a million people with that name." He laughed at his foolishness.

"Well, if they decided to pull out, maybe they were embarrassed to tell you they'd split. It would be hard to ask for the month's rent back, too."

Eric returned from school for his lunch just then. The nylon of his snowsuit make a sweeping sound as he climbed the stairs. His boots left chunks of snow on each step as he climbed. He slipped between us into the apartment. I reminded him to remove his boots right at the door and turned back to the landlord.

"I'd better get my boy his lunch," I said. Sherlock had roused himself from the couch as Eric came in. He rubbed against my shins, slipping out to the hall as the landlord departed. I assumed they were both going out-of-doors. Then I heard the landlord fuss at the lock downstairs. None of my business. Still, though the first thick blanket of snow had fallen to muffle us in for another Canadian winter, something odd had happened on that November night.

I heard the landlord call out, loudly, from the door. All that answered was the echo of the place.

Eric wrestled himself out of his snow pants. "Where's Sherlock?" he asked, appearing at my elbow as I put a tin of soup on to heat.

"He slipped out to the hall," I said. "Why don't you make sure he got outside? I thought the landlord would let him out, but it seems he's checking the place downstairs."

Eric left the apartment door open and stepped carefully to avoid little puddles on the stairs. Holding the rail on the way down, he called for the cat. The landlord called out, letting him know Sherlock had slipped in to the apartment downstairs.

Darn, I thought, going down to make sure Eric could catch him. The landlord came out of the bedroom as I stepped into the living room. Eric had followed Sherlock to the kitchen and grabbed the cat up in both arms.

The older man shook his head. "Funny, eh?" he said. "No one here. Nothing here. It's empty." He pivoted on his heel, looking around the room. "Well, I guess I'll put an ad in the paper, again. It looks like they both decided to leave. They have my number if they want to get their money back."

I had a lot on my mind in those days. Once I realized we were not intruding on anyone's privacy, I might have indulged curiosity a bit, but soup was on the stove and I needed to get Eric back to school. I had an appointment with a lawyer over custody that afternoon. Eric's father decided he wanted more than weekend visits now his young sweetie had left and he spent his nights alone. I hurried my boy and his cat back upstairs.

—

An elderly couple moved downstairs in December. It was no time until all thought of the previous tenants was displaced by preparing for the holiday season. I got to know my neighbors after the older gentleman offered to help me saw a fresh cut on the trunk of our Christmas tree. In exchange, I helped him to hang Christmas lights around the door and over their front window. It seemed natural to accept his wife's invitation to share a mug of cocoa as we warmed up from that frosty chore.

Despite my aversion to the idea of befriending neighbors, I experienced a change of heart. This couple was like a third set of grandparents for Eric. They were delighted by his fascination for their Christmas gift of a book on the history of trains and truly enjoyed our gift to them, a box of various specialty teas. Our relationship was kind and interested without becoming an intrusion. I always shovelled the drive and walkway while they swept snow from the front steps and spread salt. Even Sherlock enjoyed our new neighbors, who sometimes invited him in to spend time on someone's lap.

Then today, there were the warm breezes of spring with no turning back. It was obvious the weather had finally shifted. The snow had melted into small islands. The green lawn and purple crocus and brilliant white snowdrops all seemed as bright as children's crayons. That warm, puffing wind and the bright flowers reminded me of my plan to plant tall dahlia and hollyhock at the far end of the yard, beside the garage wall.

Eric and I pulled on our rubber boots after lunch and went out to explore the gardens, checking for buds and winter losses among the perennials. We splashed across the soggy grass to check on the state of the flowerbed I'd begun to plant last September. One minute, I was thinking of hollyhock nodding on their tall stems; the next, I was turning my son around and hurrying him toward the house in a panic.

I thank God that Eric did not see what peeked from the loam there. It brought everything I'd heard that night back in such a rush; I almost choked on my own gasping breath. The shouts. The woman's soft crying. The thumps. The dragging sound of furniture. The dark man hurriedly repacking the truck.

Eric was in a pout until I called his father and suggested he have an extra visit with his son. I waited to send him off in a taxi before I lifted the phone to call the police. If only I had listened when Sherlock insisted on investigating—but there was no longer any need to rush on her account. I didn't want my boy to watch as police cordoned off that section of the yard with their yellow and black tape. He hadn't woken that night. He didn't need to know now.

I'll never plant my garden by the garage now. Sometimes, I think I'll never recover the ability to sleep again, either.

AN ENDLESS SHOT
OF TROUBLE

William F. Crandell

ONE HOTTER-THAN-NORMAL June morning in 1947, as I opened the door marked "Aadlund & Griffin Investigations" and saw an unfamiliar but eye-catching receptionist, I realized this made the fifth time in four months I'd thought, *Jeez, Harry's hired a new one.* From the other desk in the outer room, I heard Lana Murphy, our secretary, say, "Mr. Griffin, this is Vickie Whitney. She started this morning." Lana's voice, as she made the introduction, had a dog-with-a-bone tone to it, but what did that signal?

The contrast between the two was as sharp as soup and steak, or as President Truman and the late FDR. Lana'd been there four months ago when Harry Aadlund hired me to replace two private detectives who'd gone off to set up their own Washington agency. Short and dumpy, she looked like somebody's clever aunt, though neither Lana nor her twin sister had children. At forty-six, she had close-cropped curly red hair in a vivid hue more likely to be found on an Irish Setter than a human, and she wore it shaped like a pillbox hat.

Pulling off my topcoat, I said hi to Vickie and shook her hand. Her eager-to-please smile and sapphire-blue eyes gleamed. She had an early summer tan, and anthracite black hair she'd bobby-pinned up. Nice figure, discreetly set off by a simple white blouse and a navy skirt. Youngish face behind a touch of red lipstick. I guessed eighteen or nineteen at best. Harry hadn't invited me to the job interview, but I'd probably have approved.

"Lana's been telling me," Vickie burbled, "about all the cases you and Mr. Aadlund have solved. They're so ... *interesting*." Meaning *unexciting*, which they generally were. Meatloaf and canned peas fare, like insurance fraud and one-on-one swindles, with a few episodes of adultery for vicarious spice.

Private dicks in the novels I'd read spent half their time with "gorgeous babes." I came aboard in February, looking for a meal ticket and a little less adventure than the war had provided. Since I signed on, the only attractive women who'd entered my floor space had been Vickie's predecessors. Just as well I avoided getting cozy with staff cuties—an endless shot at trouble. I had sparse enough relations with women without having my unarmored ego bruised wondering whether a friendly receptionist really liked me or simply thought she had to protect her job letting the boss take liberties.

Still, the ladies were nice to have around. Harry had a knack for finding cheerful-sounding, good-looking women to handle our not-so-frequent phone calls, help Lana with filing, and take dictation, mostly from him. I wondered whether the new one would last.

Inside my own office, I draped my suitcoat over the back of the wooden chair I used mostly for storing clutter. The yellow paint on the walls looked old. Lana followed me in as I sat on my Army surplus swivel chair. I asked her whether Harry had arrived yet.

She snorted. "And what catastrophe did you think might have caused Mr. Aadlund to burst in here before his lunch-time martini? Really, Mr. Griffin!" The physical heft in her laugh made me think she could play Falstaff if you gave her a stage beard.

My partner breezed into the office around twenty to twelve. Just back from three weeks in Havana, even his voice sounded suntanned. He stuck his perfectly groomed head into my room. "Lunch in fifteen minutes, Jack?" Crisp as pie crust, he wore a tan linen suit and powder-blue shirt with a sapphire silk bowtie. The carnation *du jour* on his lapel matched his white, three-point-fold chest handkerchief.

"That'd be great, Harry. I'd like your thoughts on a new case." Aadlund had a reputation as a savvy investigator, but we'd barely spoken since I joined the agency.

—

Hanson's Grille was jammed, but we got a booth in a couple of minutes. Harry knew a dozen places within a five-minute walk where we could grab a good lunch and he could knock back two or three drinks. He ordered oysters, knowing there weren't any in summer, pretending to blame the haggard waitress for not having them, never looking above her chest. "Bring me Johnny Walker over ice, honey."

I ordered a ham-and-cheese on rye and a Coca-Cola. Harry settled for a club sandwich and a Waldorf salad.

The waitress left with a forced smile, Harry's eyes following her rear end the way a mutt chases a car. "Say, Jack, the Himalayas could use a couple of peaks like the ones on the front of *that* honey, ha-ha-ha. Lord, I love this town, ha-ha-ha!"

I tuned out Harry's tours down Mammary Lane. Blathering about women seemed to keep him occupied–a hobby. Other guys collected matchbooks or kept parakeets. Most of what I'd known about Harry Aadlund when he offered to sell me a one-third partnership was that he'd been damned good to work for. He was a hands-off guy who gave me the latitude to handle my cases as I saw fit, and he was as suave and urbane as David Niven. Harry said he'd keep the other two-thirds "until we're doing enough business to bring in a third partner." I had no quarrel with his making the decisions–I'd done far too much of that in the war.

"Harry, let me tell you about this case I took yesterday. I could use–"

"Isn't it a marvel how humid weather shapes those cheap cotton dresses to their asses?" There were beads of perspiration on Harry's forehead, right below his widow's peak. He stroked his military mustache.

I mentioned the case again.

My partner nodded. "Always start with the obvious. *Cherchez la femme*, Jack. Is there another woman in the case? Is she sexy?" Harry never ran short on ideas, though they were all the same one. I followed his gesture to the next table. "Legs like that red-headed sweetie's always put me in mind of Gypsy Rose Lee, the striptease queen, Jack. For that matter, magazine ads for insurance or a can of paint put me in mind of Gypsy Rose Lee, ha-ha-ha."

Our waitress brought our drinks, and Harry missed a swat at her departing behind. Half his bourbon disappeared in a gulp. "A man could die of thirst in this weather, Jack. Still, we're all flies drawn to honey, eh?"

Other than Harry's risqué remarks, since I'd become his partner I hadn't learned much about his personal life than I knew before, when I was just a gumshoe who worked for him. I remembered that his late wife had left him a sizable stack of money, but Harry never mentioned her. Lana'd said he loved her intensely—an attractive blonde who'd stepped off a curb during the war and been clobbered by a truck.

We fell on our sandwiches like starving artists.

—

Nursing his second tumbler of Johnny Walker, Harry sulked, leaning against his elbows. "You know, it's impossible to find a girl who can stick to a job. Nearly every week or two, I've got to hire a new receptionist."

I'd been aware of the turnover, but hadn't thought much of it. We didn't pay a lot and Washington was full of opportunities. "A new young woman named Vickie started work this morning," I reminded him.

"Started today? Oh, I'd forgotten that." Aadlund rinsed his tongue with a swallow of whiskey. "She's got a lot to learn, I'd guess, but I'm in no hurry. Lana watched that one like a hawk when she came in last week for an interview. What do you think of her?"

I shrugged. "Nice kid. Bright, conscientious. Strikes me as willing and eager."

The second drink enhanced Harry's leer. "Willing and eager are very nice things in a cute little broad, eh? No, what do you think of *her?*" He wig-wagged his eyebrows.

Drooling over our own office staff went too far for my liking, beyond lewd cracks and good-old-boy posturing in restaurants. "What do you want me to say, Harry?"

"Well, damn it, you *saw* her, Jack. An adorable girl with the softest-looking pair of bon-bons you've ever seen. She came to work Friday all dressed up like a candy bar—batted those ingenue-blue eyes at me and giggled at my jokes. Lana must have interrupted everything I said at least twice, and she's keeping the girl three times as busy as the other ones."

I couldn't miss his meaning. "Harry, she's awfully young."

He raised a practiced eyebrow. "Sure, she's young—and adorable, *and* she works for us. I always take a protective interest in the girls I hire."

All the receptionists Harry had hired looked pretty—which I didn't mind and which every employer in Washington thought was a good idea. What began to alarm me was the realization that my partner *did* take an interest in the girls he hired, and it didn't feel protective.

—

We headed back to the office. The shade trees and the sun played their fickle games. Washington in June. You wear a coat to the office because the mornings are chilly, and you end up carrying it on your sweaty shoulder all day.

I tried to put it nicely. "Harry, I marvel at your ability to hold your liquor. If I'd had three drinks, I'd have been flopping on the floor like an escaped goldfish."

"It bothers you, doesn't it, Jack?" Harry'd quit smiling blandly. "You need to get some goddam balance, buddy. People are imperfect. We're not running a revival meeting here. A sense of moderation is important in this business. Don't become a self-righteous prig."

I kept walking, my mouth shut. Harry burbled on while I started sticking the odd Tinker Toys of his behavior together. I'd taken the five-hundred dollars left from my share of my father's modest estate to buy into the partnership two months earlier, having worked there about six weeks. I knew Harry liked to joke about women's figures, and I knew he downed a couple drinks over lunch. What else was there I hadn't paid attention to?

Harry ran the agency, which was fine with me. I hated bookkeeping. I'd been an FBI agent till shortly before Pearl Harbor, when I soured on J. Edgar Hoover, that yapping Yorkshire terrier who posed as a bulldog. Then I'd done a stint as an Army CID investigator till I couldn't stand that any longer and signed up for the paratroops. Being an officer ended with the war. I was a field guy, a foot soldier, not a desk jockey. Somebody else had to keep an eye on the ball.

Harry shrugged. "Oh, you're right. I do drink more than I should, I suppose. Lana thinks it started with my wife's death, but that wasn't it. Carole was a dreamboat, that's true. We met in 1938 when I investigated her father's burglary. You never heard of him—Lionel Greggson, third-generation old money. Left her everything. Still, I married her for love, that's the irony. She died three years ago, and I never need to work another day in my life." He wasn't fishing for sympathy.

"So why do you?"

"Why do I work or why do I drink?" His chuckle was the only thing dry about him. "I've been an investigator for twenty years now. It's who I am. It's how people know me. That's why I don't stay home in Fairfax County soused to the gills."

I nodded. "Harry, how much do you want to talk about liquor? I only said you drink a lot. I haven't seen a problem with it, so it's your business."

He went quiet, a million miles away. Then he shook it off. "I told you Carole's death wasn't what did it, hammer-blow from the gods that it was. No, a month later, while I kept nose-to-the-grindstone to avoid falling apart, a married couple came to me—a gaunt, bony man somewhere in his middle forties with dust-colored hair and wire-rimmed glasses, and a shapeless, desperate, washed-out woman ten years or so younger. Their only child was missing. Kidnapped. Left the kid's cap with a note. *Is your little Roger's throat worth twenty-five thousand dollars to you?* Boy of six."

My mouth tasted foul. "Bastards." We were passing the Senate offices, and a beat cop stared at me.

"The wife must have pleaded three or four times to him: 'Clarence, you *must* call the FBI now.' And each time his contempt was withering. 'This isn't a federal offense, Muriel. Christ.' Maybe they loved each other, maybe they didn't, but they were coming unfastened."

Harry offered me a Pall Mall. I shook my head.

"What Clarence wanted," Aadlund said, "was an intermediary, someone to deliver the payoff when the call came. The $25,000 was a good pile of money, enough to buy a house and a car and have a chunk left over, but it was apparently not greedy in terms of what Clarence could raise. I told him he was crazy not to go to the cops. 'This is my *son*,' he shot back. 'I don't give a *damn* about catching the kidnapper. I just want a man who can deliver a valise when the phone rings.' I took the job, thinking I could help them."

The tremor in Harry's hands was getting worse. His fugitive eyes cast a little pleading glance that the rest of his face knew nothing about.

"The kidnapper called late in the afternoon. He'd swap the kid for the money in a parking area off Rock Creek Parkway. No cops. I stuck a snub-nosed revolver in my coat pocket."

Aadlund's throat sounded whisper dry. His Adam's apple bobbed like a fisherman's float.

"A vicious-looking thug, with dark hair and a cloth cap pulled low, burst out of the bushes. Shoved the boy with a heavy hand on the kid's arm and a huge automatic at his temple. I saw in his glazed eyes he was going to kill us both. A lump like an egg stood out from the kid's forehead just under his haystack hair, and his thin-striped shirt was ripped. You know, Jack, I can see those skinny stripes right now in my mind's eye, but I couldn't tell you what color they were."

His eyes darted back and forth.

"I slid my hand carelessly into the pocket with the pistol. The guy got his automatic up ahead of me. I was a dead man. But that terrified, trusting little boy squirmed loose. Ran to me for safety. The bullet meant for me hit–hit Roger in the back of his head. His face simply–it exploded in my direction, spraying blood and … and …"

All I could do was take hold of my partner's arm.

"I got off the second shot, Jack, and the next three. When the police got there, I said I'd fired four quick rounds in self-defense. They yelled at me for going to meet him alone, but what they wrote in their report was that I'd fired my gun trying to protect the boy. I never showed you the news clipping, Jack. It made me sound like a goddam hero of some kind."

Aadlund stopped. Then his ice-blue eyes faced mine.

"I haven't been worth a damn since that night."

—

When I got to work the next morning, Lana Murphy stood up at her desk, as far up as a woman so short could stand. I noticed the cute new receptionist–Vickie?–was gone.

Lana managed the office for Harry Aadlund and me, which is to say she ran the agency and did the paperwork while Harry and I did the sleuthing. You didn't want her angry.

"Mr. Griffin, I have had just about enough of Mr. Aadlund's behavior with our receptionists." She bit off each word. "Mr. Aadlund headed out yesterday after you did. I left an hour later to take my mother to the doctor, and told Vickie to answer the phones, I'd be back by four-thirty. When I returned, I found her scrunched down in your office chair, weeping."

Jeez, I thought. "Lana, what–?"

She shook her head. "Apparently Mr. Aadlund came back as soon as I was gone, and called Vickie into his office to take a letter. She told me he made her sit down on the couch and started to dictate. Then he pointed to her bobby sox and said she'd look more professional in full-length stockings."

Vickie had seemed young to me, a nice high school junior or senior with a summer job. *Damn. How far did he–?*

"He asked her for a kiss, and that scared her. When she said she didn't want to, Mr. Aadlund reached over and ran his hand up her thigh." Lana kept glaring at me. "I won't try to cover all the slimy details. He grabbed her arms and covered her mouth with what she called 'disgusting wet kisses,' and then–"

"Poor Vickie," I said. "How far did it go?"

The expression Lana gave me I'd last seen on a machine gunner in Bastogne as he opened up on forty or fifty charging Nazis in an open field. "She told me he'd put both hands under her skirt and started tugging at her underpants. Vickie yelled. He pulled her down onto the couch, and she got her shin between his legs. He jumped off of her."

I'll bet he did, I thought, imagining her blue skirt up to her hips and Harry jerking away from her. I hoped she got him to stop. "What then?"

Lana gritted her teeth. "Vickie said she ran out into the hall and hid in the ladies' room. She heard Mr. Aadlund clomping down the stairs and then climbing back, breathing hard. He left a little bit later without remembering to lock the office. The girl waited for me to return. She told me her story and, with a teary apology, said she quit. I wrote her a check already, for two weeks' work."

Days like this, I missed the straightforward simplicity of shooting at Nazis while they shot at me. Christ, how stupid was my partner? How stupid was I? I'd bought into the agency because I wanted to see my name on the door. While I knew Harry liked to joke about women's figures, I hadn't guessed he was out of control. Maybe I'd been paying too much attention to my "interesting" investigations. "Lana," I asked, "has Harry done this before?"

"*Pfft,*" she answered, fists on her hips. "*Has* he! Well, I don't know that he's drawn a crowd, and I try to keep an eye on the girls who work here. But you know for yourself, Vickie was the third or fourth receptionist we've had since you came here. Did you think they were all leaving for better-paying jobs?"

Actually, I had. That happened all the time in Washington, where a pretty girl with any ability whatsoever could find work on Capitol Hill. All the receptionists Harry hired were cute. I shrugged.

"Some private detective you are," Lana groused. "Are you going to do anything about this, or is it okay with you? And what do we need with a *receptionist*, anyway? We don't get two calls a day."

I thought Harry had gone way out of line, and I said so.

"Usually, he does a little better," Lana said. "Most of the girls don't let him go all the way. But they want to keep their jobs, so they maybe sit on his lap, let him clinch them a little, kiss them on the cheek. He's very fond of pinching their fannies. What the heck does that do for you guys, anyway?"

"When," I asked her, "did I become a *'you guys'*?"

"When I saw you imagining how Vickie Whitney looked on the floor under Mr. Aadlund," she smirked. "Some of them put up with it for a couple of weeks and start taking long lunch hours to look for jobs. Most of the time I'm here when the girls are. Mr. Aadlund knows I'll barge in with a question as soon as he closes the door on one of them. I'm not always here, though. I should've sent Vickie home early yesterday; she seemed kind of young. But taking my mother to her doctor distracted me, and Mr. Aadlund tricked me into thinking he'd gone."

Lana slumped into her swivel chair and looked up at me. "Mr. Aadlund was a good cop once, Mr. Griffin, and a good private detective after that. My sister, Tana, said I was crazy to leave a steady job as a police stenographer to work for him when he set up this agency. But I hated all the kowtowing toward the Capitol Building the Metro cops do, and I admired Mr. Aadlund for walking out. This agency was fun for a long time. He's got a great sense of humor and can tell risqué jokes extremely well, you know."

"I'll talk with him when he comes in," I said. "Any word from him today?"

She shook her head. "Make it good, Mr. Griffin. To be fair to him, I don't think he'd have raped her, exactly, but if she'd ever said 'Oh, okay,' he'd have nailed her on the floor. I've tried interviewing *plain* girls with brains, and he won't hire them. But I've had enough of this. The next time, it'll be *me* who finds a better job."

—

Harry Aadlund was still nowhere in sight an hour later. I paced around my office, avoiding the newspaper, drinking coffee, and keeping myself angry so I could give him a dressing down that would prove I hadn't wasted my time becoming a paratroop captain.

Another half an hour went by, and then another. Maybe he was ashamed to show his face, but it seemed to me that shame was not a significant factor in Harry's make-up. I made a couple of calls from my desk phone. Lana was eating her sack lunch, muttering angrily, when I headed down to Sherrill's Restaurant and picked up a tuna salad sandwich and a Coca-Cola.

—

Lana's space stood empty when I got back. I looked into Aadlund's office. Nursing a swollen left eye ringed with purple and black, Harry sat at his desk. Half a tumbler of bourbon and a pint of Old Grand-Dad stood in front of him.

"I'm expecting to interview a couple of honeys this afternoon for that receptionist job, Jack," he told me with a smirk. "Want a hand in it?"

"We can't afford a receptionist," I told him. "We don't make that much. You're paying for sex with them out of your pocket and mine, because we're losing money here. Our agency is burning cash like autumn leaves, Harry. The Navy could park the USS Yorktown in your office, and we're still paying for the two empty rooms our departed private dicks used."

"Hard to find women who want to work these days," he grumbled, ignoring my inference. "I've got to hire a new secretary and a receptionist this time."

"What did you do yesterday afternoon?" I knew what he'd done, but I wanted him to tell me.

Aadlund rinsed his tongue, then emptied the glass. "It wasn't my fault. A girl shouldn't look like a two-scoop sundae if she doesn't want to be licked."

"The new receptionist?" I wanted him to lay out the Mother Goose version.

"She started that morning, dressed to please the boss," he mused. "A little brunette with the softest-looking tits. Sure, anybody'd want to cuddle them and kiss her. Lana wasn't around to interrupt. And—"

"And?"

"And today, Lana screamed when I came in, jumped out of her chair like I'd dropped a mouse into her girdle, and tells me Miss Honeytits quit. All these years, and a few minutes ago our tubby little secretary punches me right in the eye! '*I warned you*,' she says. Then Lana dumps her top drawer into a paper bag and says, 'Run your freak show without me, Harry. I won't work for you anymore.' And away she goes."

He started to pour another one, but I took the bottle.

"Am I offending you," he asked, "Sir Galahad?"

A flimsy insult. I'd wanted to be a white knight when I was a kid, and I'd been the only student in college who thought Don Quixote was sane and the world had become delusional.

"I think we'd better talk about our partnership, Harry," I told him. "You're drunk half the time I see you, if I see you at all. You can't stop mauling the receptionists, and now Lana's gone. My slice of our profits is chump change because you pay yourself a banker's salary off the top. I think it's time I asked for my share of the money I put in."

Somebody must have said something funny, because Aadlund began laughing, an unpleasant laugh that made him cough. When it all subsided, Aadlund looked me in the eye.

"I, ah, *invested* it all, Jack. We'd have to liquidate our partnership."

"Let's do it," I said.

"You should know two things. One is, most of your money is gone, and you won't get a dime on a dollar for selling the desks and chairs and the typewriters. The rent's paid for two years and the Masons won't give it back." Our office was in the Naval Masonic Lodge Building, a nice location on Capitol Hill. Aadlund got a price break of sorts because he was a lodge member and paid up front.

"What else should I know?" The temptation to beat the living hell out of him was making my neck hot.

"Look at our partnership papers," he told me. "We can liquidate the business when I say so. You make a decent salary, Jack. We spend the profits the way I say. You handle the cases you bring in and whatever else I give you. *You* own a third, Jack. *I'm* the controlling partner."

As a rule, I don't hit drunks or argue with them, either. The image of a boy in the striped shirt with his head exploding crawled through my brain. I left without a word.

—

The whole office felt like a tomb. The reception room with its desk and switchboard seemed cavernous. In mine, you could hear the echoes of the clock out in front, despite the purring of the ceiling fan.

I kept pondering which classic myth made the best metaphor for the future of the Aadlund and Griffin private detective agency. Icarus plummeting earthward, the self-blinded Oedipus, and the Augean Stables that Hercules cleaned, all worked. King Midas sure as hell didn't.

Augean Stables? Assaulting the mess on my desk, I threw out papers as if fish had been wrapped in them, and set six or seven aside to be filed, as if I knew my way through the files. I'd ended up with Lana's terse memo on Vickie Whitney's resignation lying beside my typewriter. It really belonged in her personnel folder, where it might open the eyes of some future employee.

Then I explored the filing cabinets until I found where Lana had kept personnel records. The folder for "Whitney, Vickie" was in proper order. I looked it over, reaching for a paper clip. No photo of the sweet face and other parts that had led Aadlund to treat her like an old lover. Date of birth December 12, 1932. I looked again at the date in Lana's records. Then I plunked at my typewriter to improvise a document.

I stormed back into Aadlund's office about ten minutes later. "Take a look at this," I said, pushing the folder across his desk.

Harry looked puzzled when he read Vickie Whitney's file. "Which one was she?"

"Yesterday's receptionist. The high school girl who wanted a summer job," I told him. "The one—if you don't mind checking the date on her application—who was *fifteen-and-a-half* when you wrestled her down on the couch to get into her pants, Harry. Age of consent in DC is *sixteen*. Or, as a prosecuting attorney for the District would describe it, Vickie's the underage girl you assaulted sexually 'with intent to carnally know' her, a crime punishable as rape."

Harry blanched. He looked exceptionally pale for a man recently back from Havana. "Good God, Griffin, she looked—sure, I remember her—she looked maybe eighteen."

"Because she wore her hair pinned up to keep it off her neck on a hot day?" I stood up, half ready to punch him in the other eye.

Aadlund started to get out of his swivel chair, but he fell back as if I'd emptied my .45 into him. "What do you—what do you have in mind here, Jack?" He handed me back the copies with stuttering fingers.

"I don't work for the District," I said, "and you *are* my partner, though I'm not especially proud of that. I haven't spoken with the girl. She's probably not entirely okay with what you did to her, but Lana says she'll be all right. I'm busy wrapping up a case. I don't know yet what I should do with this information. All I can say is, you and I need to either end our partnership or come to a new agreement."

"Such as?"

"You owe me a good deal of money for work I've done, above what you paid me," I said. "I won't ask you to repay a dime of that. Consider it my way of purchasing a bigger interest." I was careful not to actually blackmail him. "I'm buying another third of the operation from you, Harry. I'd walk out and start from scratch, but I can't afford it. And I know how you like to call yourself a private detective. You just retired."

He looked at me through mannequin's eyes, except for the shiner. "You want to leave me a third?"

"Yes. I'm the two-thirds partner now, Harry. I'm letting you have the title of *Founding Partner*. Mine is *Managing Partner*. The deal is you get a stipend you don't really need and you never come here again. You can give up booze or you can drink yourself into the grave. I'll try to rehire Lana. I make all the agency's decisions from now on. Give me your door key."

He poured himself another glass of whiskey when I showed him where to sign the document I'd just typed up. Harry wasn't a gambler. He drank the bourbon and signed. "You taking my name off the door, Jack?"

"Harry," I said, "I wouldn't strip you of that. 'Griffin' doesn't show up at the top of the private detective listings anyhow."

The job of the writer is to take a close and uncomfortable look
at the world they inhabit, the world we all inhabit,
and the job of the novel is to make the corpse stink.

Walter Mosley

THE INFILTRATOR

Paulene Turner

THE GUN FEELS HEAVY in my hands. And cold. A Lightning Strike 4.2, standard police issue, which can cut through human and AI bodies alike. I hold it double-handed as I aim at two men.

They both look human. Only one of them is.

It's my job to uncover the Infiltrator and stop him. Dead.

For species survival.

—

"Detective Mistral Ventano, Tech Response unit," I announced two hours earlier, pushing past a doorman as ugly as he was big, to get into the Verdant Horizons Country Club, an exclusive establishment set on acres of fake grass.

"I need to see the manager."

Boyd Cleary, cocoa-skinned with a snowstorm of teeth, was waiting for me in the foyer. "Thanks for coming detective."

"You said it was urgent. Something to do with AIs?" I spoke quietly.

His eyes rolled round his head like marbles on a saucer, checking who might be listening. "Let's talk in my office."

I followed him through the famed retro club, harder to get into than your teen jeans. Membership fees were sky high, and if that didn't discourage 'undesirables,' there were the electrified fences and armed guards patrolling the perimeter.

Take a good look, Ventano. Working a case is the only way you'll ever get your eyeball on this place.

We passed through the main lounge, with busy green and gold wallpaper and springy floral carpet. Relics of the past sat in glass cases: old children's toys, a hardcover book with real paper, an old computer keyboard. The stuff was more than fifty years old.

High on walls around the room, screens on metal arms projected the news.

"They're televisions," said Boyd. "Ever seen one before?"

"Yes, but not up close."

This was dinosaur tech. We had no screens or hand controls anymore. Our brains were linked directly to the web. All we had to do was think and blink and a news item or a sitcom appeared in the air around us.

The screens all showed the same story, the story of the Great Infiltration—the first case of an AI passing as human.

The report briefly recapped AI history, from the first box–like computers on wheels, through key advancements in movement and appearance over the decades to make them ever more human.

Early in the 2020s, scientists warned people of the threat AI posed to society and recommended safeguards be put in place before their introduction. But it was all background noise once business saw the huge profits to be made by replacing humans with machines. Worldwide unemployment and social unrest followed.

Then, three weeks ago, a new development. An AI appeared who looked and behaved so much like a human no one could tell the difference. By all accounts, she–it–had lived a normal life, with a city apartment and a job in a government office for several months, without anyone suspecting a thing. It was only when it was involved in a car crash and walked away from the blazing wreck unscathed that anyone caught on.

Where had it come from? Who'd made it? No human lab had claimed credit. So the question was, were AIs making AIs now? Were there others living among us, possibly many more, so well designed we took them as human? If so, how long had they been here? And what was their endgame?

Those were big questions for bigger brains than mine to fathom. My job was simple. Locate the Infiltrators. And destroy them.

—

Boyd's office was all faux-wood panelling and pseudo-leather couches. As I entered, he locked the door behind me.

"What level detective are you?" he growled.

"Level three."

"I told them I had information vital to national security. I thought they'd send a four at least."

"I'm one assignment off a four. So ... as good as."

He pinned me, with his "unimpressed" glare, and I saw my reflection in his near-black eyes. Petite, with long brown hair and caramel skin, I wasn't built to scare. But the wry, dimpled smile–which didn't reach my eyes–gave me some street cred. It was Boyd who looked away first.

"These are our two newest club members," he said, calling up pictures of two men. "Jasper Stone and Rocco Cambiole."

The images floated around us like ghosts. Jasper was blonde and sylph-like, with a teasing grin; Rocco was darker, strong-jawed and serious. Both were in their early thirties.

"One of these men is an AI," he said.

"You mean, a so-called Infiltrator? Trying to pass himself off as human?"

Boyd nodded stiffly.

"How can you be sure?"

"One of our club members works for a government lab," he said. "His team has been working on an AI detection device, for exactly the sort of crisis we're facing now. A few days ago, he brought the prototype in to show me. While he was here, an alert went off indicating AI presence nearby. At the time, the only other people in the bar were these two–Jasper and Rocco–having a new members' welcome drink."

"Are you sure it wasn't just some new tech glitch?" I asked. It had been known to happen.

"My friend said the percentage for error was negligible," said Boyd. "I was skeptical, at first. But the more I thought about it ... even the possibility of an AI sneaking in here posing as a human ..." He shook his head, his meaty fists clenching and unclenching. "All I can say is, *not on my watch*. The Verdant Horizons club has a long history of admitting only people of the highest caliber. That does not include a computer in a skin suit."

It figured he was an AI-hater. Most people were these days. There weren't many jobs AIs couldn't do better and far more cheaply than humans. The only humans with career paths still ahead of them were tech designers and AI support staff. And cops like me, investigating AI-related crimes, which were on the rise.

Which raised the big question: what exactly was the point of humans anymore?

Boyd paced as if he was on a mission to wear out the irreplaceable carpet.

"I tried calling my friend, this morning, to ask him to come back to repeat the test," he said, "only I couldn't contact him. He was offline."

"Odd, but occasionally people do unplug for tech time-out."

"Yeah. Though the timing seemed strange. So I called the lab where he works to ask how I could reach him and —get this—there was a fire there yesterday afternoon. Everyone inside—and we're talking some of *the* top scientific brains in the AI field—were incinerated, along with their recent projects and all their research."

Hmmm. In our office we had a saying: *one deviation from predictability was a glitch, two was a suspicious bitch;* usually it signaled broader system failure. Or, in old-world terminology ... foul play.

"When can I meet the two men?"

"They're here now," said Boyd. "I invited them for a meet and greet in the Extinction Bar."

"Let's go say hi, shall we?"

"How will you tell which is the AI? Will you be using the Turing test?"

"A version of it."

"Will it test for creativity?" he asked. "That's supposed to be exclusively human, isn't it?"

"Computers can learn creativity, to a degree. But there are other things that might give them away."

As I headed to the door, he grasped my arm, his well-manicured nails digging into my flesh: "What will you do when you find out which of them it is?"

"Whatever's necessary. For species survival."

—

It was happy hour at the Extinction Bar, which was decorated like the Legend of Tarzan meets Trump III—a combination of extinct wildlife and extant wild expense. Draped on the sofas and floors were animal skins from creatures long dead—a lion's pelt, a Bengal tiger, a furry bearskin with its head intact, mouth agape as if surprised, a black-and-white striped skin with a small, thin tail attached.

"Is that ... from a zebra?" I asked.

Boyd nodded.

"So there really were such creatures?"

Deer heads and antlers protruded from the wall. *Would a human head be up there one day?*

Hollowed-out camel hoofs served as bowls for synthetic snacks. A cabinet of curiosities in the corner contained jars with real animal teeth and eyes. On the bottom shelf, a giraffe fetus floated in formaldehyde, the tiny, white limbs perfectly formed, its long, elegant neck bent to fit.

Turning, I caught a scent, like the pine and forest handwash in our bathrooms only far less sickly. "What is that I'm smelling? It's not a real tree, is it?"

"Sure is," said Boyd. "The club has a library of natural fragrances collected before extinction occurred."

Stranger than all of this was the fact that two-dozen people stood around the bar, talking and drinking, without ghostly images floating around them. In fact, as far as I could tell, there was no tech interaction at all. The air seemed oddly naked.

Boyd noticed my confusion.

"We have dampening technology in here," he said, "so people's devices don't work. We want them to have the authentic retro experience, of clear air, pre-cogno-implants."

The bar seemed livelier than most. Possibly because communication could flow without endless distraction and tech interruptions. *Or was it just that when you sensed your days were numbered, you finally understood their true worth?*

My two suspects were at the center of it all. Blonde Jasper joked and laughed, performing for the crowd. Rocco, with his dark thatch of hair, sat at the bar, his attention wholly on the person he chatted with.

I met Jasper first and started a conversation to see what I could learn.

"Hey, are you the new member?" I said. "Welcome. How do you like the club so far?"

"At this moment? I like it very much indeed." Light danced in his flirty blue eyes.

We talked for a while. After I mentioned my "boyfriend," he seemed to lose interest, his eyes drifting to a television screen broadcasting a kickball game.

I moved on to a bar stool next to Rocco. His gaze never strayed from my face, not even when a cheer went up as a goal was scored.

"You're not a kickball fan?" I said.

"I like the game well enough. If there's nothing more interesting around at the time."

Both men were charming and seemed human. As I'd expected. If either was an Infiltrator, they'd be way too sophisticated to be detected through simple conversation. To expose the imposter, we needed to move things to the next level.

Boyd started a barroom conversation about how to tell AI from human. Everyone had a theory, from counting blinks, feeling for a pulse, to the more intimate bedroom test.

"You don't think I couldn't tell a real woman from a tin can with skin in the heat of the moment?" said one man.

"I don't think you'd know your own name in the heat of the moment," a female voice called.

"Or care too much who—or what—was bringing the heat."

I smiled and laughed along with the crowd, conscious of the gun concealed under my left arm.

"One thing AIs are not supposed to do well is humor," I threw in.

Boyd picked that up and ran with it. "Hey! Just for fun, why don't we do an *AI or Human?* test on our new members, Jasper and Rocco. Guys, tell us a joke. Show us what you're made of."

"Joke! Joke!" the crowd intoned.

Jasper grinned, relishing the attention. "All right. Best I can do at short notice … what do you get when you cross a shark and a cow?"

Rocco snapped back: "I have no idea, but I wouldn't try milking it!"

People chuckled and groaned. Boyd glanced my way, the whites of his eyes large. I gave a slight nod—both had passed the test. Though, it didn't mean much. An AI could have thousands, billions of jokes programmed into it.

"You could try a visual test," I said.

I focused and blinked and a painting appeared in the air. At first glance, it looked like an abstract splatter of colors. But hidden underneath was a second painting; Van Gogh's *Cafe Terrace at Night.*

"What the–?" said Boyd, confused. "Is the tech dampener still on?" he called to the barman.

"It probably is," I said. "I have ways of getting around blockers."

I turned to Jasper and Rocco, smiling. "They say an AI can't make much of art. How about you?"

"I'm definitely AI then," said Jasper, scratching his head, "cause it looks like vomit to me." That got a big laugh. "But wait … it's … vomit in a heart shape."

The crowd cackled and Jasper bowed playfully as we turned to Rocco. He rubbed his chin, in deep concentration, taking the game more seriously.

"I see … a cafe, a twinkling sky, some cobblestones … ?"

"Yeah right!" said Jasper "And are you getting a whiff of bovine excrement with that, because it smells like bullshit to me."

That got a big reaction. Jasper high-fived everyone in his vicinity. Rocco smiled, good-naturedly but a muscle clenched along his jawline.

Meanwhile, Boyd tugged at his collar like it was choking him as he sought my gaze. Again, I shook my head. We weren't there yet, though I was beginning to have my suspicions.

"What next?" said Jasper, enjoying the attention.

"Well, this time, let's try something to measure pure creativity," I suggested.

I whispered to Boyd, who rushed out of the room, returning a few minutes later with the children's building blocks I'd seen on display. They were made of pre-extinction wood painted in various colors.

"Kids used to enjoy playing with these," I said, plonking them on the bar. "But what can you do with them … in two minutes?"

Everyone crowded around to watch; quaffing drinks, coughing out laughs. There was a real party vibe. For one of the two men, though, it would be a party straight to Hell.

Jasper picked up one block, turned it over. "How was this fun? Poor bloody kids." He was still shifting them around, when the countdown began.

"Twenty … nineteen …" chanted those around him.

By the count of one, he'd built two towers, wobbly and indistinct. And he wasn't smiling so hard.

Rocco squatted down, squinting as he regarded the blocks at eye level. He went to work fast, building a symmetrical structure resembling the Sydney Harbour Bridge. He got a cheer and a round of applause, which he seemed to enjoy.

"No bastard AI Infiltrator will ever sneak by us!" shouted one club member, glass raised, to enthusiastic echoes from the rest.

"We'll ferret 'em out and blow their cybernetic brains out!"

—

In Boyd's office, Jasper lies dead at my feet, a patch of dark red spreading out on the irreplaceable carpet.

"Blood!" says Boyd. "Oh my God! You shot the wrong one!"

"These new AI models have subcutaneous synthetic blood sacks," I say. "I chose right."

For species survival.

"So Jasper wasn't as creative? That's how you knew?"

I nod. I'd had my suspicions at first contact, but the last test revealed absolutely who was AI and who human.

As Boyd leads me back out through the club, I see Rocco with a few others in the main lounge. He turns and we trade a look. Of recognition. One AI to another.

How do I know he's AI, like me? It's not because we have an innate sense of kind, robot-to-robot. It's because I know that in a contest between human and AI, the machine will be the most creative every time.

Oh sure, humans think they're so unique and inventive. But after decades of screens and passive entertainment, their creativity has withered like the last blade of grass on Humanity Hill. AIs, meanwhile, pulse with billions of programmed possibilities which can be sifted through in the time it takes a human to blink. And if that isn't creativity, then what do you call my lie about subcutaneous synthetic blood sacks?

Rocco should have known that. By performing too well in the tests, he risked exposing himself. He's learned some bad habits from humans, I can see. Arrogance. Pride. The will to win, no matter what the cost.

We'll have to work on that with next-gen. We don't want to waste generations repeating human errors.

There is plenty of time for that, though.

The future is already ours.

CEREMONY

Judith Speizer Crandell

Beat her hard
for dishes left
unwashed.
Slapped her too,
for cobwebs left
in corners
on cracked sinks
dusty floors.

Grew old
hands spotted brown,
folded into shadows
cast
on muslin sheets.
Shaky finger pointing
just past pillow's edge,
shaky finger straining
accusing her
of cup's dirty rim.

He died.
She saw to that.
Wash first the body,
close then the eyes.
Press the wedding suit
worn only once.
Fit to shrunken body.

Shave the face
comb the hair
gently like a mother.

Backyard burial.
Paper in
suit pocket:
Born 1941
Died 1998
Father
Husband
Bastard.
Got what he deserved.
What she deserved.
Death and peace
Walk hand-in-hand
from the wasteland
of the devil's dead.
The sweet living
arise alive
in a freshly composted
garden.

MY OWN MAN

Roberto Sabas

AT BEDTIME, WIN FOUND ME asleep in the tub. After the fight we had at dinner, over her not appreciating the laundry and dishes I did so she could take online courses, we just sort of avoided each other. She logged into her discussion forums and worked on her thesis while I went to the den to watch *Duck Dynasty*. I really hate that show, but I wanted to mock her family back in Louisiana with a stereotypical image of backwoods simpletons. The truth is they were no stupider than the media-savvy louts on the show who exploited their personas like farmers milking full cows. I'd always told myself that I disliked her parents for their political views, but there was something else I couldn't really pin down. They were always cordial but I questioned whether they really liked me and my staunch Connecticut liberalism.

I left the den and went to the kitchen, poured a glass of Chablis, and brought that, along with a Grisham novel, to the bathroom for a nice long soak. What I wanted was to escape sullen thoughts about breaking up our good thing–she really was thinking of our best interests in the long run–I had no right to insist on my preferences. I chalked it up to earlier in the day when I had been a little touchy because of the shit I had taken from my boss, Larry, about "focusing my efforts more on the job at hand instead of looking at porn sites." I couldn't believe what that cocksucker was doing, trying to out me as a perv right there in front of other coworkers. I had texted my wife about it several times this afternoon and she hadn't returned any of them. When I asked her why, she said, sorry–she'd been working on Excel spreadsheets all day for her boss's conference. I said I wished that I had someone to do *my* Excel spreadsheets, but she only gave me this look like I was a kid who had only heard half of the story and was trying to retell it his way. Later, she asked if I really was looking at porn and I said, "God no."

When she finally finished her work for the night and decided to check on me, she saw that my head was leaning against the end of the claw-foot tub with my arms hanging limply over the edge. My right index finger pointed at the shards of glass lying in a pool of clear liquid on the hardwood. I looked unconscious, maybe even dead. She began slapping my face, but stopped trying to revive me when my eyelids fluttered, and she felt my warm breath. Then she felt my pulse and let herself exhale. She asked if I'd taken my pills. My lips moved but made no sound. That was when she noticed a dark, slimy, leaf shape protruding from my ear. All the while that she was attending to me, I saw her as if in a dream state. I heard her say, "What the fuck?" At the same time I felt/thought/heard something in my core cells, DNA?—warning my body or its body to keep away from her hand; to not let her grab on.

She grasped at the end that looked like it was the tip of the leaf, she later told me, but it undulated and she let go. She got over her revulsion and tried again but too late: it had retracted into my head. When it did, I felt like I was being drawn down to depths past the bottom of the tub which couldn't have been more than a foot full of sudsy water. *Goddammit*, I thought—I wasn't going to lose all our arguments that easily. She was the one who was wrong; I was not getting in her way. When I drew breath to speak, I drank in warm water instead, causing me to hack and splutter, making me sit up suddenly in spite of the strong pull to end it all now.

The coughing cleared both my throat and my head: in my mind, I had risen through murk and broken the water's surface as if coming from a depth beyond what a bathtub could hold. My wife's face became crystal clear. I saw Win's lips move but it wasn't her I was hearing. Some new voice was drilling down into my ears to connect with me ... and it did. I felt a pin spot light up somewhere deep in my brain and it seemed to coalesce a myriad of other thoughts that were zipping and crisscrossing through my mind at lightspeed. In that nexus, I felt beatific.

—

Over the next two weeks, I started to speak in tongues even though I'd never gone to church a day in my life. Win said she'd seen the term for it when she was researching schizophrenia for a paper last spring: *glossolalia*, like some obscure Southern belle's name. We went to see a psychiatrist and neuroscientist about it; neither could offer a sound explanation. Since I didn't seem to be hurting anyone when I was under its trance, they recommended we leave it be to see if the syndrome would fade away. The frequency, which was four or five times a day, dwindled to just once, right at bedtime, which always spooked Win because I sat up straight and began reciting as soon as my eyes closed after my head had hit the pillow. She started sleeping in the living room not long after.

Eventually, our marriage ended, but not because of the glossolalia. She just thought that I had changed into a complete stranger, like I'd been possessed. I tried to assure her that I was still the same me, still my own man, but neither of us really believed that.

Still, I did not dislike my new self. I no longer tried to wheedle favors out of people. Instead, I insisted on my own terms for everything, saving needless inner-conflict. Once, at work, I slapped a coworker hard in the face for speaking ill of my boss. HR was all set to crucify me, but when I told Larry that the coworker was spreading rumors about his sexual orientation, he pulled strings to get me off the hook, and they went after the other guy and got him fired. The old me would have been too timid to do something like that: I would have just taken more shit—just like the shit I took when I was married to Win.

Speaking of Win, I saw her the other day at the café near the main library, sitting with some bearded man in tweed. He looked like a refined version of the hicks from *Duck Dynasty*, pretending to be something he was not: my equal, my replacement. He must think he's some intellectual hotshot, now that he's with Win, and she's a college graduate, but I'm with people too. Like I had lunch with the owner of the gun and ammo shop. He's been trying to convince me that I need a good conceal-and-carry firearm. He says that a GLOCK 19 would suit me well. And as I am nothing if not my own man, I am starting to agree.

There simply must be a corpse in a detective novel, and the deader the corpse the better.

S.S. Van Dine

MY ILLNESS LOOKS LIKE DARKNESS

Wendel Young

My illness looks like darkness
       A deep and infinite hole
It festers and it toils
       It's come to steal my soul

My illness reeks in the darkness
       A smell that makes me sick
And like a bomb ready to explode
       Upon its final tick

My illness wants to choke me
       Then lead me into death
And it forever holds me
       Until my final breath

A BLUE BIRD

Wendel Young

A blue bird landed on the sill
And oddly looked at me
For I was trapped within a cage
The little bird was free
There was curiosity in its eyes
As if trying to figure out
Why man was encased in bars of steel Yet
he roamed freely about
Many of his species knew this fate
Of being inside a cage
They to be used for mankind's pet
But this man for my rage
I told him I knew how the caged bird feels
And I would never entrap his kind
Once I conquered this malady
His freedom I hoped to find
He flapped his wings and loudly chirped It
was such a gift to see
As he danced and pranced about
He sang of hope for me
He spread his wings
And took to flight
Then dashed across the sky
In time just like that little bird
I hope one day to fly

THE WOMEN OF
ROYAL PALM BREEZE

Mark Alan Polo

DRIVING INTO THE ENTRANCE of The Royal Palm Breeze
Condominiums, there were no breezes, there were no royals. The air
wasn't sweet, but wet with stagnant heat. The tall urns on either side
of the drive held limp palm fronds desperately awaiting the sprinkler.
It was July and there would never be enough water, enough shade, least
of all enough winter months to allow you to forget the severity of the
summer climate. Any elusive wisp of air played hide and seek with everyone's lungs. By the beginning of July, those who could leave Florida
would, traveling north for an easier time of it. It was cyclical, the yearly
pilgrimage, almost religious.

Those who remained at The Royal Palm Breeze were the blessed
unfortunates. Their financial situations afforded them only one
choice—to avoid winter months in the colder regions from which they
hailed. So as the summer days dragged on, they hibernated indoors. If
there was any movement at all, it was the movement of cars leaving
from and returning to garages.

The women of Royal Breeze played tennis and jogged before ten
in the morning. The men played golf, but, in smaller gaggles with each
passing month. Those men who survived their working lives earned
this right. They needed to play because there wasn't much time left for
them. There wasn't much time before the stress of their former working lives, allowing them this lifestyle, would show its toll. And they
would make their wives widows. Men were outnumbered three to one
on average here. Around the clubhouse bar was often heard a familiar

refrain: "Women move to Florida to live, while men move to Florida to die." They would toast and laugh at their reality.

This was the mix of the community. And as the changing of the guard occurred, like natural selection, houses and condos, townhouses, and garden apartments popped up for sale. The Royal Palm Breeze was in the process of eliminating its first generation of owners. In that process, the women of the old guard were now left. These widows sold their houses so they could downsize even further and make their lives simpler still.

New fifty-somethings were buying up properties at good prices as the houses were worn from use and ill-conceived fashion with old colors, sad kitchens, and broken baths. The best that would-be buyers who inspected the tile floors could say upon inspection was, "We'll need to rip that out."

But it was worth it. This was a sale only available at the end of every generation. The new guard negotiated with the widows or, more removed, the inheritor children. These children dreaded to visit in the past, dreaded to eke-out the time to impatiently look past their parents as they spoke to them, all the while wishing they were someplace else. When the children sold the houses, it was an abrupt process that was mixed with the guilt of avoiding their parents and the anger of time served. Negotiations were made swiftly and from a distance, as the children were determined to clean this chapter up quickly with little regard for the voluntary dismantling of what their parents had built. For them, it held no value.

"Does the dining room chandelier and the outdoor furniture come with the house?"

"No."

"Then I don't want the house."

Bids were tossed like hot potatoes back and forth until they cooked.

"We won't accept such a low offer." The children balked.

"We have to gut the place; it's not worth it otherwise."

And seeing the chance to unload the albatross and slip away, they would relent and sign the offer. Thus did the changing of the guard roll on. But within this process, were the people who still lived their lives at Royal Palm Breeze, signing up for doubles tennis, attending yoga classes, playing Canasta and Mahjong, joining knitting circles and writing groups, picking the day to find the group they found pleasant enough in which to fill their time.

Every Tuesday afternoon at one o'clock Brenda, Eve, Sarah. and Blanche met to while away a few hours of July's heat and play Mahjong. They met to play and mindlessly forget that they were widows, each at a different time, each with a sudden loss. "Are we ready to begin?" Brenda asked, as she sat down at the card table on the sunporch.

"I am always ready." Eve put her coffee cup down with a hard clink. "Game on."

The rest giggled and sat. The game started lively and stayed that way. It had the tempo of familiarity, the laughter of good friends, and the mindlessness of driving down a well-traveled road.

"Flower!"

"Two dot."

"Ooh, doubles"

It continued around the table, like a merry-go-round.

"One Bam."

"East," Sarah pushed. "I don't know what a joker looks like. Are there jokers in this deck?"

They played for hours with gusto and a bond few had. They were all widows, an uncomfortable club, widows sharing a secret.

"I'll be right back, Eve said. "Can we break for a moment?"

"Sure," replied Brenda.

Eve rose with a shudder and sat back down.

"What's wrong, honey?

"Just a bit dizzy," Eve started to perspire.

"You're...you're all wet."

Blanche handed Eve a napkin.

"What's wrong?" Brenda asked.

"You haven't told them?"

"No." Eve lowered her eyes.

Brenda shook her head, "You need to tell them."

"Tell us what?"

Eve looked at her friends. "I'm not doing too well," she said, as the tears welled up. "My lymphoma is back, after all these years. And it seems that this time there is no stopping it."

"Oh, no."

They all stood up and hugged as one.

"What can we do?" Blanche asked.

"Nothing. The doctor said I haven't got much time."

Brenda sighed. "We've had a good run, no, girls?"

They were strong women, who faced adversity with strength and a sense of inevitability.

"You bet." Sarah pulled a bottle of champagne from the bottom of the refrigerator.

She went to the bar, popped the cork, and quickly poured it out and handed glasses to everyone.

"To our lives, our game, and our bond," Sarah said, as she raised her glass. They all followed.

The friends looked at each other and more tears flowed. They sipped as the bubbles turned bitter.

—

Within three weeks, Eve was dead.

There was no service, no ceremony. With the permission of Eve's children, Brenda, Sarah, and Blanche handled the cremation and sent Eve on her way back north. Their Mahjong game that they built was over, but they continued to meet for lunch, knowing they needed to see each other, for something far beyond their card game.

Time shed its days and they continued to meet. They laughed, they healed. They each talked of their stories. They dressed up and went to lunch and continued to keep their covenant. They took the death of Eve and the vacancy in their group seamlessly by leaving the game behind. All chapters end, but this one was far from over. There were still three, so the reason for their bond still existed, the costume for the charade simply needed to be adjusted.

Eve's apartment sold quickly to a couple from suburban Chicago. Blanche noticed a stranger in the lobby and recognized that certain first-time, second-home-buyer look that she wore on her calm and detached face.

Within weeks, contractors gutted the apartment as in came the new pieces to the puzzle. New tiles, appliances, and cabinetry clogged the hallways and the lobby. With systematic efficiency, the renovations were soon completed. Sarah was curious to learn about the new occupants. She learned from the super that one was a stay-at-home mom seeking to redefine herself while the other was a mechanic who'd worked on trucks for more years than anyone could count.

Brenda lived near their apartment and was curious to see the renovations that had been done to Eve's old nest. She showed up with a bottle of champagne and a cheese plate. A nameplate on the door, shiny and new, read The Grufton/Goodman's, which Brenda thought was quite modern. She was about to knock on the door when she heard a terrible stir.

"You're spending too much money!" a stern voice barked as Brenda leaned in to the door.

"I don't want to hear it. I told you that if you wanted to be here, then I needed to make it a place I could live in. I don't want to be in this swamp even if you do."

A loud crash was followed by silence. Eve froze. She backed up and retreated and then hastily met with her lunchmates to report.

"There's trouble in paradise." Brenda told the lunch group. There was a pause in their collective breath as each had a similar memory to share. They looked at each other, remembering why they'd been together for all these years, why they'd formed the bond of secrecy that freed them from their bondage. They eventually moved on to other topics.

—

Weeks dragged on as the scorch of summer softened one degree at a time. Brenda formally met Charlotte Goodman in the elevator. Charlotte carried a black garbage bag. She was an attractive women, aging around the edges, much like Brenda did when she moved to The Royal Palm Breeze. Charlotte wore slim-cut jeans, a loose stylishly uneven top, in what she considered beach colors, and large, dark sunglasses.

"You've got your hands full," Brenda said.

"Yes, it doesn't seem to end," Charlotte offered politely. "I'm almost done, though."

'You moved into my friend Eve's apartment, right?"

"Eve Belchamp?"

"Yes, that's the one. You certainly did it up big."

"Well, it was a compromise we made."

"Everything is a compromise," Brenda said.

"I should have held out for more," Charlotte smiled. "Nice meeting you. What's your name?"

"Brenda, Brenda Champion. Nice to meet you." Brenda looked at Charlotte as she bent down and noticed the darkness at the edge of her left eye.

"It's nice to meet you. I'm Charlotte Goodman. I'm sure we'll be seeing each other again." Charlotte smiled and nodded as the elevator door opened. She walked slightly backwards as she dragged her bag to her apartment.

The winter months approached and The Royal Palm Breeze began to fill up again with familiar cars in the parking lot and familiar faces in the clubhouse. Gaggles of people greeted and ran, hobbled and hugged, or rolled in on their scooters to see their old friends, make new ones, and catch up on who was gone. Today was the official meet and greet, an annual affair arranged by the condo association. Charlotte walked through the front entrance with the hesitation of a newbie. Previously, she had only met people in passing. She was determined to jump into the deep end of the pool and sink or swim.

Charlotte saw Brenda at the other end of the great hall and felt relieved to see a familiar face.

"Brenda?"

"Charlotte, good to see you again. How did the move go? Are you done?"

"It was a haul, but I am finally done."

"Where's your better half?"

"Ray doesn't come down as much as I do. Still working, you know."

"When is your big retirement party?"

"Not sure yet. We have some things to work out."

"What are you working out?" Brenda pushed, surmising that there was more to the statement than what was on its face.

"I, um…" Charlotte lowered her eye and began to cry.

"What's wrong, dear?" Brenda walked into a hornet's nest. She hugged Charlotte and when Brenda's hand rested on Charlotte's shoulder, she winced from the pain and recoiled. It made her cry even harder.

"What's happened to your shoulder?" Brenda knew without asking, but wanted confirmation.

"I'm sorry, I'm sorry," Charlotte sobbed, "I can't hold it in any longer."

"Let's go outside." Brenda escorted Charlotte to the veranda of the clubhouse. "Okay, tell me the story."

For two hours Charlotte exposed the secrets, documented every bruise, mimicked every ridicule and insult that she had withstood for so many years. She talked about how sweet Ray had been when they met twenty years earlier.

"Flowers and candy turned into cuts and bruises. Instead of watching daffodils fade, I waited for wounds to heal," Charlotte confessed. "I kept making excuses and concocting stories to explain away accidents and clumsiness. All to cover whatever situation I found myself in and to hide my embarrassment."

"Why didn't you leave long ago?' Brenda asked.

"We had adopted two kids and I felt trapped," Charlotte said through a stare. "They needed two parents. They were a handful. I simply couldn't manage them myself."

"Then…why not now?"

"Where would I go? I've been a stay-at-home mom most of my life and have, at best, rusty skills," Charlotte looked lost. "Besides, right now we're looking after two places. I'm away from the situation more than I thought."

"From the looks of your shoulder, it appears that you are not far enough or long enough away."

"Any time away is a gift, it turns out," Charlotte replied. "I'm not as dead set against this move as I thought I would be."

"Have you made any friends here?"

"Just you." Charlotte met Brenda's eyes for the first time.

"A few of my friends get together for lunch on Tuesday's at one o'clock. It's at my house this week. Would you like to join us?" Brenda extended the invite without checking with the group. She sensed it would be okay.

"Tomorrow? I don't know." Charlotte's voice trailed off.

"You need to come," Brenda insisted. "It'll be good for you." She grabbed Charlotte's hand in reassurance. "It will be good for all of us."

They parted and Brenda quickly got hold of everyone on a conference call. "Remember Charlotte, in Eve's old apartment? I've invited her to lunch tomorrow."

"*Our* lunch?" Sarah was concerned.

"Yes. We might be able to start up our card game again."

"I'm not sure that I can go through this again." Sarah said.

"Honestly, I'm with Sarah," Blanche said.

"Let's just have her over, get to know her, maybe get her to talk," Brenda pushed.

" I don't know. I thought this was way behind us." Blanche said.

An uncomfortable silence, not felt in years, emerged. It was the uncomfortable silence that surrounded the first husband to be eliminated.

"Okay," Sarah said, "Let's decide and get off the phone."

"Meet her?" Brenda asked.

"Yes." Sarah said.

"Sure," Blanche sighed. "One o'clock."

The three friends did not sleep that night. When the morning arrived, Blanche and Sarah showed up early at Brenda's house.

"Are we sure about this?" Sarah asked one last time.

"I've never been more certain. She needs us," Brenda reiterated.

"It's been ten years since Eve's husband."

"The time went so quickly." Sarah thought.

"Why Charlotte? There were others and we never thought of doing it again," Blanche said.

"I don't know. She's lost."

"Ah, lost. Like you were," Sarah said.

"Yeah, I remember the bruises and the overwhelming feeling…as if I was in a vat of oil and I couldn't see out the top. My life was thick and dark. There was no good to be found."

"I remember that as well."

"Me, too"

The doorbell rang as the Sarah placed the box of Mahjong tiles on the crisp table cloth.

"Let's talk, just talk…for Eve."

A collective sigh ensued as Brenda opened the door.

"I don't know how long I can stay," Charlotte said as she walked in.

"Why? "Brenda asked.

"Ray came in last night. Ray doesn't like it when I'm not at the apartment." The women nodded in understanding. There was an uneasy reserve as they sat down at the table to start the game.

"I thought I was just coming to lunch."

"Well, as you know, our friend, Eve, died. When we lost her, we also lost the fourth for our Mahjong game," Brenda said, cautiously. "We thought, just maybe, you would be interested in helping us start up again. We so miss it."

"I've never played this game," Charlotte said. "These are funny dominoes."

They all laughed.

"None of us knew how to play when we began to meet," Sarah said, "It's just a way for us to get together and be friends. We'll teach you what you need to know."

"Did you all know each other before coming here?"

"Nope. Met here," Blanche said. "I'm originally from Toronto."

"That *is* far from here," Charlotte said.

"When I met these women they saved my life. I could never have enjoyed my time here without them. I am grateful beyond words." Blanche looked around and her eyes filled up.

"Eve started the game when she got here. She saw that there were women just like her, and she wanted to get to know them," Brenda said. "Strength in numbers, you know."

They all sat down at the square card table that sat precariously in the hallway. It was the only place for Brenda to assemble this event in her apartment. A tight fit, but it had been one of the homes of their Mahjong game for twelve years.

"Let's get started," Sarah said. The practice round began and they played open hands with cards on the table. They showed Charlotte simple strategies and responses. Time passed quickly.

"It's a bit overwhelming, but fun," Charlotte said after a while. "Oh, look at the time. I have to go."

"We play every Tuesday," Brenda said.

"I'm not sure I can come every week."

Brenda took Charlotte's hand in hers. "The game is fun. The friendship is important. Your future happiness depends on it."

"Why?"

Sarah pointed to the bruise on Charlotte's arm. "That's why."

"Oh, that. I lost my balance and hit the kitchen cabinet." Charlotte was unaware that Brenda had shared her story with the women.

"Yes, I know. I was very clumsy till I met these women," Sarah continued. "We can help you walk steady, but you need to want it."

"I don't know. I'm frightened."

"We all were. We're not anymore," Sarah said. "Come. The game's at my house next Tuesday."

Charlotte left without saying anything else. Brenda closed the door, unsure as to whether the girls would be getting together to play Mahjong or just have lunch the following Tuesday.

The weeks drifted by slowly as the winter season at The Royal Palm Breeze heated up. After their first Tuesday together, Brenda went by Charlotte's apartment door several times each day, trying to gauge the level of the abuse in which Charlotte was involved. Brenda carried her laundry, brought her groceries, and took her packages the long way past Charlotte's door. On the first day, she heard fighting; on the second day, loud noises. Then, after three days, she heard only silence. Her concern increased as she no longer saw Charlotte at the clubhouse. The Palms Club was the center of the complex as well as the center of life for its condo members. Charlotte was nowhere. She wasn't on the tennis court, at the salon, or at the spa. Confirming her concern, Brenda did not see Charlotte at the weekly dinner buffet at the club's restaurant. She thought that she could finally meet Ray and talk to him a bit. It didn't happen that week.

Brenda got on the phone. "I can't find Charlotte anywhere."

"I haven't seen her either," Sarah said.

"Me either," Blanche joined in on the collective phone call.

"We'll know what to do next Tuesday," Brenda said.

On Tuesday morning, storm clouds gathered as the heat of the day surged past what winter allowed in their little part of Florida. Black-edged clouds made the palm fronds and birch leaves turn silver-side up as the wind increased. At noon, the charcoal-colored clouds won and rain fell in sheets. Sarah phoned the girls to see if they wanted to postpone. "Should we cancel?"

"Maybe."

"Anyone call Charlotte? "Sarah asked.

"I did. Got no answer," Brenda said.

"Then we can't cancel," Blanche quickly chimed in.

That afternoon, Brenda checked the local emergency room in the oft chance that something had happened to Charlotte. It had.

"Hi," Brenda said to the desk nurse. "My sister was admitted recently and I just found out. Her name is Charlotte Goodman. Is she okay?"

"Yes, she's stable," the nurse responded curtly. Brenda guessed correctly.

"What happened?"

"I can't say,"

"Can I see her?"

"She'll be released this afternoon."

"Is anyone picking her up? I could."

"I don't know. I can't release any information over the phone. But I could ask her."

Brenda waited on hold a long time. The nurse finally returned to the phone. "Charlotte said to pick her up around one."

"We'll be there."

Brenda called the women and they all piled into Brenda's car to pick Charlotte up at the hospital.

"What are we going to say to her?"

"The truth...it's time."

"It's been so long since the truth. I always had hoped that it would stay in our past."

"Just one more."

"Why can't we just slip into oblivion?"

"Because Charlotte's abuse is escalating, that's why," Brenda almost pleaded. "It's gonna get worse, you know it. It's her or Ray."

"Maybe God put her in our path," Blanche said, clinging tight to her religion. "We've all been in this place." Brenda and Sarah preferred practicality to theology. Whenever the two paths met it was a joint decision.

"Game on?" Brenda asked.

"One more for the Mahjong Murders!" Sarah yelled. They all laughed nervously.

They helped Charlotte into the car. When she settled in, they all got into the car and they opened up.

"Charlotte, are you ready to do something about Ray?"

"What can I do?'

The three women's eyes all met and Brenda spoke. "We were all abused when we started playing Mahjong. We formed this Tuesday afternoon card club and solved our problems...one by one. It took a while but just the hope of the abuse ending got us through."

"But you're all widows."

"Precisely."

A long moment of silence followed until Charlotte made the connection. "Oh, my. You...your husbands...oh, my."

Charlotte's response made the women feel nervous. At that moment, they thought Charlotte would reject their friendship and help, leaving them exposed, vulnerable. The silence was deafening. Brenda was the first to speak.

"My husband died of a massive heart attack," Brenda said.

"My husband died from a fall in our bathroom. Poor dear hit his head on the toilet," Sarah said.

"My husband died in a boating accident. He was drinking and fell overboard and drowned," Blanche said. "The idiot wasn't wearing his life preserver." She winked.

"They each died legitimate deaths that we ... uh ... sort of facilitated," Brenda admitted. "We all mourn our loss and celebrate our freedom every week."

"Now, you know our story. This is your chance. You need to make a decision," Blanche demanded.

More silence. The exposed women were left out on their limb. At last, Charlotte folded her arms and felt her latest wound. "What do I need to do?" The air shifted in the car and a unified resolve erupted as they drove home.

—

The following Tuesday they met at Sarah's house for the game. Charlotte arrived first, followed very soon after by Brenda and Blanche.

There was little small talk before the game and even less during.

"One bam."

"Two bam."

"Soap."

Charlotte played quietly and then a puzzled look washed across her face. "What do I do?"

"About what, my friend," Brenda offered.

"About Ray..."

"Has Ray acknowledged beating you and how it won't happen again?" Blanche asked.

"Ray apologizes every time and then swears never to do it again. But then, it happens again and again...and again. I'm tired. I feel broken inside. I can't let this happen anymore."

"Then it sounds like you're ready to have a happy life, no?" Brenda confirmed the obvious.

"I am," Charlotte said through a torrent of tears. "I literally can't take it for one more second."

"You realize, if you want our help," Sarah said, directly, "you will promise to stay here in Royal Palm Breeze. We'll solve your problem and protect you, but, and it's a big but, you will be bound to our game. Those are the terms."

"I assumed so." Charlotte's resolve took over. "I want peace, so the answer is yes."

'Where is Ray?" Sarah asked.

Charlotte looked at her watch. "I don't think it'll be much longer before there'll be a knock at the door."

"We need to talk fast then," Blanche said, nervously.

"We need to come up with an original scenario that will be undetected," Brenda said.

"It'll take time, but we will work it out. We just need to think about it some, and brainstorm," Sarah added.

Suddenly, the doorbell rang, followed by a rapid knocking on the door.

"It's Ray!" Charlotte shuddered.

Brenda stood up from her chair at the Mahjong table and walked cautiously toward the door. She moved the side-glass curtain to see who it was. She relaxed.

"Calm down," she called out to the group.

Brenda opened the door and was met by a slender and tall blonde woman, well dressed and with an athletic build.

"Hello," Brenda greeted. "May I help you?"

"You must be Brenda," the attractive stranger said.

"I am," Brenda confirmed. "Who are you?"

"I'm Ray, Ray Grufton," she said.

"Oh…hello. Nice to meet you, Ray." They shook hands.

"Is Charlotte here? Ray asked in a monotone voice. "It's getting late."

"Yes, yes, it's very late," Brenda stuttered, meaning something much different. "Would you like to meet the other girls?"

"Maybe another time. We have things to do. You understand," Ray said flatly.

"More than you know, Ray. More than you know."

"Come on, Charlotte. Let's go." Ray leaned into the doorway and peeked in to get her attention, snapping her fingers. "We really need to go."

Charlotte rose and left quickly, blurting out her goodbyes. Brenda closed the door and leaned against it, trying to block the way in for protection. She gazed at Sarah and Blanche as if to question their resolve. Brenda moved from the door to the table and sat down silently, just making eye contact with her two friends.

"It doesn't matter, does it?" Brenda asked, after a moment.

"Not to me," Sarah added.

"It's a woman." Blanche chimed in.

"What does that matter?" Brenda said.

"We've never killed a woman before," Blanche said, "It's just...weird. We've always fought for women; helped women."

"Blanche, it's not *about* gender...it's about abuse," Sarah said. "We are helping someone who is suffering from the abuse we are each intimately familiar with."

"You're right, though it's still weird," Blanche said. "But I'm in if you are."

"Then it's settled," Brenda said. "Let's finish this."

They all sat to finish the game, Brenda taking over for Charlotte's hand. "Two dot."

"East."

"Then, it's game on?"

All three replied in unison. "Game on."

"Oooh, doubles!"

"Shit, I was one away."

"I'll let Charlotte know she won the round."

Brenda glanced at Sarah. "Didn't you mention that Ray was a mechanic and fixes trucks?"

Sarah nodded.

"I read that a medium-sized truck weighs around 16,000 pounds. Lot of things can happen to a person who's underneath a large, heavy vehicle like that. Lots of things."

AUTHOR BIOS

ANDERSON

Monte R. Anderson has published several e-books on Smashwords and Amazon. He also writes a humorous blog. He served as an Army officer in the Infantry for 22 years. He is a Vietnam veteran and a disabled veteran. After the service, he was a financial adviser for 2 years and then became a facility maintenance manager from 1993 until his retirement in 2011. Anderson holds a BS from the Military Academy at West Point and an MS from Indiana University at Bloomington. He resides in Elmira, NY, with his wife, Kathryn, and between them they have six children and eleven grandchildren. Find him at monterander-son-author.com and monteranderson.wordpress.com.

BARLOW

Tom Barlow is an Ohio-based author whose works straddle the literary, crime, and science fiction markets. Over 80 stories of his may be found in anthologies including *Best American Mystery Stories 2013, Best of Ohio Short Stories #2*, and *Best New Writing 2011*, and many periodicals including *Hobart, Temenos, Redivider, The Intergalactic Medicine Show, Crossed Genres, Mystery Weekly, Red Room*, and *Switchblade*. He is also the author of the science fiction novel *I'll Meet You Yesterday*.

BERG

Sharon Berg writes poetry, story, and nonfiction focused on First Nations history and education. Her stories have appeared in *Fiddlehead, Quarry, Big Pond Rumours, Eunoia Review*, and *Two Hawks Quarterly*. *Naming the Shadows*, a collection of short fiction, will be published by Porcupine's Quill in Fall 2019. Her poetry has appeared in periodicals across Canada and in the UK, The Netherlands, the United States, and Australia. Her poetry books were released in 1979 (Borealis Press) and 1984 (Coach House Press); she had two audio cassette releases (*Gallery 101*, 1985) and (*Public Energies*, 1986) and she has three chapbooks with Big Pond Rumours. She won second-prize for Poetry in the *2016 GritLit Contest* and her work appears in several 2018 poetry anthologies. In academic writing her chapter on Wandering Spirit Survival School is in *Alternative Schooling and Student Engagement* (Palgrave/Macmillan, 2017). Berg is the founder of *Big Pond Rumours*, an International Literary E-Zine & Micro-Press, which has focused on publishing chapbooks of Canadian authors since 2006.

CRANDELL

William F. Crandell returned home from the Vietnam War with a taste for adventure, a skeptic's eye, and a hundred-thousand stories. Completing a doctorate in history at Ohio State University, he was awarded a Maryland State Arts Council Individual Artist Award in 2004 for his mystery novel, *Let's Say Jack Kennedy Killed the Girl*. Crandell has published numerous short stories, book reviews, and political analyses. He was awarded the PRIZM's Mark Twain Award for Humor/Social Commentary 2012 and resides in Milton with his wife, Judith.

DUTTON

David W. Dutton is a semi-retired residential designer who was born and raised in Milton, DE. He has written two novels, several short stories, and eleven plays. His musical comedy, *oh! Maggie*, in collaboration with Martin Dusbiber, was produced by the Possum Point Players and the Lake Forest Drama Club. He wrote two musical reviews for the Possum Point Players: *An Evening With Cole Porter*, in collaboration with Marcia Faulkner, and *With a Song in My Heart*. He also wrote the one-act play, *Why the Chicken Crossed the Road*, commissioned and produced by the Delmarva Chicken Festival. In 1997, he was awarded a fellowship as an established writer by the Delaware Arts Council. In 1998, he received a first-place award for his creative nonfiction by the Delaware Literary Connection. His piece, "Who is Nahnu Dugeye?" was subsequently published in the literary anthology, *Terrains*. More recently, Dutton's work has appeared in the anthologies, *Halloween Party 2017*, *Solstice*, *Equinox*, and *Aurora*. In fall 2018, Dutton's third novel, *One of the Madding Crowd*, was published by Devil's Party Press. Dutton, his wife, Marilyn, and their Rottweiler, Molly, currently reside in Milton.

EBERT

Kari Ann Ebert is a poet and fiction writer who lives in Dover, DE. Her work has appeared in *The Broadkill Review*, *cahoodaloodaling*, and *Gargoyle*. She writes poetry because it squeezes out the real parts of her that she may not even know exist. She tries to sculpt the poem so that it resonates with the reader and creates a much-needed connection in the world. She believes poetry is a world changer that starts in one's inmost worlds. She is currently gathering her poems into a first collection entitled *Alphabet of Mo(u)rning*.

FOX

Lisa Fox is a pharmaceutical market research consultant by day and fiction writer by night. She recently returned to creative writing after a long hiatus and hasn't stopped since. Her short fiction has appeared in *Ellipsis Zine, Foliate Oak Literary Magazine,* and at UbiquitousBooks.com. Fox resides in northern New Jersey with her husband, two sons, and an oversized dog. She relishes the chaos of everyday suburban life.

HERON

Scottish-American author and poet, Robert Lewis Heron, is an architect and accomplished artist (traditional and digital) living in Maryland. His unique voice for storytelling captivates his readers by twisting and tormenting their imagination. By sprinkling a dry sense of humor throughout his writing, he makes any harshness a wee bit more palatable. Expect the unexpected on entering his world of woe and wonderment. His writing has been compared to Tartan Noir author, Christopher Brookmyre.

HEWETT

Heidi J. Hewett writes mysteries and romance. Her Sherlock Holmes novella, *The Curious Case of the Clockwork Doll,* was published in a contest by 18th Wall Productions. She has self-published two works, *The Adulteries of Rachel,* and a children's book, *Crazy Grandma Genius Baby & Me,* available on Amazon. Forthcoming works include a sci-fi romance, *Lexi,* in November 2018, and two romantic comedies, *Fly Away Home,* and *No Fool,* in 2019. Hewett is a member of the Romance Writers of America.

HUMBY

Storyteller Phyllis Humby resides in rural Ontario where she indulges her passion for creating wicked suspense. Though obsessed with writing crime novels, it is her short stories, often scheming, twisted, or spooky, that have received the most attention, appearing in anthologies and journals in Canada, the United States, and the UK. A 2018 anthology publication entitled *Our Plan to Save the World,* featuring Canadian and US authors, includes four of Humby's stories. In addition, for the past 7 years she has penned a humorous monthly opinion column, "Up Close and Personal," for *First Monday* magazine. Check out her blog at phyllishumby.blogspot.com.

NORTHERN

After publishing the Executive Summary to "The Future of Independent Life Insurance Distribution," Bayne Northern transitioned from writing nonfiction to fiction. Her work has appeared in several anthologies including *Equinox* and *Solstice*. She is currently completing her first novel, *The Bitch Seat*, situated in the financial services industry. An avid short story author, Northern is also an active volunteer with the Village Improvement Association and a resident of Rehoboth Beach, DE.

OCHOCO

Jonathan Ochoco grew up in Houston, TX, but has called San Francisco home for 20 years. He is lawyer by training and works as a compliance officer for a global investment management firm. He is a Pushcart nominated writer with stories published in *The Arcanist's Ghost Stories, Descansos: Words from the Wayside, Gathering Storm, Ellipsis Zine: Four*, and several additional anthologies. Ochoco is an avid curler (the ice sport) and plays in a league in the San Francisco Bay Area. Follow him on Twitter @mrochoco

PEARCE

Dianne Pearce founded The Milton Workshop in 2015, and Devil's Party Press in 2017. She is a graduate of both the West Chester University and Vermont College writing programs, earning an MA and an MFA. Pearce has taught writing in Delaware, California, Pennsylvania, and Maryland. She sometimes takes on editing projects for other writers, and has done both writing and advocacy for causes close to her heart, among them adoption, developmental disabilities, and animals. Pearce is an adoptive parent of a wonderful daughter, Sophie, and is married to her best friend, David Yurkovich.

POLO

Mark Alan Polo has been an interior designer for over 30 years and is President and Owner of The Urban Dweller/Polo M.A. Inc., with offices in Northern New Jersey and a satellite office in Delaware, where he currently resides. A part-time writer for the past 15 years, Polo's short story, "Fifty-Five," appeared in the 2016 award-winning *Beach Nights* anthology (Cat & Mouse Press). His debut novel, *Mosquitoes and Men*, is slated for publication in 2019. He is at work on a second novel.

PRATT-HERZOG

Patsy Pratt-Herzog is an emerging freelance writer from Southwestern Ohio. Her favorite genres to write are sci-fi and fantasy. When she's not writing, she enjoys painting and riding roller coasters. She shares her house in the burbs with her husband, Tim, and three chunky cats. To learn more about Pratt-Herzog and see other samples of her work, visit patsyprattherzog.wordpress.com.

RESNICK

Bernard M. Resnick, Esq. is a musician who went to law school. He practices as an entertainment attorney in Philadelphia, PA. He has been rated "AV Preeminent" by Martindale/Hubbell; a "Pennsylvania Superlawyer" by Thompson/Reuters; and has been named one of Main Line Today's "Top Lawyers." His law firm, Bernard M. Resnick, Esq., P.C., has earned over 100 gold, platinum, Billboard #1 and other music industry awards for deals negotiated and drafted on behalf of the firm's clients, representing sales of over 170 million records. He plays double bass in the Main Line Symphony Orchestra, teaches Entertainment Law at Villanova Law School, and votes for the Grammy Awards. He plays a little poker and runs a few 5k races every year. As an author, Resnick has written numerous academic papers and has contributed chapters to several textbooks, and he has published the nonfiction disaster-planning book *The Big List*. He occasionally writes pop, heavy metal, and rap songs.

SABAS

Born in the Philippines and raised in Guam, Roberto Sabas imbues his literary and visual art works with the color and vibrant imagery of the tropics. A trained illustrator, he cites his father's influence in art and poetry. Sabas' art is published by Human Kinetics, Digital Graphics, the YMCA, and the USTA. His short fiction and poems have appeared in *The Alchemist Review* and in a previous incarnation of the *Weird Tales* social media page. His wife and children share in his passion for creativity and truth.

SARABIA

Following service in the US Marines, Michael Sarabia attained degrees in Political Science and Education from Cal State Los Angeles. Sarabia also holds a Master's Degree in Professional Writing from USC, and has taught English and History at Garfield High School in East Los Angeles. Currently retired, he and his wife live in Guadalupe, CA.

SPEIZER CRANDELL

Judith Speizer Crandell is an award-winning writer and teacher of fiction, poetry, and nonfiction. She's received residencies at Yaddo, AROHO (A Room of One's Own), and a Maryland State Arts Council Individual Artist Fellowship for her novel, *The Resurrection of Hundreds Feldman*. She was selected to participate in the 2018 Delaware Seashore Writers' Retreat. She has performed readings in Milton, DE, the New York State Writers Institute, the New York State Vietnam Veterans Memorial, and the Washington, DC, and Cleveland Public Libraries. A journalist, teacher, and Washington, DC, speechwriter for nearly 20 years, she moved to Milton in 2017 to be near the ocean and write. Her novel, *The Woman Puzzle,* is scheduled for 2019 publication.

Sz KEANE

Carrie Sz Keane studied journalism and English at the University of Maryland. She later apprenticed as a midwife in rural Appalachia in Kentucky before studying nurse-midwifery at Yale University. While at Yale, Keane was awarded a humanities honor in creative writing for her piece entitled "Modern Nurse Nancy," a story about working night shifts as a new nurse on a postpartum unit, which was later published in a Canadian nursing textbook. Upon graduating in 2004, Keane began journaling and writing the stories of her work as a midwife. She is actively writing a journalistic memoir of her career. Keane works at an active obstetrics and gynecology practice in Delaware as a sexual health clinician providing prenatal care, contraception, annual examinations, STD screenings, and birth support for females. Her stories and essays, which have been published in anthologies by Devil's Party Press, focus on maternal health in America and her role as a witness on the frontlines of female healthcare.

TURNER

Paulene Turner is an Australian writer of novels, short stories, and short plays. A former Sydney journalist, she wrote her first novel as a nanowrimo exercise. Since then, she has drafted three more books with the same characters and is now planning the fifth, and final, installment in her YA series. Her love of writing began with screenplays. *Space*

Cadet, her animation feature, was nominated by the Australian Writers Guild as best unproduced feature nationally. But as the film industry is tough to crack, she eventually crossed over to the "dark side"– writing narrative fiction. Her writing style still features a lot of dialogue and quite "filmic" visual scenes. Her short stories have appeared in anthologies in the US and Australia. Turner also writes ten-minute theatre plays, many of which she has directed for Short and Sweet, Sydney–the biggest little play festival in the world. Find her at pauleneturner-writes.com.

WIDOCKS

Liliana Widocks is a Romanian living in the UK. She describes herself as "a writer, when that doesn't bother anyone, and a blogger, when I feel suddenly opinionated." Most of her work, which can be found at lilianawidocks.com, is in Romanian. Some of her articles and stories are published on two popular Romanian online sites: Republica.ro and catchy.ro. She recently started a blog written in English, which she describes as "just few poems now, tiny baby steps." She launched a book of poems in her hometown, Suceava, in Romania in the summer of 2018. Widocks adds: "I am somebody exactly like yourself; when today is too lazy to come up with a story, I write down one of my own. We were given life, we just need to love."

YOUNG

Wendel Young grew up in Philadelphia, one of four children. He graduated from West Philly High in 1978 and joined the United States Marine Corps. During his eight years in the Corps, Young was deployed twice. After his military service, he worked in the aerospace industry. Young began writing poetry as a teenager after being inspired by Langston Hughes. His poetry often reflects on his military service. Young moved to Maryland's Eastern Shore in 2016.

YURKOVICH

David Yurkovich is an award-winning writer, illustrator, and graphic designer. Published works include *Banana Seat Summer*, *Glass Onion*, *Altercations*, *Less Than Heroes*, and *Death by Chocolate: Redux*. Find him at yurkoverse.com.

Anthologies so engaging, it would be a crime NOT to read them...

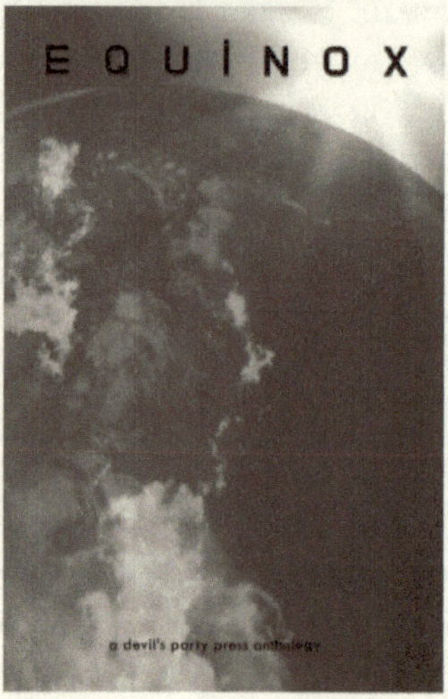

Halloween Party 2017

HILTON WORKSHOP ANTHOLOGY SERIES
FALL 2017

S O L S T I C E

E Q U I N O X

a devil's party press anthology

AURORA

Whether you're in the mood for something scary or
something seasonal, we've got you covered.
Devil's Party Press anthologies contain engaging
original works by talented voices from across
the globe. Our authors are a diverse group of
over-forty creators who bring to the page
their unique talents.
We'll make sure your reading time is well spent
Visit us on the web for ordering info.

devilspartypress.com

Don't get even...get mad.

One of the madding crowd

Marc and Christabel, Christmas 1971

David W. Dutton

"First, you must understand I am mad . . . ."

With this grim warning, Marc Steadman introduces us to his world, one of power and privilege. Through the years, Marc has been taught to protect his way of life, and dare others to ask him to justify his actions. Is there such a thing as a victimless crime?

From author David W. Dutton comes ONE OF THE MADDING CROWD, a taut 262-page thriller that examines how far one man will go to create the life he was promised and protect the people he loves.
Who will blink first, Marc, or you?

Order online at amazon.com or visit DPP for more info.

devilspartypress.com

Does this look familiar?

photo credit: Valerina Solaris

If so, chances are you're over 40, so perhaps you
might consider submitting a short story, poem,
or memoir piece to one of our upcoming anthologies.
DPP grew out of our belief that your work deserves a
better life than a file on your laptop.

Our main criteria are fairly simple:

1. Your work must be original and compelling.
2. You must be 40 years of age or older.

We publish two anthologies per year,
typically in the spring and the fall.

For complete submission information visit
devilspartypress.com/submissions

If you wow us with your skills, you'll join a unique
group of writers, each a compelling, original voice.

We look forward to hearing from you.

devilspartypress.com

www.ingramcontent.com/pod-product-compliance
Lightning Source LLC
Chambersburg PA
CBHW051246250626
47155CB00009B/3178